DAMAGE DONE
M.J. Schiller

Part One

"Indifference and neglect often do much more damage than outright dislike."

-J.K. Rowlings

CHAPTER ONE

C ork, Ireland~1960
   Teddy Passmore McKee was born in Cork, Ireland, with a limp
and a chip on his shoulder that threw his balance off all the more.

In actuality, the chip grew there.

One day, five-year-old Teddy was taken to the park by his Auntie Mary. Auntie Mary would sit on the bench talking to the other moms, keeping half an eye on Teddy, as she was responsible for returning him at the end of the day, to her brother Noah. Not that Noah paid an ounce of attention to the boy anyway, since he blamed his son for his wife's death in childbirth. Nevertheless, there would be hell to pay for sure if anything happened to the boy on Mary's watch.

Teddy was busy in the sandbox making long, curvy hills that all led to a tall blob in the middle in a circular fashion. Another child came and sat on the side of the sandbox observing the construction with interest. After watching for several minutes in silence, he finally asked, "Whatcha buildin'?"

"A sand octopus." Teddy wrinkled his brow. That was the silliest question he had ever heard. Wasn't it obvious? The boy glanced from his project to a seven-towered monstrosity that a little girl in a red dress was making at the other end of the sandbox. With a slight nod, the boy seemed to decide that castles were for girls, and sand octopi were extremely fashionable, for he came over, plopped down next to Teddy, and began to dig.

The two worked together without speaking for a bit before Teddy's tagalong belatedly asked, in his thick Irish brogue, "Say, what be your name anyway?"

"Teddy Passmore McKee," he responded, sticking his hand out like he'd seen adults do.

The other boy stared at his hand blankly. "What's ya doin'?"

Teddy looked at his hand. After a beat, he shrugged and wiped it on his shorts. "Darned if I know."

From that point on, the boys were chums, working side-by-side and stopping occasionally to make sure they still had only eight tentacles. Teddy had heard his Uncle Phineas tell many a tale of the wide blue seas, and he knew, for a fact, that octopi had only eight tentacles. Phineas was rather an odd bird. An old sailor, he lived on the outskirts of town in a lighthouse he built himself, despite the fact that they were miles from the coast. He was the one person who was kind to him, and Teddy loved his uncle dearly and had built the wonderful octopi in his honor.

The boys stood back for a minute to admire their handiwork. Teddy's gaze slid to the girl's sandcastle, which now boasted a large red flower on one of its many parapets. "Needs somethin'," he commented. "I know." He hobbled off to a pathway made with a wide array of stones. Scooping a handful of the colorful rocks, he alternately stomped then dragged his malformed leg, all the way back to the sandbox. "See," he continued excitedly, "they're like suction cups." He laid them out in a measured pattern on each tentacle. He'd finished two legs before he realized his friend hadn't rejoined him. He turned to see the lad still standing a distance away, a look of horror on his face. "Well now...ain't ya gonna lend a hand no more?"

"What's wrong with your leg?"

He looked at his two legs. "Whatda ya mean?"

"Your leg, your leg." The boy gestured. "What happened to it?"

Realizing, suddenly, why his friend was gawking, he responded, "Nothin'," with an edge to his voice.

"Somethin' musta happened to it," the boy insisted logically. "It's gammy."

"Nay. It's always been this way." Certain he had given a satisfactory answer, Teddy turned back to his sea creature.

The boy still stood off for a minute. When Teddy glanced up, he was peering in the direction of the pretty little girl. She had run off to a nearby bush to pick more blossoms for her palace. After another moment's thought, the boy chased after her.

Teddy sat back on his haunches awkwardly. He wondered what he had done to make his friend mad. He reviewed their conversation and grasped with sudden clarity why he had been left alone.

And the chip began to grow.

TEDDY RECEIVED NO COMFORT at home, living with his eleven older Passmore cousins. In fact, they all seemed to resent his presence and the idea that his father had insisted he get his own room. The family lived in a large, rambling home outside of Cork that their Uncle Noah, Teddy's father, had paid for, unbeknownst to the cousins, while he, himself, continued to live in an aging boarding house in town.

None of them questioned that strange arrangement; it was simply how it was. Noah would join them every once in a while for dinner, but it was almost as if he were not there at all. They would carry on a polite, stilted conversation, and everyone would be relieved when he finally left, Teddy most of all.

The boys spent most of their energies thinking up ways to make Teddy unhappy without being so obvious they incurred the wrath of their Uncle Noah, or, God forbid, their mother. The girls, for their part, had decided some time ago to ignore Teddy, to act like he didn't exist; and this was the cruelest treatment of all. At least when his boy cousins were up to something, they would interact with him to a degree, usually to suck him in and catch him off guard, but at least they spoke to him. Auntie Mary may have been his only saving grace. She treated him as poorly as the rest of her children; would smack him with a wooden spoon without the slightest provocation, for example, but he took comfort in this warped equality.

By the time Teddy McKee reached the age of twelve, the chip was the size of a monolith, and equally unmovable. He began to get in fights on almost a daily basis, unable to stand the taunts and jeers of his malicious classmates.

On one particular day, the principal called his father to come and take him home. His father left the principal's office, grabbed Teddy by the collar, and dragged him out to his car in front of all of the other students, without a single word. When they returned home, his father sent him to his bedroom. Twenty minutes later, Noah ascended the stairs and entered the room, pulling a desk chair to the middle of the floor and straddling it backward. He rested his arms coolly on the back of the chair before addressing Teddy, straightening out the line of his sleeves a little as he did so. His father was always impeccably dressed, starched, and polished, and decidedly unwrinkled.

"What, pray tell," he said, biting off his words, "did you get yourself into a fight about this time?"

"Oh, the same ol' stuff," Teddy answered rashly. "Those bastards makin' fun of me leg."

He took great pleasure in the way the curse word seemed to affect his father like a slap in the face. There were some advantages to living in a household of older cousins.

"Teddy." His father visibly struggled to retain his temper. He would deem it undignified to lose control in a situation such as this. "Teddy," he said more evenly, "you can't hit someone because they don't take a shine to you."

"Why not?" Again the boy reveled in the lovely shade of purple his father was turning.

"Because, Teddy..." Noah tossed up his hands with a sigh, and then he shut down, like a pub at closing time, and took on his standard reserve. Noah McKee's ability to be absolutely unapproachable was astounding. He had never even given his son a hug, could hardly even bear to look at him. Teddy knew it was because he bore a striking resemblance to the woman he'd been told his father had loved with all his heart—although he found it hard to believe Noah had one—a woman whose death he felt, however irrationally, Teddy was responsible for. "This is unacceptable behavior, totally unacceptable." Noah paused, shaking his head. He cleared his throat. "I have decided to remove you from the school, Theodore, and send you to a trade school. You will go there, and you will not become involved in any more shenanigans. Am I understood?" he added, his voice stern, forestalling all objections.

"Aye," Teddy responded, dropping his customary "sir". He didn't care anymore.

Noah stood and pushed his chair into the desk, straightening a book on the table that was not perfectly aligned with the others. He turned from the desk and marched to the door, his attitude brusque, pausing in the doorway to say, "You're incorrigible, Theodore." Noah's voice was saturated with the disappointment he must have felt. He didn't turn around. He didn't even look at Teddy. He simply left.

"Ehh...and how would you know?" Teddy muttered to the closed door, his deep-seated bitterness toward his father tasting like metal on his tongue.

CHAPTER TWO

L ife at the trade school was similar to life at his former school...only worse. The trade school tended to be populated with a rougher, meaner crowd, and each passing day made Teddy harder inside.

"Say, gimp. Be careful with that table saw. It'd be a shame for you to drop it and chop off your one good leg. Har. Har."

"Gee, Ted. You'd make one hell of a pirate. All you'd be needin' was a parrot for your shoulder."

"Hey, crippled boy. Is it true you ain't got no mam?"

"Aye. Maybe she left the wee mite because of his ugly, crooked leg."

This one would invariably get Teddy into a fight. Apparently a friend of one of his cousins knew his history, and it became a subject of interest for those in the school whose very existence centered upon making his life a living hell.

About a week after his arrival, another new kid enrolled in the school. Seamus Brady had been the chubby kid on the playground, the one who others picked on, until he reached puberty. Now Seamus looked more like a walking post box and hit harder than a freight train. He began to assert his dominance at once.

Teddy was walking to class and didn't even see the bigger kid near the lockers. Seamus stuck a foot in his path, and he went sprawling. His books skidded across the floor, and a pencil slid almost all the way down the long hallway. The wind was temporarily knocked out of him and his chin bloodied. But Seamus wasn't through with him yet. He hopped on the back of Teddy's legs then tried to jerk him around by his jacket to get a better shot at his face. Teddy saw a pair of boots approaching him from the opposite direction.

"Hold this, will ya?" a calm voice said, and he looked up to see the booted newcomer handing books to a bystander. Before anyone knew what was happening, the boy's lightning fists laid Seamus Brady out cold. "Thank you kindly," Teddy's savior said to the other boy as he took his books back, proceeding down the hall without further comment.

"Wait! Wait!" Teddy yelled, scrambling after him. When he caught up he asked, "How'd you do that?" with a hint of awe and reverence.

The blond-haired boy opened his fist to show a crude set of brass knuckles in his palm. "Made 'em in shop class. Nice to see me education comin' in so handy and all." He grinned.

"Great saints alive! Do you think you could show me how to do that?"

"Sure, lil' man. Sure," he answered, putting an arm around Teddy's shoulder jovially. From that day on Teddy McKee and Sean Hennessey were inseparable.

SEAN HENNESSEY WAS a bit of a ladies' man. Girls described him as having "thick hair the color of sunshine, wavy in all the right places, and dreamy green eyes." He could have any girl he wanted, and he wanted many. Teddy benefited from his friendship by scooping up the crumbs. Sean's girlfriends' girlfriends would often give him a pity date, just to remain close to Sean and observe his every move. Sean wore his self-confidence as he wore his trademark leather jacket, his tight black jeans, and calf-high boots; and it was equally attractive to the girls. In addition, he never sent them away unhappy.

Even adults seemed drawn to him. Before he was sixteen he was a regular at the pub.

"Hey, Seanie. Let me buy ya a pint."

"Thanks. And how's about me buddy, Ted, here?"

"Oh, sure, sure. Two pints, then."

So no one was surprised when, one day, a man named Patrick Bradigan waved from across the pub, asking Sean to join him at a corner table. He approached Bradigan skeptically, as he wasn't a regular in the pub, and stuck out in his cashmere coat and expensive loafers. He had well-groomed, curly, grey hair and large, slender, manicured hands. The smudgy grey of the bar haze, cigarettes mixed with peat smoke, didn't seem to touch him somehow, and Sean could even smell the expensive cologne the man wore over the smoke. The older man gestured to the bartender to send over drinks for them both.

"Sean. It is Sean, isn't it?"

He nodded.

"I've been watching you. I've noticed you're very popular around here. Got lots of friends, don't ya?"

He nodded again, still reserved.

Bradigan smiled smoothly. "I'm looking for a kid like you...good lookin', smart... How'd ya like to earn yourself a lot of money? When you have money, people respect you, son."

He considered this. He was impressed by Bradigan's luxury car and thick wad of cash, and before long he was reaching across the table to shake his new boss's hand.

Sean was smart enough to know that having a person around who was completely devoted to him, like Ted, could be very beneficial. Teddy was always willing to do the dirty work for him, which, when they were sixteen, was not too serious. But once the relationship was established, he had Teddy under his thumb for the rest of his life, and they both knew it.

SEAN ALWAYS SEEMED to have money, lots of it, without any visible job to produce it. Teddy, on the other hand, worked hard as an apprentice at a woodworking shop, but rarely had more than a couple of dimes to his name. He had learned a lot at the trade school about woodworking, but it was at the shop that his true craftsmanship came to light.

Sean and Teddy were leaving the pub one evening, Teddy climbing on the back of Sean's motorbike, when Teddy saw her through the haze of gas fumes. She was the most beautiful girl he had ever seen in his life. She had long, dark, curly hair, bronzed skin, and deep brown eyes. She wore a simple white linen dress, not really the typical style girls at that time were wearing, but she was able to pull it off seamlessly.

"Who's that?" he said, awestruck. Sean turned around to gaze at her, too.

"That's the new gal. Her father is takin' over the bank. Moved here from Limerick, I hear. Mam's supposed to be completely Spanish, speaks nary a word of English," he added thoughtfully.

The girl glanced in their direction. Sean revved the engine of his bike as a sort of come on, but she turned her back and continued down the street. They made a big loop and sped past her, kicking up dirt in their wake. Teddy held on tight, but turned his head, making eye contact one last time before they headed out of sight.

TEDDY SWUNG OFF THE back of Sean's bike.

"Good luck," his friend called, no doubt thinking to himself, *you'll need it.*

Teddy walked resolutely into the store. He saw her behind the counter, and hobbled over. "Hi," he said, hoping he projected a confidence he didn't feel, something he had been practicing with Sean.

"Hello," she said, dropping her eyes. She spoke so low he had to lean closer to catch it. "Can I help you?"

Her voice was as beautiful as she was, sort of melodic, with a hint of an accent, a charming combination of both Spanish and Irish. "Aye. I'm lookin' for..." He glanced around quickly. "...perfume. I'm looking for some perfume."

"I see, for your girlfriend?"

"Nay." He chuckled, his cheeks growing hot. "I don't have one."

"Oh, for your mother, then."

"Nay. Don't have one of those either."

"Oh." She put a hand to her heart, seeming a little taken aback by his forthrightness. After a beat she recovered. "I'm so sorry. Then it is for...?"

Teddy fished for an answer. "My auntie. Aye, my auntie."

"Very good." She smiled. "What kind of perfume do you think she would like?"

Teddy didn't want to even think about Auntie Mary wearing perfume. "I don't know. Maybe perfume is not the right thing at all. Gee, I don't know. What would you like to receive as a gift?"

"Me?" Her eyes widened. "This certainly seems like an unorthodox way to shop for your auntie." She tilted her head. "Then again, in my experience men are fairly helpless when it comes to shopping for women, or for anyone else." They chuckled. "Well..." Her gaze flitted about the room. She leaned closer, and he could smell the scent of roses. "You know what I'd really want," she said with an air of confidentiality.

"What?"

She flew around the counter to a round table. Various scarves were fanned out on the surface, turning it into a pinwheel of color. She withdrew a black, intricately woven shawl with fringes along the end. Throwing it around her shoulders playfully, she looked in a floor-length mirror nearby as she danced to and fro. Teddy was captivated. "Isn't it beautiful?" she sighed, and then seemed to remember herself, laughing. "Beg your pardon. I must surely be gettin' a little punchy. I've been here all day."

"Nay. Nay." He chuckled. "How much does it cost?"

"It's dear." She sighed. "Three pounds."

Teddy had exactly three pounds he saved from running errands for Sean. Oh, but tax...

"Actually, it's ten percent off the top. It's on sale right now."

"I'll take it, then."

"Really? Well, I'm sure your auntie will love it. Let me put it in a box for you."

"I'm Teddy by the way. Teddy McKee."

"Gabrielle," she said, placing her slender hand in his.

"Gabrielle," he repeated slowly, holding her hand for a beat. "That's a lovely name."

"Thank you. Not your average Irish girl's name. But then again, I'm not your average Irish girl," she added with a twinkle in her eye.

You're certainly not.

Gabrielle fluttered behind the counter again to retrieve a box. She was so lively and graceful; he could not take his gaze off her. She folded the shawl with great care and laid it in the tissue paper. He handed her his money, and she moved to the cash register to get his change. In minutes the transaction was over, and he stood uncertainly with his box.

"Would you be needing anything else? I don't mean to rush you, but we are about to close for the evenin.'"

"Oh, nay." Teddy stirred himself. "Nay. Have a lovely evening, Gabrielle."

Her warm eyes stayed on his for a second. "Same to you, Teddy."

He waited outside the shop on the sidewalk. After about ten minutes, Gabrielle stepped out with an older woman, who turned to lock the door, eying him.

"Hello, again." He shifted his weight.

"Gabrielle, would you like me to walk you home?" the older lady said pointedly.

"Nay, Mrs. Connelly, you don't have to trouble yourself. I'll be fine." Gabrielle turned to Teddy. "You were waitin' for me?"

He nodded. "I wanted to give ya this." He handed her the box.

She looked him in the eye, studying his face in the streetlight. "The shawl? For your auntie?"

He looked at his feet for a second. "It wasn't really for me auntie."

"Nay?" She ran her hand across the lid of the box longingly, but then held it out. "I'm sorry, I can't take it. We don't even know each other."

"I know your name is Gabrielle," Teddy argued. He screwed up his courage. "And...that I'd like the pleasure of taking ya out sometime." The words came out in a rush.

"Teddy, ya don't have to buy me things in order to ask me out."

"I know. I know. But pretty girls should have pretty things. And I want ya to have it, please."

"I don't know." She hesitated.

"How 'bout I come over tomorrow morning, and you'll favor me with a walk," he said, changing the subject. "I'll show you some things. You bein' new in town and all."

"Oh, I can't possibly tomorrow. I have church. It's Sunday."

"Oh, aye, I forgot," he lied. "Well, I'll meet ya at church then. Which one would you be attending?"

"St. Finnabar South."

"Great. I'll meet you at..." he took a stab in the dark, "...nine, then?"

"Nine-thirty."

"Oh, right. Right. It's the other church that'll be startin' at nine. Nine-thirty. I'll be there with bells on."

"Okay." Her voice wavered.

He stepped off the curb and ambled across the street. Glancing back, he saw her remove the shawl from the box and place it around her shoulders. She strolled down the sidewalk toward her home.

SEAN SAT ON HIS BIKE, backward, making out with a waitress from the bar. He raised his eyes when he heard the jingle of the shop bells across the street. Without breaking his lip-lock, he observed Teddy handing the girl a package then heading back across the street in his direction. Sean pulled back but continued to watch as the girl put a shawl around her attractive shoulders. "Why, you lil' drubber," he said in surprise as Teddy waltzed up.

His eyes burned brightly in the light from the pub. "I've got a date tomorrow."

The waitress hopped off Sean's bike and blew him a kiss as she headed inside. "See ya, darlin'."

"Well, Jesusmaryandjoseph!" Sean quipped with feigned enthusiasm when she was out of hearing. "Let me buy you a pint." He put his arm around Teddy's shoulder, but cast an eye back at Gabrielle's shapely figure, silhouetted in a streetlight. He didn't know what it was about the girl. She was different somehow. He would discover for himself what that difference was.

CHAPTER THREE

Nerves forced Teddy to get to the church ten minutes early. When Gabrielle finally came into view, after climbing the sloped parking lot with her parents, Teddy stood at the bottom of the stairs waiting for her. He swept the cap from his head and nodded at them, extending a bumbling hand to Gabrielle's father.

"Glad to make your acquaintance, sir," he said, his voice strained, but he gave her father a hearty handshake. "Mrs. Quinn." He nodded, taking her dainty hand in his large one. Mrs. Quinn was a taller, statelier version of Gabrielle, with the same flowing dark hair and eyes, and graceful bearing. A tortoise shell comb decorated her hair with a short, black veil flowing behind it. She smiled, nodding at him, even though it was abundantly clear that she didn't understand a word he was saying. Though her father was shorter and balding with a bushy mustache, his conservative banker's suit reminded Teddy at once of his own father. His palms began to sweat. He stole a furtive glance at Gabrielle.

"Ted, I presume? Gabrielle told us she met you yesterday at Mrs. Connelly's shop. Are you a churchgoin' boy, Ted?"

He peered into Mr. Quinn's keen eyes. Gabrielle's father seemed to be gauging him, reading his face. Teddy dropped his head a second and made a decision. He looked the man squarely in the eye. "I'm afraid I can't say that I am, sir. Me father never took me. I went with me auntie a time or two, though," he added in a rush. "And it was surely enjoyable."

"Good, good," Mr. Quinn said, chuckling and thumping Teddy on the back as he turned to climb the stairs into the church. "We'll make a churchgoer out of you yet, son."

Teddy was pleased to be accepted and stood tall next to Mr. Quinn in their pew. Gabrielle's father did not join the majority of men in the back of the church, choosing instead to stand at his beautiful wife's side. From time to time, Teddy shot Gabrielle a secretive glance down the row, where she stood beyond her mother. His heart raced when she caught his eye and smiled, and he quickly looked away, heat rising in his face.

Gabrielle slipped her arm through her father's on the way out of church, and Teddy was surprised when Mrs. Quinn's arm slid beneath his. He looked at her, and she smiled easily, giving his arm a squeeze. He liked her on the spot, though they had not exchanged a word. When they reached the bottom of the steps, he turned back and retrieved a package he'd hidden in the recess where the church wall met the steps. He handed Mrs. Quinn the beautiful bouquet of daisies and pink and purple carnations with a grin. Her face lit up, and she exclaimed in Spanish, breathing in the flowers' sweet fragrance.

Mr. Quinn raised a brow. "Well, now. Would you be stealin' my best gal, Teddy McKee?"

Teddy was startled, and shook his head, about to deny the charge vehemently, when he caught the teasing twinkle in the banker's eyes. He chuckled. "Nay, sir. Not at all."

Mr. Quinn spoke a few words in Spanish to his wife, smoothly transitioning from one language to the other. He held a hand out to her, and she took it, moving to his side. They both looked at Teddy, appraising him. "*Si, si.*" She took her husband's arm. Gabrielle moved to his side and peered up at her father.

Quinn waited a heartbeat before saying, "We-e-e-ll, don't you two have some place to go?"

Gabrielle beamed and dashed forward to give him a peck on the cheek before taking Teddy's arm. As they turned to walk off, he called after them in a stern voice. "Take care of her." His message was clear, though he offered Ted a final smile.

"Yes, sir. I will," he returned solemnly, and then they were off.

They spent several hours strolling through the town, Teddy keeping up a running commentary on each location they passed. "...and that there is Hurley's Pub. It's a fine lil' place...sometimes they have dancing...and this is Mrs. Connelly's dress shop...oh." He chuckled. "Of course, you know that."

Gabrielle squeezed his arm. The way Teddy gazed at her made her feel like a princess. Stealing a glance at him she noted his short, soft, brown hair, the handsome, if somewhat plain lines of his face, and his muscular build. *He has the sweetest lopsided grin,* she mused. He had a definite charm, stemming from his complete lack of self-awareness. His actions came without pretense, or even forethought, rather they simply stemmed from the depths of his genuine emotions.

Later, when he walked her home, she let him steal a kiss. He controlled his passion, kissing her instead with tenderness. He was a good kisser, and a happiness welled up inside of her that she had never felt in the past. Before parting they made plans to meet the following day.

THE NEXT DAY GABRIELLE left the dress shop with a package in her arms containing a dress her mother had ordered. As the door closed behind her, she noticed the boy across the street on the motorcycle. For a change, he was alone, no girl draped ceremoniously across his lap. Catching her eye, he revved his motor. She turned, laughing. *Does that really work on any girl?* But at the same time, her heartbeat quickened. When she was halfway down the street, she heard his bike zip along to her side. She continued on, pretending not to notice him. He walked his bike along the road next to her until she could no longer ignore him. She stopped and turned to look at him, a hand on her hip.

He gave her an easy grin. "How 'bout a ride?"

Gabrielle frowned at him. "Aren't ya Teddy's friend?"

"That I am," Sean said, completely without remorse. "And you are, too, aren't ya?" His tone was suggestive, and her face warmed. His voice, for a minute, had a strange edge to it; but then he suddenly lightened his tenor. "It might be good for us to get to know one another. Come on." He patted the seat behind him.

Gabrielle hesitated. "Oh, but I have this," she finally said, indicating her package, fumbling for an excuse.

"No problem, love." He held out his hand for the package, and again she hesitated. "I'm not gonna steal it," he insisted.

She relinquished the package, and he strapped it onto the back of the bike with some elasticized cords. He turned and held his hand out to her without a word, looking unreservedly into her eyes.

She stared at him. Her composure abandoned her. His sexy green eyes pulled her in, and she placed a hand in his. It was completely beyond her control to do otherwise. He helped her onto the seat.

"Hang on," he said over his shoulder. She hesitated but was forced to slip her hands around his waist, gliding along the smoothness of the supple leather jacket he wore. They took off with a jerk, and she tightened her hold. "Where'd ya live?" he yelled over the rumble of the engine.

"Oh, you can't take me home!" she cried in alarm. Her mother would kill her if she knew she was on a motorcycle.

"Okay, then." Sean's voice held an air of satisfaction, and he veered off on a road that would take them out of town.

They flew through the countryside. She was exhilarated by the wind whipping her hair and the heat and vibration of the powerful machine between her legs. She laughed, feeling free, and all at once the smell of his leather jacket became heady. The heat of his body as it radiated out from him, separated as they were by only three layers of fabric, both soothed her and made her nervous. She found her hands slowly traveling from his waist and over his broad chest. She examined his expansive muscles, and her arms tightened of their own accord, pulling her closer to him. *My God, he is gorgeous!*

He accelerated, and the wind tore at her hair, beating it back into her face. She was afraid to let go in order to push it away, so she instinctively ducked her head behind his back, laying a cheek on the cool leather. The audacity of the move suddenly struck her, but she didn't change positions; it felt too good.

Sean had been watching her face in the rearview mirrors. The wind sent her long, curly, black hair flying behind her. Her eyes were bright with pleasure, and she laughed out loud. Her hands ran over his chest, and his desire increased. Reveling in the way she laid her cheek on his back, he placed his hand on her leg and pushed her skirt up, rubbing his hand along the back of the thigh. She tensed and jerked her leg, every muscle suddenly rigid. He moved his hand back to the handlebar, confused.

Finally Sean slowed the bike and steered it off the road, bumping over the uneven ground, alongside a creek. He stopped by a tree and shut the engine off, dismounting. He turned to help her off but she already stood on the opposite side, wringing her hands. He was bewildered by her behavior. This was generally the time the chosen girl of the afternoon would strip to her skivvies, and they would do it in the grass, or if she was really desperate for him, up against the tree.

"I need to be getting home now," she said without looking at him.

His mouth hung open until it was able to form the word he wanted, "Why?"

"My mom doesn't know where I am," she said quickly. "She'll be worried."

Well, that makes sense. He gazed at her a moment longer then moved around the front of the bike to touch her arm. "Are you sure?"

She backed away from him, and he could see that she was trembling. Baffled, he turned and got back on the bike.

On the way home she kept her hands, noncommittally, on his shoulders, keeping a wide distance between them. When he came within a few blocks of her home, she screamed, "Pull over. Pull over." He did as he was bid, and she practically flew off the bike. He loosened the ties on her package and handed it to her, slightly dented where the cords had crossed it and crushed the lightweight cardboard. She stared at it a moment, probably wondering what she would tell her mother about the damage. "Th-th-thank you." Again, she refused to look him in the eye. "It was a lovely ride." With that, she was off up the street. He sat dumbfounded, staring after her. He didn't understand her, and for the life of him, he didn't know why that mattered to him.

TEDDY ARRIVED THE FOLLOWING Sunday for dinner at the Quinns', uncomfortable in the coat and tie he wore. He dropped his fork twice.

"So, young Ted, Gabrielle tells us you do woodwork."

Teddy swallowed his food hastily so that he could answer. "Aye, I do, sir."

"That's a fine trade. Did Gabby tell you I dabble in woodworking myself, in my free time? Nothing like you can do, I'm sure. But I rather enjoy it." He sighed. "I tell you, son, I envy you. Don't get me wrong, being a banker is perfectly agreeable. We have a nice house..." He gestured around the room. "I'm able to keep Gabrielle here, and the missus, in fancy clothes, and believe me, that's quite a feat." He chuckled.

"Oh, Da." Gabrielle laughed and swatted her father's arm with her napkin.

"Hey, hey. It's true. Sure as that pretty shawl around your shoulders." She blushed, and Teddy squirmed. Mr. Quinn didn't seem to notice and continued speaking. "But truly, it must be a blessing to work with wood all day. The feel of the smooth surface after you sand it...the smell of the sawdust..." He pretended to take a deep breath. "Ahh. And the satisfaction you get out of creating a well-crafted piece of furniture. Aye, I envy you."

Teddy marveled at his insight. "Aye, 'tis a good line of work, to be sure."

Although the conversation was pleasant, Teddy was relieved when they finally excused themselves from the table and headed outside to sit on the porch swing. The night was mild, and he enjoyed Gabrielle's closeness. He put an arm across her shoulders, and she leaned in, resting her head on his chest from time to time. They talked quietly and laughed, comfortable in each other's presence.

Gabrielle studied Teddy as he talked. He was, really, quite handsome, with beautiful hair that she would love to run her fingers through. He had an honest, strong face, and kind brown eyes that softened when he looked at her. With Teddy she felt secure, and, as her father's job had moved them often when she was younger, security was something she craved.

When the family waved goodbye from the front steps at the end of the evening, Gabrielle's mother spoke to her in Spanish, "Now that one, Gabby, is a fine boy. He would make somebody an excellent husband," she added pointedly, eyebrows raised. She turned to head into the house. Her father nodded his agreement and followed after his wife. She breathed in the night air, which had turned a little cooler, content, wrapping her shawl more tightly around herself and humming a happy tune.

CHAPTER FOUR

When Teddy arrived the next Saturday night to pick up Gabrielle for their date, he was nearly bowled over by a rushing Mr. Quinn as he was leaving the house. He seemed unusually flustered and carried a small suitcase that had clothing sticking out of it in places.

"Oh, Teddy. I'm sorry. Gabrielle asked me to contact you, and it completely slipped my mind. She's in the hospital. She's quite sick, the poor angel...something she contracted in Spain before we left, a serious strain of influenza. I'm going there now."

Teddy's heartbeat accelerated. "May I go with you?"

"Of course, of course."

When they entered the hospital room, Mrs. Quinn was draped over a small couch in the room, apparently exhausted from watching over her daughter. Teddy rushed to Gabrielle's bedside. She had on a white nightgown with an elastic neckline. Her hair was splashed across the pillow, and her usually bronzed skin was drained, almost making her melt into her sheets. Her brow beaded with sweat, and strands of hair stuck to the sides of her face. His stomach tightened. He was rarely sick, and his Passmore cousins were also of sturdy stock, so he had seldom seen someone who was ill. Her hand was outside the covers. He reached out and brushed his fingers across it. Gabrielle's father gave out a cry of shock. He was speaking his wife's name and shaking her but she was not responding.

Teddy dashed out into the hall and grabbed a passing nurse.

"Young man!" she snapped.

"She needs you," was all that he could muster. He led her into the room by the elbow, where the nurse rushed to Mrs. Quinn's side. After examining her she stated, "It's likely your wife is suffering from the same strain of influenza your daughter has. We'll need to get her into a bed and have a doctor examine her. But I'm short of help. I have a room open, but I'll need some-one to assist me with getting her onto a stretcher."

Teddy crossed in front of the nurse, bent and lifted the patient. Her height made it a little awkward for him, but she was light.

"Right this way."

After she was settled into a bed, Teddy excused himself and returned to Gabrielle's side. He sat still for hours, barely daring to touch her hand. Occa-sionally, he would see a nurse hurry by in the hallway, but they were left alone. Toward two o'clock in the morning, Gabby became restless. She moaned and shook her head from side to side. He found the nurse, and was told someone would be with them as soon as possible. He returned to the room, standing by the bed, unsure of what to do. After some time had passed without a sign of any help coming, he stole into the bathroom and got a washcloth wet with cold water. He began to bathe her face, and eventually she settled back into a more peaceful sleep, much to his relief. He stayed by her bedside all night long, continuing to care for her. Finally, around dawn, the nurse came back to check on them.

"The fever seems to have broken," the nurse said, sounding pleasantly surprised. "Whatever you've been doing to take care of her seems to have worked," she added, smiling at him.

"Teddy?" Gabrielle mumbled weakly from behind her.

"Aye. I'm here." He flew to her side, his whole body sighing. "How are ya feelin'?"

"Weak as a kitten," she mumbled, closing her eyes.

"You rest then." He patted her hand.

Her eyes flicked open. "How long have you been here?"

"Oh, I don't know. Awhile, I guess." He shrugged.

"He's been here all night," the nurse commented with a smile.

"You have?"

Teddy shifted his weight. "Aye. I suppose so."

"That's nice," Gabby said, sighing and closing her eyes again. She drifted off to a comfortable sleep, a smile on her face.

SEAN HENNESSEY HAD edges, edges he kept well hidden. His mother had left his father, sister, and him when he had been only four, because of his father's drinking, and because she was what his grandma always referred to as "a bit of a free spirit." His father was a cruel man, who had taken great delight in ridiculing him and his older sister, Keira. They were the only bits of his wife he'd had left to torture. He'd had no qualms about smacking Sean around if he dared to talk back and had bloodied his lip and blackened his eye on more than one occasion. But it was not that; rather it had been the constant belittling and demeaning that had broken him down.

When he was thirteen, he had run off to live with his sister, who had moved out several years before, but the damage had already been done; a once-vibrant young boy'd had his heart hollowed out and filled with molten lead.

But from the day he had first laid eyes on Gabrielle Quinn, something had begun to stir inside of him, something that made him quite uncomfortable. Desire. Not the Friday night, had-a-few-and-found-a-willing-barmaid kind of desire, but something strong and unnerving.

Now, as he finished a transaction with a customer in the alleyway behind Hurley's, he heard her familiar laughter. Stopping at the sound, in the middle of thumbing through his bills, he stuck his head around the corner of the brick building, searching the sunny spot where the yawning mouth of the alley opened to the street.

They stepped off the curb. Gabby had her arm through Teddy's, and he was talking to her animatedly. She wore a dress, as she always did, something else that set her apart from the other girls in town, and a breeze from the alley made it flutter and rise several inches above her knees before she pushed it down. The length of leg he glimpsed there made his mouth run dry.

"Who's that?" the stiff he was with asked.

"What? Huh? Oh, nobody. Nobody. Go on now."

"But you 'aven't counted me money yet."

"I trust ya," Sean said quickly, nudging the man with his elbow as he pocketed the wad. "Get going."

The customer needed no further urging and took off down the narrower, darker end of the alleyway, away from Hurley's.

Sean trotted along the lane in the opposite direction, sticking close to the edge of the building. His boots made scratchy noises as he kicked the loose gravel and broken glass that always ended up on the edge of the alleys. He slowed when he neared the street, not wanting the noise to attract anyone's attention. Stepping out into the bright sunlight he squinted, throwing a hand up to shade his eyes. Teddy and Gabrielle were about a block away, still on his side of the street. He increased his speed.

Now his boots made clomping noises as he stomped across the wooden floor in front of Hurley's, part of the half porch, half covered walkway that spanned the front of the building and a few of the attached establishments to the north. He was not worried about being detected anymore as people swarmed the sidewalks tonight, it being a mild evening. He dodged in between people, every once in awhile catching someone's eye and giving a nod and a smile, but for the most part his eyes were riveted on Gabrielle's back. If he would lose sight of Gabby when someone cut in front of him, he would immediately seek her out when the path became clear.

He was so focused on her that he made the mistake of stepping out in front of a car that was turning onto the street he was about to cross. The car honked, and he had to do a little dance to get out of the way, slapping the side and raising his hand, acknowledging his mistake.

Gabrielle turned her head casually at the honk. He saw it in slow motion. She was in mid-sentence, her mouth open. She caught his eye. Without his permission to do so, his heart raced. She blinked, and it seemed everything was frozen for a beat. Then it returned to normal speed, her mouth moved as she finished what she was saying, and her head whirled back, turning to Teddy again. His heart sank, but the next second he bolstered it with unreasonable hope. Hadn't there been a spark of somethin' in her eyes?

He crossed the street, hoping his following would appear less obvious from the opposite side. He kept his eyes forward for the most part, but would occasionally swing them sideways to observe the couple. He would lose them at times and have to stop to scan the sidewalk, catching their happy reflection in some shop window as they passed, oblivious to everything other than each other.

He cursed himself for caring. Told himself to stop, to turn around, go back to the pub. But his feet and a burning inside propelled him forward.

They came to the end of the sidewalk at the same time, but, where Sean's was a dead end, Gabby and Teddy were able to turn on a side street and head toward the Quinns' home. He swallowed, watching as the couple grew smaller and smaller, dust rising from their feet as they continued along the road. When they climbed the steps of Gabby's front porch he turned away.

Sean jabbed his hands into his pockets and walked back the way he came at a much slower pace. His head was bent, and he acknowledged no one, only plodded on. His temples began to throb. He realized his jaw was tight and consciously relaxed it. Gabrielle seemed to have forgotten their bike ride. But he couldn't stop thinking about her. Like a mosquito's bite, she had gotten under his skin, and no matter how hard he tried not to scratch, the bite was broken open over and over again.

Why? Women were usually his strong suit. When he had come of age, women had begun to throw themselves at him. At only fourteen he had lost his virginity to an older woman. He had given her back her youth; she had given him the sense of being loved that he'd never felt before. But he was nothing if not smart, and he soon understood the woman did not really love him; she merely desired him. That had hurt him at first. But ever ready to make the most out of a bad situation, he had derived pleasure in his power over her. She'd needed him desperately, which had given him the upper hand, and he had kept it that way.

Gabrielle Quinn, however, refused to fit into his mold, and this perplexed and infuriated him. She was poles apart from any other girl he had ever met and thus a complete mystery to him.

By the time he crossed the street and returned to Hurley's, he had decided that it would be best to bury himself in work to distract his mind from thoughts of her. He entered the pub and found an empty stool at the far corner of the bar. He didn't feel like company tonight, didn't think he could muster up small talk with the headache that had grown behind his eyes. He lifted his head after a bit to find a pint of ale frothing onto a napkin in front of him and was surprised he had not noticed the barkeeper placing it there. He searched for the bartender to thank him, but he was already at the other end of the bar. He raised his glass and let the coolness of the ale soothe as it slid down his throat. Exhaling loudly, he relaxed his shoulders. His mind turned to Teddy.

Sean had discovered over the years he was actually quite fond of Teddy. Their hatred for their respective fathers was a common bond, and he would occasionally enlist Teddy to make his deliveries, and then share a pint when the job was done. Lately he missed Teddy's company on the evenings when his errand boy was off with Gabrielle. He found himself, most illogically, feeling betrayed by his friend. He would tell himself, *You're the bastard that tried to take away his girl.* But it didn't make a difference. His heart, once cracked open, was a confused place.

"I'M SORRY I'M LATE, Gabby," Teddy said one evening. "I had to make some deliveries for Seanie." She stood by the sink, finishing some dishes for her mother. She seemed to bristle at the mention of Sean's name.

"What is it that ya deliver for Sean?" she asked with a hint of irritation.

"Oh, I don't know. Packages."

"Well, obviously, Teddy. But what is it that is *in* the packages?"

"I don't know. Stuff for his clients, I guess. Stuff he's selling."

"Umm-hum," Gabrielle responded skeptically, but Teddy changed the subject by slipping his arms around her waist and whispering in her ear.

"Do you know what Friday is?"

"No. What is Friday?" she returned, sounding curious.

"It's our one year anniversary. Don't tell me you didn't remember."

"Oh, of course I remembered." She turned around to give him a kiss.

"Well, I want to take you out somewhere special to celebrate, all right?"

ON THE APPOINTED NIGHT, Gabrielle was to meet Teddy at the pub across from the dress shop after she got off work. The pub was celebrating its thirtieth anniversary and had hired a band and pulled back tables to allow for a dance floor for the evening. He fidgeted impatiently, bursting at the seams to see Gabrielle.

"Say, what's with you tonight, Teddy?" Sean asked.

He had borrowed a suit coat, which was slightly too big for him, and had his hair slicked back.

"Ya promise not to tell?" Teddy asked, but didn't wait for an answer. "I'm gonna propose to Gabrielle t'night. I already asked her father earlier, and he gave me his blessin'." He beamed at Sean.

"Ah." Sean studied his glass for a second. "Well, this calls for a drink. Barkeep, pour me buddy here a good, stout ale." When Teddy turned back he was swirling a glass, which he handed to him. "To Gabrielle." Sean raised his glass.

"To Gabrielle," he said tenderly, drinking.

Sean lifted his hand. "Get us another, Sam."

Gabrielle arrived about an hour later. She had changed into a stunning red dress she'd purchased at the shop for the occasion. Her shoulders were bare, showing off her glowing skin, and the bodice was cut lower than what she normally wore, accentuating her figure. The fabric was gathered across her flat stomach and wound tightly around her hips. Mrs. Connelly and another woman who worked at the shop had helped her to twist her hair into an ornate clip, and wispy tendrils hung about her face.

"Hey, baby. You look great." Teddy whistled appreciatively. The band started a new song. "Let's dance." He took her hand, but when he stood, he began to sway. "Whoa!" He fell into his seat, one hand going back to grasp the edge of the bar. He cleared his throat then, chuckled. "I guess the drinks really hit me funny tonight." When she looked at him with concern, he added, "I'll be all right." He shook his head to clear it. "You dance with her, Seanie. A pretty gal like that needs someone to dance with." His words were slurred, and he seemed to have trouble focusing. She was about to protest, but Teddy interrupted her. "No, go on, honey. I want you to have a good time tonight. I'll get some fresh air, and that'll sober me." He stumbled toward the door as Sean stepped into her path.

"What do you say, Gabby?"

She gazed into his eyes and saw something she didn't expect, desperation. It distracted her from her worry over Teddy's state for a beat, and that was all it took. Before she could say a word, Sean took her hand and led her out onto the small dance floor. He stood for a moment gazing at her with those penetrating eyes, and she was spellbound. What was he up to? Then, ever so slowly, he slid his hand around her waist. They stood transfixed for a moment.

All at once, he pulled her to him. Their faces were inches apart. His hand was held firmly on the middle of her lower back. She felt controlled by him, and the feeling was magnetic. She was no longer thinking about Teddy. No longer worried about his well being.

They swayed together, never taking their eyes off each other. Gabrielle's heart raced, and although they were in a crowded place, she began to feel a sense of panic. He moved his hips for a moment in a way that made her weak. Then he bent in, one painful fraction at a time, until his lips claimed hers. The whole room fell away, and all that remained was the two of them.

Passion surged through every part of her. Helpless, she gave into the feeling, her mouth, disconnected from the shouted warnings of her brain, sought his with equal hunger. He maneuvered her over to the wall and pressed her against it with his lower body. His hands were on the bare skin of her shoulders then sliding under the fabric. His mouth and tongue were on her neck. She could barely breathe.

She opened her eyes. They were in a dark corner of the pub. People carried on raucously around them. No one seemed to notice them. His hands were on her breasts now, and he brought his mouth to her ear. "Gabby...let me take you home," he said huskily, his warm, moist breath so close it seemed to come from inside her. She moaned and found his lips again. Her body was pressing against him; she wanted him so badly it ached.

"I..." Her breath was coming in pants now. "I..."

"Yes?" His voice begged her.

"I..." She was lost, but her mind was calling her back. "I...no...this is wrong." she at last blurted out.

"Oh, no, baby. This is *so* right." He leaned against her harder forbidding her to escape.

"Sean, stop!" she cried out, trying to push him away. She had regained her clarity, and with it, a need for distance.

"Oh, come on." The pleading tone in his voice was mixed with irritation. He tried to kiss her again.

"Stop!" she said loudly enough that some heads at nearby tables began to turn. He would not let her go. "Sean!" Desperate, she raised her hand and struck him across the face; the sound of it seemed to take the noise out of the room. He grabbed her arm, squeezing it painfully. She let out a small gasp of fear.

The violence of the slap made his hair fall into his face, and he shook it out of his eyes. She could feel the stares of other patrons. He gave her a little push into the wall, but released her, storming out the back door.

Eyebrows were raised at her in mute accusation. All the faces said the same thing. This was Seanie's place. She straightened her dress and pushed back the hair that had fallen loose from her clip. With as much dignity as she could muster, she forced herself to put one foot in front of the other and walk toward the front door. She blinked back the tears that stung her eyes.

Once on the street, Gabrielle found Teddy and told him she wasn't feeling well, and she had to go home. After some time she managed to convince him to let her walk home alone. She hustled down the street, glad she no longer had to face Teddy's innocent face.

SEAN BURST OUT INTO the alleyway and turned to bang his fist against the brick wall. "Dammit!" he screamed. He shook his hand. "Dammit! That hurt." He laughed with a wild desperation at himself. *Yeah, you idiot. Pounding your fist into a solid object hurts.* He shook his head then clasped his hands behind his head, throwing it back as he paced around in a tight circle. He came to a stop in front of the wall again and slowly placed his clenched fist on the bricks. He lowered his forehead against the coolness he found there, framed in the blaring light of the caged bulb above the door.

Then he heard her voice. He stepped around the corner and saw the two of them in the streetlight. Gabby squeezed Teddy's arm, and then she walked off, the sound of her heel clicks echoing back to him through the still night air. When she had gone out of sight beyond the neighboring building, he turned to look at Teddy, whose hopes for what could have been the happiest day of his life lay dashed upon the sidewalk. He stared after her a few seconds then turned and reentered the pub, still having trouble walking.

Sean hustled to the end of the alleyway. He stepped out and heard again the faint sound of Gabrielle's footsteps in the distance. He hurried after her.

Gabrielle walked in a daze. Her aimless wandering led her to the foot of the steps of St. Finnabar. She stopped. Sean halted as well, diving into the protective shadow of a storefront, trying to still his breathing so she wouldn't detect him. Slowly she climbed the few steps and entered the building.

Sean rushed ahead, closing the gap between them. He opened the door a crack and slid in, grateful the ancient door didn't creak loudly on its hinges. He spied on her from the foyer of the church.

She drifted along the main aisle. A huge cross was elevated behind the altar. The blue-and-purple stained-glass windows behind it shone despite the dark outdoors, illuminated somehow from the other side.

Sean watched her from his hiding place; she had taken a seat and was totally still. He wondered for a minute what she must be thinking. Then he saw her shoulders begin to shake, sobs escaped from her and echoed hellishly around the church. His heart gripped him in a way he would not have thought possible.

He had rarely seen a woman cry. His sister had become hardened by his father's cruelty at a very young age. Any women whose heart he had broken in the past, he had never felt sorry for. They should have known what they were getting into; he had never made false promises. Besides, he figured the world owed him, and if a few hearts got broken in the process, so be it. Guilt was not an emotion he possessed.

Now, though, as he watched Gabrielle being torn apart by her own guilt, he felt ...something. He took a step toward her then stopped. He wanted to go to Gabby, to swoop her up in his arms, to be whatever it was she wanted him to be. But he knew he didn't have the power to love her as Teddy did; whatever capacity for love he'd had once, had long ago evaporated, like the holy water missing from the holder in the entryway. He squeezed his eyes shut, unable to bear the sight of her sorrow any longer, and unconsciously his hand went over his heart. It burned inside him, threatening for an instant to consume him. At that moment, he knew he had to leave her alone; he was no good for her. He could not give her what he himself no longer possessed. With one last, longing look, he turned on his heel and strode out the door, letting it slam closed behind him, just as he was, once again, slamming the door of his fractured heart shut.

Gabrielle jumped at the sound of the door closing and stabbed at the tears on her face, trying to calm her breathing. She turned to see who was there, but found the church empty.

The following week, Teddy again suggested meeting in the pub before heading out to dinner.

"Will Sean be there?" she asked tentatively.

"Nay, I'm sorry, honey. He said he was going to be away on business for awhile now."

Luckily, Teddy didn't sense her relief.

CHAPTER FIVE

Gabrielle was stunned when she entered the pub on Saturday to find Sean sitting on the stool next to Teddy. She almost turned around and walked out, but Teddy spotted her and waved her over. She wore the same red dress as the week before, but this time, the black shawl Teddy had given her hung loosely from her shoulders. As she approached, the two men gazed at her. Teddy's face was as open and trusting as always. She glanced at Sean. When his eyes first fell on her they widened. He sat straighter, his mouth hanging open a second. Then his whole face tightened, starting at the jaw and moving to his eyes.

She pulled the shawl closer, feeling suddenly exposed. Teddy kissed her, and she kissed him with more ardor than she would have normally displayed in public.

Teddy gave her that lopsided grin of his. "Wow!"

Gabrielle turned to Sean with more coolness than she felt inside. "I thought you were to be out of town tonight."

"My plans changed," Sean said, an edge to his voice.

Teddy leaned in. "How 'bout a dance before we get going?"

"I'd be delighted," she said, slipping her arm through his, not taking her eyes from Sean's. She turned after a second or two and smiled sweetly at Teddy as he led her onto the dance floor. She glanced back at Sean over her shoulder. He was watching them, but after a minute he turned and spoke to the bartender.

Strangely enough, what grace Teddy lacked whenever he walked, was there in abundance when he danced. Soon people had stopped to watch. Gabby was astounded by what a good dancer Teddy was. She released the tension that was like a vise around her chest. She laughed as Teddy spun her around, letting the lightness she felt when she was with him make her giddy.

His face was glowing as he gazed at her, and she wrapped his love around her like a favorite jacket, keeping her safe from the heat that Sean's presence inspired. She looked at him now over Teddy's shoulder. He was talking with a vivacious blonde, but he still kept his eye on them.

The song ended, and Teddy said breathlessly, "I'm dyin' of thirst. Wanna get a quick drink before we go?"

"Sure." She grinned. He drew a seat out for her at a nearby table then sauntered up to the bar.

As he was waiting for his drinks, the blonde Sean had been talking to approached him. To Gabby's shock, Teddy bent to kiss her. The woman pulled him in tightly, running long fingernails through his hair, her lips ardent on his. Gabrielle watched in disbelief, feeling her face, which was already flushed from dancing, becoming hot. As she stood, her eyes lighted on Sean. He was watching her with bemused delight. *He* had put the girl up to this. Feeling humiliated and virtually exploding with anger, she snatched her shawl and flew across the room and out the front door.

She could hear Teddy calling behind her, but her only thought was of escape. She rushed out into the street but then stopped in the middle of the road as if the emotion propelling her there had suddenly lost steam. She closed her eyes, but all she could see was Sean's taunting face. Fists clenched by her sides, she wanted desperately to scream, but she refused to give him the satisfaction. Teddy rushed out behind her.

"Gabby, honey. It was only a birthday kiss, I swear. You don't think I would—"

"Nay, Teddy, I don't," she said with a sigh, releasing, in part, her rage.

He smiled, and his shoulders relaxed. He steered her onto the safety of the sidewalk. "Come on, honey. Let's take a walk." They strolled silently for a time, leaving the pub and its noise behind them as they headed down the deserted street.

Finally, Teddy seemed to find his voice. "Gabby, I want you to know that I love you."

Gabby was struck with remorse. "I love you, too. It was just seeing that girl all over you..."

"Aye. I don't know what got into Deidre. Maybe she had too much to drink."

"It doesn't matter. I know it wasn't your fault."

He stopped and took her in his arms under a streetlight and kissed her. "I know I'm not a perfect man," he said earnestly. "But since you've come into my life..." His voice broke for a second, then he regained control. "I feel like I'm no longer a lost cause. With you, I have been found at last. I don't know what I'd do without you. I know this may not be the right time, but this is the right place." And with that, he knelt on the sidewalk on one knee. They had stopped in front of St. Finnabar's. "Gabby, would you do me the great honor..." He fished a ring box out of his pocket. "...of becoming my wife?" He held the box up to her, his hands shaking slightly. She was stunned. "You don't have to answer right now," he said hurriedly. "But I want you to know, I did ask your father's permission, and he said..."

She no longer heard him, her mind running. Once she took those vows, she could put all this nonsense with Sean behind her once and for all, and, in that moment, that was her fondest wish. Besides, she loved Teddy. He made her feel happy, secure, safe. And Teddy needed her. "Aye, Teddy," she said quietly, tears running down her face. "I want nothing more than to marry you."

GABRIELLE STOOD ON her front porch in a beam of moonlight. Teddy waved a final goodbye and turned the corner. She sighed happily, leaning against a post, and stretched her left hand out in front of her to admire her new engagement ring. The light danced off the tiny gem.

A heavy noise behind her made her jump. She whirled around. A dark shape crouched on the top porch rail then leapt lightly to the floor. The figure stepped toward her, and she backed against the porch rails, bringing her arms up in a defensive position. Light from inside the house illuminated Sean's face. She was surprised by the tortured expression he wore.

"So that is all you see Teddy as, a lost cause?" Tears glittered in his fierce eyes. He paced back and forth in the tight space like a caged panther. "Someone you have to save?"

"No, of course not."

"Of *course* not," he mocked. "Ach." He turned from her to lean heavily on the porch rail, his arms spread wide. Hanging his head for a moment, he stilled himself. He sighed and asked quietly without moving, "And this is what you want?"

Gabrielle couldn't find her voice.

"Woman!" he yelled, still not looking at her. "Is this what you want?"

"Aye," she squeaked.

Without another word, he catapulted over the porch rail. With a scuffle, his feet landed in the loose rock surrounding the porch, and he ran off, disappearing into the night. She stood stock still for several moments, her heart beating furiously in her chest, and then she fell to her knees, sobbing, not understanding why she was so overwrought. She was glad for the darkness so no one could see her. She drew her knees in to her chest and rocked back and forth while the tears streamed down her face. This was to be the happiest day of her life, and somehow Sean had managed to destroy it like a bully smashing a sandcastle. She looked at her hands, still clutching her knees, and the glint of her engagement ring brought on a new set of sobs.

SEAN RODE THE FREIGHT elevator in the warehouse up to the floor where he made his home. When it came to a stop, he threw open the metal gate with a loud clang and strode into his apartment. Brick walls and long narrow windows enclosed the large room. A blaring light hung the long distance from the ceiling, centered over a small, wooden, kitchen table. One corner of the room was elevated several inches above the rest of the floor to set it off as its own area. Mattresses lay on a black platform, covered in black satin sheets and a burgundy comforter.

Sean crossed purposefully to the kitchen table then stood like he didn't know what he'd come there for. A rectangular, brown paper package sat on the table. Wooden crates were scattered about the room, one open near the table, with its pried-off lid leaning against it. He drew a switch blade from his pocket and opened it with a satisfying metallic *click*. He stuck it into the wood of the table fiercely, the blade vibrating as he let it go. He fingered the brown package, his mind occupied with an internal struggle. In a flash he yanked the knife from the table and buried it in the package, ripping a large hole in it. White powder spilled upon the table like a collapsing snow bank.

In that instance he had decided to break the main rule of drug dealers: never use your own stuff.

CHAPTER SIX

Almost a year had passed since Gabby and Teddy's wedding. That day Sean had donned his tux, played his part as best man, polite, charming, and ever the gentleman. That was, up until the point he was discovered stoned, in a very compromising position with the coat-check girl, on the guest coats. Since then, he'd spent his time trying to avoid the happy couple as much as possible. It had been months since he had seen Teddy, when he finally waltzed into his woodworking shop. Sean gave him one of his now-rare smiles and clasped him in a bear hug, both men thumping the other on the back loudly.

"Hey. Where've ya been, Seanie-boy?"

"Oh, around, around. How are ya? I heard you're runnin' the place now." Sean swept his hand through the sawdust accumulated on the worktable Teddy had been sitting at. He brushed his hands together, knocking the sawdust off in a splintery cloud, then brought them to his face to smell the sweet pine.

"Aye." He stood straighter. "Old Man McKinney finally retired and sold me the place."

"No kiddin'?" He raised his eyebrows. On one end of the table Sean's hand found a small figurine. "You makin' kids' toys now, Teddy?"

"Nay." He hurried over to a shelf and pulled down an ornate carved wooden box. He slid the lid off and inside nested a half-dozen wonderfully wrought statuettes, hand painted and inlaid with some sort of white stone. "It's a nativity set. For Gabby."

Sean reached into the box and drew out a camel. He turned it over in his hand thoughtfully. It was easily the most beautiful thing he had ever seen. Small "gems" bejeweled the saddle and the reins, and the lifelike expression on the camel's face left Sean expecting it to spit into his hand. He knew Gabby would be enchanted. "Boy, I don't know, Teddy," he said slowly. "I think girls kind of expect something big, like jewelry or something, on their first Christmas as a married couple."

Teddy looked crestfallen as he handed him back the piece. He, too, turned the object over in his hand, studying it sadly. "Aye. Maybe so." He shoved the camel into the straw in the box, slid the lid shut, and re-situated it on the shelf.

Sean regretted his words, chastened by the disappointed look on Teddy's face. "Don't get me wrong, these are beautiful and all. They're just not the kind of thing a woman goes ape for."

"Aye. I guess you're right."

"Anyway," he said, changing the subject. "I'm here on business, me friend."

"Business?"

"Aye. My boss, Mr. Bradigan, needs some coffins. Ten actually."

"What? Are you in the mortuary business now?"

Sean studied him. "Aye, something like that. And I need them to have false bottoms."

"False bottoms?"

"Aye. It's...the new style. People like to take stuff with them, ya know," he added with a wink.

Teddy shrugged. "All right."

"YOU'RE QUIET TONIGHT." Gabrielle ruffled Teddy's hair before setting his dinner plate in front of him. He grabbed her hand and kissed it before she headed back to the counter to fill her own plate.

When she returned to the table, she sat and waited expectantly.

He sighed. "I saw Sean today."

"Sean?" she repeated, taken by surprise.

"Aye."

Gabby sawed at her steak. "How was he?" She tried to sound as casual as possible.

He shrugged. "Aw, you know Seanie." He took a drink of his milk and set the glass down. "I was thinking, why don't we have a party before we move?" He had recently inherited a house from his Uncle Phineas. He was slowly making repairs to the unique lighthouse-shaped home and hoped to be finished soon.

"A party? Sure. That would be fun," she answered absentmindedly. She put a hand over her middle. The mention of Sean's name had made her stomach roll.

THE NIGHT OF THE PARTY had come. Gabby rushed around with plates of appetizers as Teddy made sure that everyone had drinks. The doorbell rang. Gabby, who was on her way back into the kitchen, called out, "I'll get it."

She opened the door with a smile ready on her lips to greet her guests. On the doormat stood Sean, dressed in a long-sleeved, button-down black shirt and jeans. For a second, she was caught off guard, but she recovered her equilibrium, swallowing and then saying genuinely, "Sean, it's good to see you."

He stood on the doorstep with a bewildered look for a minute, but then his face broke into a broad grin. "Good to see you, too, Gabrielle," he responded, though perhaps a bit too formally.

She stood aside to let him in. "Welcome to our home."

They stood awkwardly in the hall for a second. She gave him a perfunctory hug. "It's been so long," she said as she pulled away, with more emotion than she would have liked.

"Aye, too long." His voice was neutral. "Nice place," he added without taking his eyes from her.

"Thank you. Teddy and I are happy here." The last came out unexpectedly.

"I'm glad for you," was his flat answer.

"Well, look who's here. Seanie!" Teddy roared as he entered the hallway. He punched Sean in what, she was sure, was supposed to be a gentle manner. Sean rubbed his shoulder. Gabrielle smiled at him apologetically; it was obvious Teddy had already had too much to drink. Married life had kept him out of the pub, for the most part, and his tolerance for alcohol had diminished. She sighed in relief as he took Sean off to introduce him to some of the neighbors.

As Teddy was definitely three sheets to the wind, she had her hands full taking care of her guests. In fact, it had been over an hour since she had seen Sean when she passed the bedroom and heard his voice. She put her hand to the doorknob and was about to turn it when she heard the unmistakable sound of coquettish female laughter. She released the doorknob like it had burned her, remembering the scene in the coatroom on the night of their wedding. She hurried down the hall, her face hot.

SEAN HASTILY CLEANED his mess, slipping the rest of the package into his pocket.

The girl was stoned off her gourd, giggling behind him on the bed. He lay next to her, his hands folded behind his head, staring at the ceiling. She sat up on one elbow.

"Come on, baby." She grabbed his shirt and began to unbutton it. "Let me show you a good time."

He looked at her blankly, his eyes coming in and out of focus, but all he could think of was Gabby. The girl suddenly slumped across his chest, and he pushed her aside.

Turning over, he buried his face in the pillow. Aye. It smelled like roses, like her. She had looked so lovely when she opened the door, even more than the night he had kissed her. And what about that night? She acted as if nothing had ever happened between them, as if she'd forgotten it, as if it meant absolutely nothing to her. *Well, it meant nothing to me, then. She would have been another roll in the hay, nothing more.*

He looked around again. *This is where Teddy makes love to her.* Sean's face screwed up, but then he ran his hand under the sheets longingly, wishing she were there with him. Why was she acting so ambivalent toward him? She made sure to tell him she and Teddy were happy here. She must have intended to anger him. The drugs began to make his skin crawl, and the blood in his veins seared. The more he thought about her distant manner, the angrier he became. *I could have her if I wanted her*. He imagined what it would be like to be with her, her silky hair gliding over his skin, those full lips pressed to his as his tongue explored her mouth... His hazy mind began to formulate a plan.

FORTY-FIVE MINUTES later, Sean entered the living room where Gabby was busy cleaning plates. She couldn't help but notice his shirt was unbuttoned more than when he first arrived, and the neighbor's daughter, who entered behind him, had somehow mussed her hair.

"Seanie, come here," Teddy demanded sociably, patting the couch next to him. "Let's catch up on old times." His speech was slurred, and he didn't seem to notice the inconsistency of his statement.

Sean accommodated him, with a wink to Gabby, sitting by his side. "How 'bouts we catch up on what's been goin' on with each other first? *Then* we'll talk about ol' times, partner."

Teddy laughed. "Sh-shure. Sh-shure. Whatever you say."

Gabby collected the plates, embarrassed, and headed for the kitchen. She had finished washing the last dish and was drying her hands on the towel when Teddy bellowed, "Gabby. Gabby. Come here."

With a what-now feeling, she returned to the living room. Sean had disengaged himself from Teddy and now stood outside on the patio with the neighbor girl, the sliding door open behind him. "Come here, sh-shugar. I haven't s-seen you for awhile." When she got close Teddy grabbed her, knocking her into the coffee table and onto his lap. He kissed her sloppily, running his hand without grace or subtlety up her leg, hiking her dress to her thigh.

"Teddy!" Gabby scolded, prying his fingers from her hem and yanking it down. She stood, wiping the back of a hand across her mouth. "You've had too much to drink."

"Nay. I've had just the right amount. Like freakin' Goldilocks," he said, laughing at his own joke.

Sean had entered behind her. "Gabrielle," he said, rubbing his temples. "I have one hell of a headache. Would ya have any aspirin?"

She tore her eyes from the slouched image of her husband on the couch with a sigh. "Sure, right this way."

She led him through the hallway to a small bathroom and opened the medicine cabinet. Rifling through packets of pills without their boxes, she tried to figure out which was which. Sean was behind her. She heard the click of the lock a second before he slid his hands around her waist. His mouth was on her neck, the sound of his breathing in her ear. His kisses were not the clumsy kisses of a drunk, rather, the expert kisses of a man who'd bedded many women.

"Sean. What are ya doin'?" She wriggled out of his grip, nearly stumbling over the toilet in her effort to get away from him, but righting herself on the edge of the bathtub. She put her hands out in front of her. "Sean," she pleaded.

Guests were right outside the door, not to mention her husband. But she could not deny the physical attraction. She gazed at him now, his thick blond hair was ruffled, but it still managed to be sexy. His smoky, green eyes seemed to be undressing her already. He didn't look at her with the puppy-like adoration that Teddy did, but rather with a raw desire that made her heart race.

He grabbed her hips, and while she protested, the words were hardly audible. He pushed her against the wall opposite the sink. Her body made a loud noise as it hit the wall, and they both stood still, breathing heavily. His lower half pressed against her as they listened for a response from outside the room. Hearing none, he slid a hand behind her hair, lifting it, appearing to test its weight. He brought his lips to hers, kissing deeply.

She could feel the weight of his hard body. She thought about Teddy outside, thought about his sloppy kiss, whiskeyed breath, thick, clumsy hands. Yet in her mind she called out to him. *Teddy, come save me.* A desperation she had never felt before seized her. She had to gain control of her runaway hormones, but even as she wished it, she doubted her fortitude, and nipped at Sean's sensual lips.

He lowered his hand to her breast and caressed her, gazing into her eyes and grinning smugly. That look made her stomach roll. Her hands, which until this point had been unengaged, came to rest on his hips. Voices in her head screamed, *you are a married woman.* But an even louder voice said, *but*

I need this! My God, I'm only human! Her hands slid to his firm ass, and she squeezed it, arching her back in pleasure.

He tugged the cloth away from her breast and closed his teeth around her nipple. This time she couldn't help but moan. Fueled by this, he slid his hand behind her leg along her bare skin and lifted it to wrap around him. He put his other hand on the leg supporting her and found her panties. He grabbed hold of them with both hands, ripping them with unexpected violence. She listened again for a noise outside the bathroom, but she suddenly realized she didn't care anymore; she was too far gone. She ran her hands under his loose shirt, feeling his muscular chest, and he spun her, lifting her at the same time onto the counter. He reached and unzipped his jeans and before she knew it, he was in her, pumping so hard her back hit the faucet, but then he eased her to the edge of the sink until they were finished. Sweat ran down their faces. He pulled away and zipped his jeans with a smirk.

"So you did want me after all. *Gracias, señora.*" He left the bathroom before Gabby even had time to catch her breath.

She turned to look at herself in the mirror, still flushed, and began to shake, sobbing. She never left the bathroom. People knocked on the door every once in a while, but she didn't respond; only sat on the toilet seat, head in hands, weeping. Finally it was quiet. She opened the door to find she was alone. Teddy had slid off the couch, and was lying on the floor, with a stupid grin on his face. "Damn you, Teddy!" she cried, a few final tears sliding out. She stood astride his limp body, her guilt ripping her in two. "Damn you."

CHAPTER SEVEN

Teddy and Gabrielle shared Christmas together in their apartment. They slept in late, exchanging presents the second they woke up, without even getting out of bed. He was surprised by the sweater she knit for him in secret; he hadn't even known she could knit. Gabby loved the delicate bracelet that Teddy had given her, and they sat admiring the way it looked on her tiny wrist.

"There's something else," Teddy said abruptly.

"Oh, nay, Teddy. This is enough."

"I know. I know. This is something small."

"Okay," she said, grinning. He loved how she was like a little girl with her presents.

"I didn't wrap it. I wasn't even sure I was going to give it to you."

"Why?"

"I dunno." He shrugged and handed her the wooden box.

She ran her hand over the beautiful carving, sitting up to study it. "Oh, Teddy!" Tears filled her eyes. "It's beautiful."

"Open it," he said, suddenly excited by her reaction.

Gabby slid the lid back gently and removed the figures one by one, exclaiming over the exquisite details. "Oh, Teddy! I can't believe you made this for me." Her eyes shone. She returned each piece safely to its bed of straw and laid the box carefully on the floor. She turned back to him and smothered him with kisses, pushing him back on the bed and laughing. They made love as the first snowflakes began to fall, blanketing them in for the day.

IN THE DAYS AND WEEKS to follow, even though Sean tried to keep it together, his behavior became more and more erratic and unpredictable. Despite this fact, his business thrived. Unfortunately, it took increased amounts of his own supply to numb him, so the profits were soon spent. He thought that once he had her, she would be out of his system. But quite the opposite was true. His desire for her maddened him.

He began bringing home a different black-haired beauty every night. He would chase them, bed them, then berate them for being easy and kick them out. One evening, when he was flying higher than usual, he even dragged one of the girls from his bed and threw her, naked, into the freight elevator. Cursing, he threw her clothes in with her, in his confusion calling her Gabby. He slammed the gate shut as she begged him to let her get dressed, and pressed the button sending her to the street. From the window he watched the distraught girl hail a cab, rubbing her arms, her breath freezing in the air, but he felt nothing. He paid for that one, though, as the girl's three brothers visited him the next night and beat him to unconsciousness.

One day he chanced to see Gabby through a department store window. He rushed inside, nearly knocking someone else through the revolving door with him, and hiding behind racks and posts. He watched as she held up a baby outfit with a smile. When she stepped out from behind the rack he saw the distinctive rounded shape of her stomach. She was having a baby.

She was having *Teddy's* baby.

He told himself the pregnancy no longer made her attractive to him, but it was a lie. In fact, that night he had dreams of the two of them lying on a blanket in a meadow, he caressing her sizable tummy as she smiled at him. Then the image shifted, and he was holding a baby as they lay on the blanket. He lifted the baby over their heads, and it cooed, the sunlight fanning out behind the small head like a halo. He had never been so happy.

But the dream soon faded, and the reality hit him, she would be having that baby with another man. He popped another pill, donned his jacket, and headed to the pub.

GABBY STUCK HER HEAD in the door of the carpenter's shop, her pretty face flushed.

"It's time."

"Time for what?" Teddy asked, looking up from his work with a frown. She simply smiled and he jumped to his feet, rushing to her side. "Oh. Oh!" he cried. "Are ya okay?"

"Aye, Teddy, but I think we'd better get goin'."

"Of course, of course. Let me get the door." He fumbled with the handle.

"It opens in. You have to pull it," she said, finally.

"Right, right."

She didn't have an easy time of it. Her small frame hindered the baby as it tried to pass through the birth canal, and the labor dragged on for hours and hours. Teddy was beside himself, remembering his own mother's death giving birth to him. Seeing Gabby in so much pain and not being able to do anything about it was almost more than he could bear. But at last, at 4:30 on a clear summer's morning, Michael Patrick McKee was born, and with much relief, Teddy welcomed his son into the world.

He decided then and there he would never allow Gabrielle to be put in that position again, and a few weeks later, despite the fact he knew she wanted to have more children, he invented a business trip to Dublin and secretly had a procedure done.

FOR YEARS GABRIELLE longed for another child, and Teddy bore the weight of knowing he was the reason she'd never have one. After a time she seemed to console herself by pouring all her love and devotion into Michael. One evening, when he was eight, he rushed in the house, blood dripping from his knee.

"Mam!"

Gabby turned from the sink, where she and Teddy had been doing the dishes together.

"Oh, Michael! What happened?"

"I scraped my knee on—" His gaze darted to Teddy. "—a piece of wood."

He read his son's eyes. "Were you messing with that horse again?"

Michael licked his lips, but then nodded, his eyes welling up again. "Aye. I just wanted to brush him."

Teddy took a step forward. "I told you not to—"

Gabby steered her son with a hand on his shoulder to the sink. "It doesn't matter how it happened. Let's get it cleaned up."

Teddy sighed, laying his towel over the back of a chair. So much for a little time alone with her. "The boy needs to learn to listen, Gabby."

She crouched to dab at Michael's knee with the end of a towel she had run under the faucet. "You do listen, don't you?" She smiled up into his face. "'Twas only an accident."

Teddy's chest tightened. He knew it was unreasonable, but he resented the closeness she shared with Michael.

She turned her head. "Could you get us a bandage?"

He frowned, but moved toward the bathroom. "If I told him once, I told him a thousand times..." he muttered, but no one seemed to be listening.

When he returned, Gabby took the bandage from him without a word. Once it was in place, she hugged Michael. "Now, why don't you hop on up to bed, son." He smiled and nodded. With one last glance at his father, he climbed the open stairs to his bedroom. Teddy watched until his feet disappeared.

"You've got to quit babying the boy, Gabby."

"Nonsense. I don't baby him." She frowned and placed a hand on her hip. "Why are you always so hard on him?"

"Hard on him?" Teddy sputtered. "I'm not hard on him." Wanting to avoid her gaze and the inquisition they were now headed for, he grabbed his jacket off a hook. "I'm going to go make sure those stables are in order and he didn't leave the corral open or something." He felt her gaze on him as he sped out the door, but she didn't say anything further. He paused on the other side, shaking his head. They had been laughing before the boy entered. Gabby had been flirting. Now she was angry with him. He trudged toward the barn, although he knew Michael would have bled to death securing everything rather than incur his wrath. He exhaled, his shoulders slumping. *Maybe I'll never be a good father. It's not like I had the best example.*

When he got to the barn, he twisted around and saw Michael's figure silhouetted in the upper window. His jaw tensed, and he ground his teeth together, turning his back.

TEDDY BEGAN TO SPEND more time at the shop. Sean continued to order large quantities of coffins with false bottoms, and he had time for little else.

One day, Sean's delivery man was late picking up at the shop. He called to tell Teddy he'd fallen down some stairs.

"Sean is gonna be so ticked, man."

"Nay, Shane. What for? 'Cause you hurt yourself? Ach," he said dismissively.

"Nay, Teddy. You don't know him anymore. He explodes for the slightest reason. And if you give 'im reason, look out. He found out some guy was stealin' from him, and that guy ended up in the hospital with a concussion and six broken ribs. I swear, Sean's crazy. But don't tell him I said that."

"I won't. I won't." This didn't sound like his best friend.

"I don't know what he'll do when he finds out I didn't pick up from you."

Teddy could almost hear him shiver over the phone. "I'll run the stuff to him."

"Ya will? Man, I'd owe ya."

"Don't ya worry about it, now. I'll take care of it. You get better."

"You're a peach, Teddy. A real peach."

"Yeah, yeah," he mumbled.

He hung up the phone and sat for a moment in thought. He grabbed the furniture-truck keys and began loading the coffins one by one. By the time he had finished, the physical work had burned away his worry. *The kid must be exaggerating. Seanie's not like that.*

He drove the short distance to the building that was both Sean's warehouse and his home. The guy at the door recognized Teddy and waved him in. He walked into a room humming with action. Coffins lay stacked around the perimeter of the room. People busily unloaded boxes from the back of trucks and pried open crates with crowbars. Strangely, a desk stood all alone in the middle of the room. Sean leaned against the desk with a clipboard in his hand, paging through invoices. He wore an expensive-looking, red silk shirt and tan pants, juxtaposed with all the others who wore jeans and t-shirts. As Teddy walked toward him, he passed two men working together to take brown, brick-shaped packages, like the kind he had delivered in the past for Sean, out of a crate marked with the name of some wine company. They laid them in the bottom of a coffin, covering every square inch. Sean looked up from his work as he approached.

He looked different, thinner. Red eyes told him he hadn't slept well in a long time, and his face was tense as he snapped pages back and forth.

"We-ell," Sean exclaimed as he drew near. "If it ain't Teddy McKee?" His jaw was tight, clearly aggravated by the interruption. He sighed. "So what can I do for you?"

Teddy took in the package opened on the desk behind Sean, its powdery white contents still spilled carelessly across the wood.

"Sean," Teddy said in disbelief and shock. "What are you doin' here?"

He laughed mirthlessly. "Well, what is it you think we're doin'? Mortuary work?"

The men around him laughed.

"Seanie," he begged.

Sean turned his back on him and set the clipboard down. He began to walk around the desk, but Teddy grabbed his arm. "This isn't right."

Sean looked at Teddy's hand on his forearm with raised eyebrows, as if in wrinkling his shirt he was accusing him of the worst vulgarity. The others straightened, readying themselves for his reaction. Teddy released his arm, and he shook it, running his other hand over the sleeve to smooth out the fabric.

"Maybe so, Teddy, maybe so. But it pays the bills." He picked up another invoice and began studying it without looking up.

"P-p-pays the bills?"

"Oh, now don't go gettin' all indignant on me. It's kept your pretty little wife happy."

"Nay, nay. I had nothin' to do with this." Teddy gestured at the room in general.

"The hell you didn't! Come on, now. You didn't really think I was in the burying business, did you? A guy like me hangin' around a bunch of dead stiffs?" His men jeered.

"Sean," he spread his arms wide, pleading with his friend, "this isn't you."

"Bullshit!" He slammed his fist on the desk. "You've never known me, Teddy. You've seen what you've wanted to see. You're a...a big fool."

Teddy clenched his jaw, staring at him. "I guess I have been, but that's over now. I ain't gonna do it no more, Seanie." He whirled to storm out, only to find his way blocked by a couple of thugs. He slowly turned around. "Come on. I'm a father now. I can't be gettin' involved—"

"Oh, aye. How is the boy?" Sean straightened. "He's what...eight or nine years old now?"

"Ten."

"Aye, ten. And Gabby, how's Gabby?" he added with an edge, and his implication was clear.

"What are ya gettin' at?"

He strutted around the desk to stand in front of Teddy. "You aren't gonna be walkin' out on me now."

"Are ya threatin'in' my family? 'Cause I don't think it would be wise—"

Sean raised his hand sharply, and the man on his right punched Teddy hard in the stomach, knocking the wind out of him. Two men grabbed his arms as he bent over, wheezing.

Sean circled around him. "I won't take any more of your guff. I need those coffins. So you turn yourself around and hobble on back to your little shop, and no one will get hurt. And don't think that I'll have second thoughts about it just because I've slept with your wife."

Teddy's head snapped up. "Slept with my..." He laughed jaggedly, still catching his breath. "Oh, right. Be serious."

"The night of your party at that little apartment you rented when you were first married. You remember? You were passed out on the couch, and your little Gabby was doin' me in the bathroom."

He lunged at Sean but his cronies tightened their grip. "You son of a bitch! You're lying!" he spat.

"Son of a bitch, huh? Well, you might be right about that one. But I'm still the son of a bitch that did your wife on the bathroom sink. How else would I know Gabby has the cutest little heart-shaped mole on her ass?"

Teddy was lightheaded and suddenly his difficulty in breathing had nothing to do with the blow he received. He broke away from his captors and tackled Sean into the desk. The others struggled to haul him off, but when Sean finally stood, blood trailed from his nose. He wiped it with the back of his hand and examined the blood distastefully.

"I'll forgive ya that one for ol' times' sake. But you had better toe the line, Teddy-boy. Throw him out," he added to the men who were holding him. They dragged him out to the back alley and flung him against his truck. The men who had finished unloading the coffins scurried inside, not wanting to be part of whatever was going on with Teddy.

He groaned as he slid behind the wheel, an arm over his stomach. Seething inside, he turned over the engine and started to back out, churning up white dust among the rocks in the alleyway. As he did, a man rushed out the door wearing overalls over a loose cotton shirt. One of his straps swung behind him, the button missing to latch it in place. He put his hand on top of the partially rolled-down window, jumping on the running board. "Teddy."

He recognized the tall, skinny man as Colm Finnegan. He had lived next door to his Passmore cousins and attended the same trade school as he and Sean. "You've got to listen to him and be careful. Those thugs he hired would slice their mam open and go bowlin' after. He's not the same Sean, Teddy," he heard for the second time that day.

He patted the taller man's hand gratefully, and Colm jumped off. Teddy backed out of the alley and looked toward the building before changing gears. Dirt swirled in the sunlight as Colm stood watching the truck leave.

WHEN GABRIELLE OPENED the door, Teddy could see Michael behind her at the kitchen table, surrounded by text books and papers, chewing on the end of a pencil. She looked at him and then tried to peer around him "Teddy!" She laughed. "What are ya doin'?" She scrutinized his face as he fought to control his emotions. "What's wrong?" Michael came up from behind her.

"Hello, son," Teddy said in a kinder voice than he usually reserved for Michael. He realized now how silly it had been for him to be jealous of the love Gabrielle had for their son, when he should have been worrying about the feelings she had for his best friend. "Got a lot of homework tonight?"

Michael nodded slowly, no doubt wondering why his father rang the doorbell instead of coming in and why he was acting so agreeably toward him. Teddy reached out and rumpled his hair. "Can I talk with your mam a minute?" Michael gazed up at her, and she nodded. He looked back at Teddy, hesitating a moment, then turned to head inside.

Gabrielle stepped out and closed the door behind her. "What's wrong, Teddy? You're scarin' me."

He lowered his head a moment. When he lifted it, tears filled his eyes. "Why'd you sleep with him?"

"Wh-what? What are ya talkin' about?"

He glanced away briefly then looked her in the eye. "Sean," he said with difficulty.

The blood drained from her face. It all came rushing back at her. Sean walking his motorcycle alongside of her in the street, dancing with him at the pub, the expression on his face as he stepped into the light on her front porch, the way he looked at her in the bathroom, the feel of his hands on her breasts, the mockery in his voice as he zipped his pants, *Gracias, Señora.*

She choked out the words as tears spilled down her face. "I'm sorry. So sorry." She reached out to steady herself on the door frame.

"Gabby..." He struggled with his speaking, too. "You were the only one. I trusted you."

She wrapped her other arm around her stomach like she had received a blow. "I know," she said feebly. They stood in silence, unsure of what to say or do next. "I do love you, Teddy."

He sighed, lowering his head. "I know," he said tiredly. "I know."

He turned around without another word and trudged to his truck. She stood on the doorstep, tugging the shawl she wore more tightly around her. The wind blew her hair as the last rays of the sun shone. He pulled away and headed down the road.

TEDDY DROVE AIMLESSLY. His truck, however, knew the way, and he was soon parked outside his shop. He entered and sat behind his bench without moving. Hours may have passed when he finally looked up and noticed two of Sean's men approaching from across the street. They opened the door, the bell ringing above it. His eyes stung as he glowered at them.

"Sean wants those coffins," one said, trying to sound tough.

Teddy reached for a piece of wood that was being formed into a table leg and rose slowly from his seat. "Get. Out. Of. My shop. NOW!" he raged, advancing on them.

They scurried out the door, calling to him, "We'll be back, Teddy."

He returned to his bench and sat. He wiped his fingers through the sawdust; it was the only thing he understood anymore. He picked up his tools and began to work.

He labored feverishly into the night, fashioning coffins hour after hour. Catching his reflection in the window, he froze. He had been running his hands through his hair making it look wild, and it was peppered with flakes of wood. He looked every bit the madman he felt he was. Finally, exhausted, he lay down to sleep on the floor amid the coffins.

CHAPTER EIGHT

A ll week long Teddy worked and slept in the shop. He would occasionally see Gabby passing by on the street, but she left him alone. When Friday came, Shane showed up as usual to load coffins.

"Hey. Thank ya much for takin' me load last week. I hope ya didn't have any trouble with it?"

He snorted. "Nay, Shane. It was fine."

"Are you okay? You look a little...tired...or something."

"I'm right as rain."

Shane studied Teddy quizzically then dropped it. "Okay, then. I'll be off."

After loading Shane's truck, Teddy returned to the shop and quickly gathered a pile of invoices into a folder. He grabbed a little wooden box that had been sitting on his work bench and left the shop without even stopping to lock the door.

Gabby was out hanging wash on the line when he tore into the dirt lane leading to their unusual house. He threw it into park but left the engine running as he hopped out. He ran to her and threw his arms around her. Astonished, she froze at first, then clung to him. He held on to her for a long time before he drew back.

"Gabby, please take this and keep it safe." He handed her an ornately carved box with a white dove of stone inlaid on the lid. Before she could say anything he kissed her long and hard. He pulled back. "Where's Michael?"

"Well, he's at school, of course."

His face fell. He hadn't thought of that.

"What's this all about?"

He kissed her again, and stroked her cheek. "I've got to go." His voice was hoarse. He jumped back in the truck and started to turn it around.

Gabby ran alongside the truck. "Where are ya goin' to? What's goin' on? For God's sake, tell me!"

He sped away, looking at her in the rearview mirror, tears in his eyes. Her cry faded on the wind.

"Teddy, please..."

He searched for Michael on the playground. The raucous sounds of laughter and shouting filled his ears as he caught sight of him playing catch with another boy. He was laughing, having a good time. Teddy decided not to spoil his fun. He watched his son for another fifteen minutes then started the engine and left.

ACROSS TOWN, SEAN SAUNTERED in the door of the warehouse.

"Boss, there's a problem with the coffins we got in today."

"A problem? What problem?"

"They don't have no fake bottoms."

"Oh. They're really hard to see. Teddy's good at that. Let me show you."

He ran his hand over the bottom of the coffin. Not feeling the little slide catches Teddy usually installed, he tapped on the bottom. A solid knock was returned to him. Suddenly, he understood. "Why, that JACKASS!" In a rage, he grabbed a crowbar and everybody near him ducked as he buried it in the coffin, sending pieces of debris flying everywhere. No hidden compartment was revealed below.

Sean thought quickly. "Is there anything Teddy has that would connect these coffins to me or Bradigan?"

"Well, yeah. There's the invoices he has us sign. They have both of your names on them."

Sean slammed his fist into the side of the broken coffin. How could he have been so dense? He was always so careful. He had underestimated Teddy. His eyes blazed. "Find him," he said precisely, anger giving his voice a dangerous edge, "and bring him to me."

THE PHONE RANG, JOLTING Sean out of an uneasy sleep. It could only be one person. No one else would dare to wake him at...he searched for the number blaring at him indecently from his alarm clock, *four-thirty in the freakin' morning!* He reached for the receiver, but his hand was asleep and senses not quite sharpened yet, and he sent the whole thing crashing to the floor. The receiver landed several feet away, beyond the shaggy, round carpet surrounding the bed, lying on the hardwood. He reached over, nearly tumbling out of bed, but got hold of the curly cord, reeling in the phone like a late-night fish. Loud noises emerged from the phone as he dragged it nearer.

"I want out."

"You stupid bastard!" he yelled into the phone, yanking on the chain to turn the bedside lamp on. "You think you can order *me* around?"

"Aye, Seanie. This time I do." He sounded plastered. Teddy must be calling from inside a pub somewhere. With a movement from the other side of the bed, a rumpled head emerged from the covers.

"Huh?" The woman yawned. "What's goin' on?"

He kicked her sharply to hush her. Throwing off the covers and swinging his legs over the side of the bed, he sat, fully awake now. The girl tried to yank the covers back over her half-naked body. "It wasn't very smart of ya to leave your little family unprotected," he hissed into the phone.

"You shut up! You don't mention them. So help me, Sean, if something happens to them...well, you know then I'd have nothing to live for and I sure the hell would take you down with me."

Sean fumed silently. He didn't doubt Teddy's words. It infuriated him not to be in charge of the situation.

"I've got the papers in a safe place. Somewhere where you'll never find them, so don't go tryin' to."

Sean's mind raced with the possibilities. They hadn't been at the shop when his men had gone back to search it, and he didn't think Teddy would have been foolish enough to leave them at his house. "All I want is some time. Some time to earn me some money and get us a place here. Then I'll send for Gabby and Michael. When I have them safe and sound, I'll send the papers back to you. They're my guarantee, Sean. I'm not interested in bringing you down. I only want out. I want something better for my family. I want to start over."

He closed his eyes and sighed. It sounded like Teddy was near tears.

"You need to get out of the business, too. It's no good for you. You look terrible and—"

"Shut up! Just shut up! You don't know what you're friggin' talkin' about!" He rose, snatching the base of the phone and pacing back and forth on a short path along the bed, wondering what the hell Bradigan was going to think when he found out about the missing papers.

He heard a voice in the background. "I said 'last call' a half-hour ago. You've got ta get outa here."

"I'll leave Gabby and the kid alone for now. But if I find you, all bets are off. And I *will* find you." He heard a click, and the line went dead. He couldn't tell if the pub owner had ended their conversation or if Teddy had hung up on him. "Damn!" He slammed the receiver in its cradle, and put the phone back on the bedside table. He sat staring at the bed for a minute then kicked it savagely. "Get up! Get up and get the hell out of here! I'm done with you."

The girl slinked out of bed and quickly gathered her remaining pieces of clothing from off the floor. She had been with Sean before and knew when he was serious. She zipped her skirt.

He tugged on his jeans and stood staring out at the city, one hand reaching up to lean against the tall glass windows.

She crossed to him. "Come on, baby," she said, stroking his shoulder. "Come back to bed. I'll make you forget it," she cooed.

He shrugged off her hand without turning and continued to peer out over the black night.

She left.

WEEKS HAD PASSED, AND Gabrielle had seen no sign of Teddy. His shop was broken into and trashed on the day he came to visit her, but she felt certain he was safe. Because she had to believe that. She thought about him constantly, missing his gentle sense of humor and what had, at one time, been his perpetual confidence in the two of them. *That's probably gone forever. I destroyed it.* If she hadn't known it before, now it was patently clear to her what a mistake she had made all those years before. She knew, too, she had been neglecting Teddy and had become too fixated on caring for Michael, and that had been an injustice to them all. The only thing worse than watching Michael grow up without a father, was knowing she was the cause of it.

When she opened the box he gave her, it contained what had to have been nearly all the money he possessed. She stood awash in confusion. Why had Teddy left her? If it was because he found out about her affair, why leave her the money? And why did he kiss her like he had on the day he left? If he forgave her for the affair, why leave at all? And how had he found out about the affair to begin with? The only other person who knew about it was Sean. But if he told Teddy, why did he wait all these years to spring it on him? Was he somehow to blame for Teddy leaving? After a time, she could stand it no more; she went to see Sean for answers.

She found him in the first place she looked for him, in the pub across from the dress shop. He sat at a table with four other men, a wide array of glasses covering most of the surface of the table. She stomped toward him without hesitating.

Sean saw Gabrielle the minute she walked in the door. She wore black jeans and a red, button-down silk blouse with a matching lacy camisole beneath it. Her hair was shorter than it had been in the past, a little past the shoulders, but she was still absolutely breathtaking. His heart tightened in his chest as it did whenever she was near, reminding him that he did indeed still have a heart. His mouth hung open a moment, stopped in midsentence as he told some bawdy tale to his friends seated around him. His listeners followed his gaze, giving him a chance to recover while they examined her.

As she approached the table, he stood and moved toward her, calling out derisively, "Why, look boys. If it isn't 'Our Lady of the Lost Cause.'" They laughed loudly, clearly not knowing why they did it, but perhaps feeling that it was nevertheless called for. He stepped closer to her, the question that followed concealed from the others by the noise of their laughter. "What about me, Gabby? Aren't I a lost cause?"

She flinched, but then straightened her shoulders. "I want to know where my husband is." She said it with a conviction she lacked that night on the porch, when he had asked her if a life with Teddy is what she wanted.

"Well, so would I, darlin'. So would I." His friends laughed even more boisterously than they had before. "But if he does chance to come back, you be sure and let me know, would ya?" Again they laughed at his comment.

What does he mean by that? She looked around the table hoping to find someone sympathetic to her cause, but all she saw was coldness and come-ons. Sean held a drink in his hand. He swirled the ice casually then tipped the glass to drain it, setting it back on the table with a sharp *clink.*

"Go home, Gabrielle," he said harshly. "There's nothing here for you."

Her face burned with anger. Though humiliated by his dismissive tone, she could see she was getting nowhere. She turned on her heel and marched out of the room, feeling his gaze and hearing the laughter at her expense.

THE WEATHER BECAME cooler, and Gabby was buried in bills. The furnace had picked the worst time to break down, and the beleaguered water heater followed suit a week later. The money Teddy left them had run out months ago, and she was forced to work long hours to keep food on the table. She eventually had to sell Teddy's workshop, but she kept his tools, even though they could have fetched her a pretty penny, in hope he would someday return to use them again. Michael never asked her about his father's disappearance and seemed to take becoming the man of the house in stride.

She saw Sean in town from time-to-time, always sauntering around with his entourage, and she wondered what became of the man who once rode, so carefree, around these very streets, with Teddy on the back of his bike.

One day Sean was out walking by himself when the mention of Gabby's name made him tune into the conversation of the two women strolling in front of him.

"I feel so sorry for that lil' Gabby McKee."

"Oh, I do, too. Such a beautiful girl. But she's working herself to death. And now her little one is in the hospital, she's beside herself." He recognized the taller woman as Mrs. Connelly, the owner of the dress shop Gabby worked at. "You know, I caught her the other day in a dressing room crying her little eyes out. Poor thing felt bad she couldn't visit Michael in the hospital because she had to work to pay the bills, so I told her to get herself on down there, she'd put in more than a day's work, and she needed to go. ...Oh, isn't that a cute hat." He hurried past as the two women stopped to admire items in a shop window.

He quickened his pace, stepping off the curb to change direction and head for the hospital. He saw her as soon as he entered the building. She was down the long hallway right inside the door, sitting in a chair with her feet out in front of her, head leaning against the wall behind her, staring at the ceiling. He stood between the double lobby doors, stepping to one side, concealed by the thick door frame. She remained frozen in this position for several minutes; then sat, putting her elbows on her knees and head into her hands, rubbing her temples. A nurse approached Gabby with a box of Kleenex and spoke a few kind words. His curiosity getting the better of him, he stepped inside the door, flipped his collar up to hide his face, and bent over a drinking fountain. He could hear the nurse now clearly.

"Is there anything more I can do for you, Mrs. McKee? I know this is a difficult time for you."

Gabrielle was dabbing her eyes. Now she squeezed the nurse's hand. "Nay, nay, Beth. You've been great. I want to pull meself together a little bit before I go in to see him. I guess I'm tired tonight."

"Of course you are, dear," she said, in turn patting Gabby's hand. "Take your time. I think he's sleeping, anyway." She headed away, leaving Gabby to compose herself.

She stared at the closed door across the hall. After several minutes, she stood and took a deep breath, steeling herself for what was to come. Sean watched, fascinated, not even remembering to keep himself hidden; but it didn't matter. She was oblivious to anything but what lie in front of her. She crossed the hall and pushed open the door, slipping inside.

He pondered what he had seen and heard. Giving the doorway Gabby entered a wide berth, he hastened to the nurses' station.

"Can I help you, sir?"

"Aye." He hesitated. "Michael. Michael McKee. I was wondering if you could tell me what his condition is."

"I'm afraid I can't, sir. Not without permission from his mam. But she's right down the hall. Would you like me to go get her?"

"Nay. Nay," Sean said quickly. "Perhaps you could tell me how to get to the billing department instead."

CHAPTER NINE

The next day, Sean sat sipping a whiskey at the pub with Patrick Bradigan. It had taken him a long time to smooth things over with his boss after Bradigan found out about the invoices Teddy stole. But slowly the man had restored his faith in Sean. They sat sharing the customary drink after discussing their business, debating who they thought would come out on top in an upcoming rugby match.

Without warning, a large stack of money held together by a rubber band was slapped onto the bar beside them.

"We don't need your money, Sean."

He glanced up and caught Gabby's furious look in the mirror behind the bar. He had never seen her this angry. Bradigan watched, his eyes wide with curiosity. Sean coolly took another sip of his whiskey. "I don't know what you are talking about, Gabrielle."

"Oh, ya don't? So you wouldn't be the 'handsome young man in a leather coat' who paid off my bill yesterday?" She hit him on the shoulder, the leather making a smacking sound.

He shrugged. "There are plenty of people with leather jackets. Any of them could have paid your hospital bill."

"Ahh. But I didn't say nothin' about any hospital, Sean." She turned to leave; then whirled back. "If you really want to do something for me and Michael, why don't you bring Teddy home to us?" Her voice cracked, and she choked back a sob. He spun around to stare at her. "And don't ya go tellin' me you had nothin' to do with it. I know better. Teddy would never have left—" Her hands flew to her face, and she broke down.

He reached out to grasp her shaking hands. "Gabby..."

She stepped back, dropping her hands, her eyes flashing. "Don't touch me. Don't you touch me!" The volume of her statement drew the attention of others. "You don't think I know who you are, Sean? Mr. Big Man, right? Right?" she screamed, her voice becoming hysterical. "Stay away from my family—or what I have left of it—ya hear?" She turned and ran out of the bar, knocking a drink from a bystander's hand and all over the front of his shirt as she did so.

"Shit, woman!" the man yelled, his jaw tensed.

Sean hopped to his feet and drew his money clip from his pocket, peeling off several bills. "This is for your drink, and your dry cleaning." He scrambled out the door after her, but by the time he hit the street, she was nowhere in sight.

Bradigan raised his head when he returned to his vacated stool.

"Sorry about that."

Bradigan finished his drink thoughtfully then spoke up. "I've been very patient with this situation." He set his glass down and twisted to face Sean. "This whole McKee thing. You made a mistake, and I cut you some slack. But you can't let this woman come in here and make a fool out of you in front of people," he said, his voice low and lethal. The implied threat hung in the air. "It's not good for business."

He stood, donning a pricey tweed jacket. Sean took another pull on his drink. Bradigan turned to leave, bending first to whisper near his ear. "And if you don't do something about it, I will."

SEAN SAT AT THE EDGE of his bed for hours, thinking about what a mess his life had become. He finally lay and folded his arms behind his head, staring at the ceiling. After a while, he drifted off to sleep.

He was on his motorcycle, and he could feel Gabrielle's arms around him. He pulled over by the tree and helped her off the bike. She was smiling as she reached for his face, kissing him tenderly.

And then he woke with a start. He was alone in the big, empty apartment.

He reached into the drawer of the bedside table, taking out a bottle of pills. He spotted a key Teddy had given him a long time ago, and he lifted it out, turning it over in his hand. Picking up a glass of water sitting on a notepad beside the phone, he downed a handful of pills and again lay back against the pillows. As the drugs took effect, his anger grew.

What the hell had he done, anyway? Paid her freakin' bill! She had no right to be mad at him. Why did he care about her anyway? Why, after all these years, could he not rid himself of her? He was like the boy on the playground trying to run away from his ever-present shadow. Everywhere he turned, she was there. Every breath he took, he longed to mingle it with hers.

He was squeezing the key so tightly in his fist he could feel it cutting into his skin. He opened his hand to see the imprint of the key in his palm. He stared at it in wonder. The only two people he had ever opened his heart to, and they had both betrayed him.

The drugs he started taking years ago to numb himself had begun to rob him of his reason and make him paranoid. The ceiling came into and out of focus. A long crack became Teddy's jeering face...and then Gabrielle's. He remembered now how she yelled at him in front of Bradigan and potential clients. Looking weak? That was bad for business. And the only thing that had ever made any sense to him, the only thing he had ever been any good at, was his business. He simply could not let her get away with that. She must be put in her place, and before Bradigan decided to take action. Jumping up, he grabbed his jacket from the foot of the bed and headed for the elevator.

HE SLID THE KEY INTO the lock, and the door opened, granting him permission to take whatever he found inside. He saw her right away. Her bed was not far from the stove. A thin curtain hung down to separate kitchen and bedroom, but it was drawn back. He walked across the floor and stood over her. She had on a white linen nightgown with wide straps and an em-broidered bodice. The brightness of the clothing set off her brown skin. He watched her as he slowly unbuttoned his shirt and laid it over a kitchen chair. She breathed steadily, unaware of his presence. He knew the boy was upstairs, but it didn't concern him. He touched the end of the thick braid hanging be-low her shoulder then climbed beneath the covers.

She woke with the weight of his body leaning against her. He rose on one elbow, looking at her smugly. She screamed.

He laughed. "Darling? I'm home."

She was frozen in shock for a second, staring at him, wide-eyed, but then she became a blur of action. She drove her fists into his chest, pounding on him as hard as she could and cursing at him in Spanish.

"Whoa, whoa, little lady. What's the problem?"

His acting as if this invasion of her home, of her bed, was a minor transgression enraged her, and in a fury she dumped him out of the bed.

"GET OUT!" she screamed shrilly. "GET OUT OF HERE!"

He scurried to his feet, his eyes wide, appearing unable to react at first. She came at him like a hell cat and was able to push him the short distance to the door, open it, and thrust him across the threshold. At the last minute he regained his equilibrium and grabbed for the handle. He was almost able to wrestle his way back into the house, but with a final effort, she bolted the door. Outside, he screamed.

"You stupid little half-Spanish whore!" He banged on the wood. "I'll be back for you, woman! Don't you worry. I'll be back for you, all right."

She sat with her back to the door, trembling.

"Mama," Michael called from above.

She saw his white face, peering down between the railings. She prayed he was too asleep or still too young to understand what happened; but she could tell by the look in his eyes he wasn't.

SEAN ROARED INTO TOWN on his bike and swung haphazardly into a spot in front of Hurley's Pub. He yanked his helmet off his head and, in a fit of anger, threw it across the sidewalk, where it bounced against the side of the pub. Two of his friends barged out the front door. Seeing it was Sean who had caused the noise, they seemed to bite back the tongue-lashing they had been about to give the person who disturbed their peaceful imbibing. Collecting the black helmet, they slowly brought it over to Sean and handed it to him.

"This whole McKee thing is out of hand," he growled. He looked at them, his eyes blazing. "I want you to pay his house a little visit. Not when his missus or his kid are around or anything...but make it clear they've messed with the wrong guy, understand?" The two nodded mutely, and he dismounted from the bike. "I need a drink." He marched into the pub.

GABRIELLE BOLTED THE door and set her keys on the table wearily. Michael sat poking at the coals in the big potbellied stove standing in the middle of the room, it being the only heat they could afford at present. He still wore his hat and coat and seemed lost in thought. He came from school to the shop to walk her home, something he had never done before. Mrs. Connelly gave her permission to leave early when she saw that he was there.

She looked at his back as he stood outlined in the firelight. He had not mentioned the scene last night, but, instead, was unusually quiet on the way home. Should she discuss it with him and try to put all of his fears to rest?

But how could she, when she herself was still shaken by the strange encounter in the middle of the night? Her eyes shifted to the still unmade bed. Even now, as she thought about how frightened she had been, waking to find someone lying next to her, she shivered. It was when she realized it was Sean that she became incensed. How dare he come into their bed.

Sean's eyes at first seemed so unfocussed as he had stared down at her. When she attacked him, they widened with shock. But as she struggled with him at the door, his eyes burned with an intensity that was truly terrifying. The drugs and the rage distorted his features so badly it was like looking into the face of a complete stranger. His muscles had instantly tensed, like steel cables, and he fought with a ferocity she had never seen before. She didn't know how she managed to force him out the door, but she was thankful she had.

Her eyes returned to Michael as he sat slowly stirring with the poker, staring into the heart of the stove. She walked over and stood in front of him, waiting for him to speak. The light illuminated his fair face, but gave her no clues as to what he was feeling. Was he, too, thinking about last night?

"Michael..." she began gently.

"I'm going to bed."

She didn't want him to leave and go upstairs to his room. "No cards tonight?" she cajoled, but he simply hung his coat next to a tattered one Teddy left on a peg under the spiral staircase leading to his room. He started to climb the stairs. Pausing for a moment, he looked down into her worried face. "I'm just tired, Mam."

It had been a sleepless night for both of them. "Me, too, Michael," she admitted. "I'll turn in then."

She saw her white nightgown lying at the foot of the bed and for a moment thought of crawling into bed with her dress on, rather than to clothe herself as she had the night before. But in a singular act of defiance, she put the nightgown on and slipped under the stack of quilts on her bed.

They went to sleep before the sun even set, but soon she could see the red glow of the oven through the dark shadows of the night surrounding her. She sat on her side with the blankets drawn to her chin and watched the coals burn to nothing. She thought about Teddy and how she missed him and wondered if he were staying warm wherever he was at the moment.

CHAPTER TEN

S ean straddled his bike on top of the hill overlooking Teddy and Gabrielle's house. His helmet rested on the seat in front of him. On either side a biker mimicked his stance.

"You're sure no one is home?"

"Aye. We've been here since six. Gabby works 'til six, and we've seen not hide nor hair of her. She and the kid must have eaten in town."

Sean frowned. "It's pretty late for them to still be out to dinner."

The man on his right shrugged. "Maybe they're visitin' friends or family or something."

"You're absolutely certain the boy didn't return from school, and the house is empty."

"As sure as my Granny's fanny."

"All right." He sighed. "Let's get this over with then." He wasn't enjoying this as much as he wanted to.

The two donned their helmets and rode down the gentler slope to the right then circled around to the lighthouse. The only windows in the strange house were tiny and high. Higher even than the second floor, so no one could have seen them even if they were home. They doused the base of the house and as high as they could reach with gasoline tanks they had strapped to their bikes. When the tanks were empty, they leaned them against the frame of the house. Finally they lit wads of newspaper they had rolled into a cone shape and threw them on the house. They took off in a cloud of dust, their engines' high-pitched whining cutting through the night. They returned to Sean's side to watch their work.

At first the fire was disappointingly small. It didn't look like much damage was going to be done to the house as the little flames took their time at climbing the walls; but a sudden burst of wind sped the fire along, the big flames pushing the littler ones like a big brother pushing his kid brother on a bicycle. With a loud whoosh it seemed the whole place was ablaze in an instant.

From the top of the hill, the men whooped with satisfaction as the old, dry wood of the building fed their bonfire. When they stopped shouting, an echo could be heard in the night. Sean froze. Was it merely an echo or had he heard something? It took him a minute to realize it was a human voice; a terrified human voice. Now he could hear it clearly.

"Michael!"

While Sean had been still, listening intently, his cohorts had backed their bikes away without speaking. They started their engines and took off, driving as fast as they could away from the scene.

Sean started his own engine and barreled down the steep embankment. The ground gave way underneath his wheels and he half-slid to the base of the hill, falling with his bike on top of him. He heaved it off and abandoned it, but had only run a few feet toward the glowing building when the door opened, and a figure appeared. For a moment she stood motionless as the wind rushed into the house, the flames racing into the interior. Her arms outstretched and her sleeves ablaze, she looked like some sort of fire angel. Shocked, he stood shielding his eyes from the intense glow, the heat threatening to incinerate him. Then the boy came flying out, tackling his mother to the ground and wrapping her in a coat.

It became eerily quiet. The only sound that carried back to him was the sound of the boy's sobs and the crackling of the wood as it was consumed. The boy didn't seem to see him; maybe he was blinded by the sudden change in lighting. Then Michael jumped to his feet and ran toward the barn.

What was he doing? Why had he left her? Sean started forward but was arrested by the sounds coming out of Gabby's throat. She moaned in agony. He rushed to her side and bent, peering into her face.

"S-sean?" she rasped. Strangely her face had been untouched by the fire. Her eyes were dazed, and he could see the life ebbing out of them.

"Oh, God, Gabrielle! I'm so sorry," he sobbed, overcome with emotion. She only stared at him with a look of utter confusion. He heard the barn door creak, and on reflex he turned and ran. He stumbled blindly, tears streaming down his face. He stopped several yards away but still in plain sight. Luckily Michael had eyes only for his mother. Moments later Sean could hear Michael's "Hyah!" as he snapped the reins and drove the horse he had coaxed out of the barn forward, hitched to a wagon. But in his heart, he knew it was too late.

TEDDY WAS SO HAPPY, he felt like running the last mile to his house. How long it had been since he had seen Gabby and Michael. He had thought about them constantly, but dared not contact them for fear Sean would discover where he was hiding in Limerick. But now, at last, he had gotten a job at a mill that would support them, and he was anxious to take them and leave Cork for good, leaving all their troubles behind them.

In his hand he held a box containing a dress he picked out for Gabby.

I hope she's still the same size, he worried. *But even if she's not, even if she's as round as the little nun at St. Finnabar's, it won't matter. To see her smile again…*

He chuckled warmly, imagining the look on her face when she saw him. In his other hand he held a package of wooden soldiers he had carved for Michael. He had worked on them every night he was away; it made him feel close to Michael in his absence. But he had not expected to be away so long, and the little army he started off making had grown into several large regiments.

Toting his cumbersome packages he at last breasted the hill on the dirt pathway leading to his property, anticipating the view of the crazy, old house he had yearned to return to for so long. He saw, instead, only charred rubble. He froze, his heart caught in his throat. It took several seconds for his mind to digest what he saw. The little lighthouse where he and Gabrielle spent most of their married days lay burnt to the ground. Dread washed over him. He dropped his packages in the road as he broke into a run. Then, as he neared the remains of the house, he saw it, rising out of the ground like a demon, the white stone bearing his wife's name. He fell to his knees in front of it, running his hand across the letters and weeping. *No* his heart cried in the vacant stillness.

How can this be? How can this be? My Gabby...gone? This can't be right. She was supposed to be waiting here. We were going to start over, she and I and the boy.

The cruelty of it all, of his waiting, dreaming of her every night, and now she was gone?

He lay in the grass, thinking for an instant about it being the only thing separating them. But all too soon his mind understood a great chasm had opened between them; one he could never cross.

PATRICK BRADIGAN LEANED back in the leather recliner in the corner of Sean's bedroom, smoking his cigar in the dark. Two of his men stood on either side of the elevator, waiting to jump Sean the moment he returned. It was unfortunate. Sean was one of his finest dealers, turning a profit in times when no one else could. But, alas, he had heard, like so many others before him, Sean had become an addict. Stoned out of his mind while conducting Bradigan's business. Reports were in the last several weeks things had become worse; that he was out of it most of the time and didn't seem to give a shit about the business.

Bradigan sat, letting his ashes litter the floor. Where once Sean had been an asset, in recent days he had become a liability, a casualty of the drug business, a risk he was no longer willing to take. Truly, it was regrettable. Now he would have to train someone new...

He heard the distinctive sound of the old elevator beginning to rise. He watched with interest as Sean wrestled with the gate, stumbling into the apartment, barely able to stand. If he had any doubts about the reports of his unsteadiness, they were vanquished now. His men grabbed Sean's arms, and he let them lead him over to his bed without struggling.

"Well, hello, boys," he said, smiling at them stupidly and examining them with bleary eyes. He caught sight of Bradigan sitting in the corner. "Ahh, Patrick..." He had never called his boss by his first name before, "...to what do I owe the pleasure of this little visit? I hope you made yourself at home. I can turn on some lights for you."

"That won't be necessary," Bradigan returned coldly, standing and grinding his cigar into the wooden floor. His cohorts pulled out pieces of plastic tubing and began to tie Sean's arms to the bedposts. A third section of tubing was produced and cinched tightly around his upper right arm.

"Hey, fellas," Sean said with childlike curiosity. "What are ya doin'?"

Bradigan crossed the room and towered over him. He slid out a package from his inner pocket and laid it on Sean's lap. It was a piece of soft leather tied with a strap, which he loosened. He unrolled the leather. The insides contained several loops, each holding a syringe in place.

"Are ya goin' to kill me now, Mr. Bradigan?"

"I'm sorry, Sean," he replied sincerely as he stuck the needle into the vein.

In the last moments he seemed to decide he wanted to live after all and fought to free himself, but his efforts only spurred the poison through his system more quickly.

TEDDY WOKE IN THE GRASS. Mud, created by his tears, smeared across his cheek. He was numb. How long had he been lying there? The sun had gone down, and night was beginning to form in the little hollow which had at one time contained his home. He sat up stonily and began to think. How could this have happened?

And then slowly an idea began to form on the edges of his mind and march resolutely inward. Sean. Sean, who had stolen his love from him once, had come to make it final. A rage filled the emptiness that had been part of him all afternoon. He rose and plodded toward town, forcing one foot in front of the other.

BY THE TIME TEDDY REACHED town, darkness had fully developed. It hid him as he stood in the alleyway across the street from the warehouse. He heard the familiar creak of the elevator as it began its descent. Three people stepped out of its door as he slinked back into the shadows, and they hurried off down the street. No one else was around.

He took the elevator to its preordained destination. The room was black, except for where the streetlight fell across the bed, spotlighting a body tied to the bedposts. He hesitated for a moment then rushed forward. Sean's eyes were wide, but unseeing. A single tear still clung to his face. A needle hung from him. Teddy withdrew the syringe and reached over to close the eyes of his friend, a new ache growing in his heart. He was so overwrought, he didn't even hear the sirens coming.

Part Two

"The damage done in one year can sometimes take ten or twenty years to repair."
-Chinua Achebe

CHAPTER ELEVEN

O ld Head of Kinsale, Ireland~1999
      Even through bloodshot eyes, Michael could see she was different. She walked in, unsure of herself. Her long red hair shone despite the smoky haze in the pub; it was thick and wavy. He watched her curiously as he tuned his guitar. The redhead crossed the floor to the bar and started talking to the boss, Tad McGregor. McGregor planted his meaty fists on the bar, leaning toward the girl, shirt sleeves rolled up, accentuating his beefy arms, a bar towel slung across his shoulder. He was flashing the girl his dazzlingly white smile, *something you might find charming, if you didn't know the s.o.b.* She left, looking a little disconcerted, it seemed; but then Molly crossed into his line of vision, blocking the redhead out.

"Michael, darlin'." He turned his attention to her, and she went on. "Will ya be singin' me a song tonight, luv?" She smiled at him, displaying the gap between her top two teeth. She was a nice enough girl, and although she wasn't exactly a looker, she sure knew how to pleasure a man, he remembered.

"Of course," he returned jovially. "What would you like to hear?"

"Oh, you know me, anything." She winked at him as she bent over a table, clearing a platoon of dead soldiers onto her tray and giving him a nice view down her blouse of her ample breasts.

Some girls make it too easy.

"Hey, Molly. Could you get me another?" He raised his empty bottle in the air.

"Sure, sugar."

TESS PACED ALONG THE sidewalk. Music and laughter filtered out of McGregor's Pub, growing louder, then fading again each time a patron stumbled out. She needed a job badly, but had it really come to this? She marched determinedly toward the door, but at the last minute turned and crossed the street, heading in the opposite direction. The fog that had begun to appear at sundown was thicker. She crossed another street and turned to head up the hillside toward a grotto.

Shoulders slumped, she sat on the cold stone bench in front of the statue of Mary. She had never felt so lost. Looking into the face of the statue, she searched for an answer. She hoped for some kind of miracle; for the statue to come to life and give her advice and comfort. It was a crazy thought, but she couldn't help herself. Mary's face was serene, but, alas, unchanging. She became aware of heavy footsteps on the pavement behind her. She realized she had been hearing the noise for several seconds without it totally registering in her mind. She turned to see who was approaching. He stepped out of the fog, setting off so many emotions in her she couldn't possibly sort through them all.

"Ah, Tess." Jacob's voice was painful to her. "You're lookin' lovely tonight, darlin'," he said with calculated casualness.

Tess jumped off the bench and backed away from the man, wide-eyed. "Y-y-you s-stay away from me." Her sentence started out barely audible but worked into a shriek.

"Easy. Easy, now." He held his hands out in front of him. "I'm going." He continued on down the hill, chuckling to himself.

Tess turned back around and collapsed on the bench. She gathered her heavy sweater around herself even more tightly against the chill. She rubbed her arms and rocked back and forth, tears starting to roll down her cheeks. Someone came from behind her and grabbed a handful of her hair. An arm came around in front and pulled her forcefully back against her attacker's body.

Jacob hissed in her ear, yanking her hair to emphasize each word. "What? You think you're too good for me or somethin'?" The smell of whiskey was heavy on his breath. "Don't you forget, I know what a tramp you are." He ran his tongue along her neck, tasting her. She closed her eyes, concentrating on disconnecting from him; not feeling his tongue on her neck, not smelling his rancid breath, not hearing his words. "Ach!" he said angrily, shoving her to the ground in front of the bench. "No one will have you now, Tessie. You're soiled, and no man will want you in his bed." She didn't turn to look at him or lift her head, leaving her hair to fall around her like a curtain between them. "So don't you be so high and mighty with me. You'll be beggin' for a piece of me down the road. You can bet on that." Her hands on the cold stone pavers trembled. She cringed, waiting for him to strike her. The fog turned to a cold drizzle. After several long minutes, she finally dared to turn her head. He was gone.

MICHAEL WOKE. THE ROOM was dark. One beam of moonlight filtered in the dirty street-level window high on the wall and illuminated his path to the john. He grabbed his underwear, which had somehow landed on the small, battered TV set, pulling them on. He staggered across the room to the bathroom and relieved himself without fully opening his eyes, yawning. *Damned ale never gives you a good night's sleep.* He shuffled wearily back into his bedroom/kitchen/dining room/den. He opened the refrigerator, staring into its depths a minute before choosing one of his last three pints, the only contents of the refrigerator other than an uncovered bowl of soup, a tub of butter, and half a loaf of semi-squashed bread, which didn't exactly need to be in the refrigerator, but it discouraged the roaches. He popped the bottle open on the side of the counter skillfully, even hitting the trashcan with the top, he noted with pride.

He stumbled to the only chair in the room, patched in some places, in need of patches in others. Leaning back, he kicked his feet up on the particle-board coffee table and knocked Molly's panties to the floor. He watched her a moment as she lay on the bed on her stomach, completely in the nip, snoring. Her diagonal positioning across his small bed unintentionally denied access to anyone who might be over the height of two feet. Her jumbled dirty-blond hair hung down, partially concealing her face. *Poor thing. Nineteen years old and out on your own 'cause your daddy caught you messin' around with his best friend. Tch."* He took another swig of his libation. *'Course I was younger than that when I was first out on my own...*

And look at how you've ended up now, a nasty voice in his head sounding curiously like his father's, told him. He took another long pull on his bottle, musing. *Twenty-six years old and not a dime to your name.* He kicked his blue jeans off the table, stubbing his toe in the process. The belt buckle clanked heavily on the floor, making a loud noise in the almost empty room. Molly stirred and somehow managed to claim even more of the bed before drifting back to sleep. He downed the last of his beer unhappily and set the bottle on the floor next to the chair. He raised the lever on the side of the chair and the foot rest came partway up, blocked by the table. Turning on his side, he spied a towel on the floor. He reached over to get it, almost toppling the chair, but he pushed himself up, covered his nearly naked body with the towel as best he could, and closed his eyes.

Sunlight threatened his eyelids but he left them closed. The sound of water running through the gutters mixed with the damned birds chirping on the sidewalk. He sat, groggy and stiff. A torn piece of paper fluttered off his chest, to the ground. As it flipped over and over in its descent he saw it was an old receipt with some writing on the back. He retrieved it and read the simple message, "Thanks for last night, Molly."

Oh, yeah. That explains the towel and the chair and all. He got to his feet, knocking the empty bottle from the night before, sending it skittering across the floor and under the bed, where it clinked against a sibling. "Shit!" he cursed, stretching his sore back. He attempted to ruffle away the bedhead from his short brown hair. Stepping forward, his hands fumbled around the bedside table, knocking over a bottle of aspirin Molly must have left there, and finally discovering his wire-rimmed glasses. Putting them on, he shuffled again to the refrigerator; reaching in, after a few seconds of staring, for the half-eaten bowl of soup. Then he changed his mind, pushed it back and took out a beer instead.

"YOU'RE LATE, MCKEE," Taddy McGregor yelled across the bar.

"Dock my friggin' lousy pay," Michael countered.

"Don't think I won't." Abruptly his demeanor changed. "Well, now. Hello, Miss Tess. Don't you look the picture of pretty in your uniform?"

Michael turned to see the girl from the night before, this time in the standard peasant's blouse, with its off-the-shoulder elastic top, and the short green skirt, her hair in a thick pony tail. She caught his gaze and didn't look away for a moment. Her eyes were startlingly green, her face fair and freckled, the cheeks rosy from outside; and that's when he realized what it was that made her so different. She had a soft, innocent, fresh look, while all the other women around there, even the nineteen-year-old Molly, had a hard, weathered appearance. He stood frozen a minute by her eyes. Then she hastily dropped her focus to the floor. Becoming aware of his racing heart, he grabbed a handful of peanuts off the bar, hoping the ordinary gesture would calm his nerves. "Hey, Jimmy." Michael tried to sound casual as he tipped his head in Tess's direction. "Who's the new girl?"

The bartender smiled, drying a glass as he gazed at her, too. "Name's Tess Flanagan." After a moment or two he turned back. Michael was still watching her. "She's not for you, Michael," he warned. "The boss has an eye for her."

Tess was saying nervously to McGregor, "I'm sorry I'm late."

"No problem, darlin'," Tad answered, winking at Michael.

He turned his back in disgust and walked away.

TESS SERVED DRINKS and wiped tables until her back was sore and her dogs were barkin'. As she worked, the musicians tuned their guitars and performed after a break. The music drew her in. The band played mostly familiar rock tunes, and yet she had never heard them sung with such passion and intensity. The lead singer's voice was sometimes throaty and rich, sometimes high and breathy. At times it seemed husky with holding his pain in; at other times it was like he was trying to shout it out of himself. His voice reached inside her and tugged at the pit of her stomach.

Tonight it triggered a memory of her father.

One of the things she and her father once had in common was a love of music. After her mother passed, it had been only melancholy songs he sang as he worked on the farm. Then one night, when he came in from the fields, he heard her singing one of the songs as she milked the cows, unaware that he was there.

"Why, Tessie, dear. That was lovely."

She jumped, startled, then laughed. "Oh, Da. You frightened me. I thought I was alone."

He looked at her fondly. "You have a fine voice. Like your ma." His voice cracked and he turned and hobbled toward the house without another word.

She stared after him as he was framed in the doorway, the sunshine swallowing his slight figure as he went. He had aged before her eyes. The work was hard, and she sometimes wondered if perhaps he would have preferred a son in her place. But no, he insisted, "You're the apple of me eye, Tessie-girl."

"Tess." McGregor's stern voice ratcheted into her revelry. "That table's good and clean now. How's about movin' on to another?"

She nodded and started on the next table.

Hours later, last call had been announced and the only remaining drunk had been dumped out on the street with a sort of routine callousness. McGregor was counting his pennies in the office, and Tess was on her way out the door. As she left the break room adjacent to the office in the rear of the bar, she heard piano music. Startled, she crept out of the back hall and into the main room. She had thought she and the boss were the only ones left in the building. In the glow of just one remaining light, the lead singer sat at the keyboard. All the nights she paced the sidewalk outside trying to gather the courage to come in, she had heard him and his band playing, but she had never heard him on the keyboard before. He started singing quietly. His voice was husky, choked with emotion. Her heart caught in her chest. The pain she heard she recognized.

Without realizing it, she moved closer. She must have made a noise because he turned. She drew in a breath and backed up. In her haste, she bumped into a table and knocked over a glass that had gone unnoticed. It began to roll toward the edge of the table. Panicky, she grabbed at it, but too late, it spun out of her reach and went crashing to the floor.

"Oh!" She stooped to hastily collect the shards.

He jumped off the stage. "Are you okay? I'm sorry. I didn't mean to scare you." He bent to help her. She drew back, sucking her breath through her teeth and squeezing her hand. Drops of bright red blood peppered the floor. "You're hurt."

"M-mm," she groaned. "It's my own fault. I'm so careless."

"Hold on. I'll get a towel from the bar." He was back in seconds with a rag. "Here, let me help." He wrapped her hand with the towel and applied pressure to stop the bleeding. "I'm Michael, by the way."

She nodded. "Tess. Oww!" she said involuntarily.

"Did I hurt ya? I'm sorry."

"Nay, nay. 'Tis my fault." She peered into his face. She had never thought brown eyes could be so expressive. At present, as they looked at her with concern, they reminded her of melted chocolate. She was amazed by how tenderly he now held her hand. "I'm sorry...I shouldn't have been listening in on your playing."

"That's all right." He shrugged.

Almost without thinking she blurted out, "That was a beautiful song."

He smiled warmly. "Me mam used to sing it to me," he admitted.

"Ahh. Is that where you got your musical gift from then?"

"Maybe. ...My father used to sing some, when he'd been drinkin'...not as pretty though." He winked at her and she laughed.

Michael liked the sound of it. She looked different without her apron on. She had let her hair down and it hung below her shoulders. It looked so soft; he resisted with effort the urge to reach out and touch it.

"What the bloody hell's going on here? Who broke that?" McGregor roared, coming in from the back.

"I did," they said in unison. Tess stared at him in surprise; he continued to look at McGregor and didn't return her gaze. "It was my fault. You can take it out of my check."

She turned her head slowly to McGregor. "Nay, Mr. McGregor, 'tis not Michael's fault, 'tis mine. I backed into a table and knocked it off. I'm sorry. I'll pay for it."

"You say you did it...he says he did it..." He looked from one to the other, baffled, shaking his head. "What did you do to your hand?" he said as if just noticing it.

"Uh," she said, staring dumbly at the bloody rag on her hand. "I cut it on the glass."

He shook his head again. "Ach! Get the hell out of here, the pair of ya!"

Michael grabbed her elbow. "Aye, sir," he said contritely, tugging on her. They turned and rushed out the door. As soon as it closed behind them, they burst out laughing.

When their laughter subsided, Tess looked at her shoes and said quietly, "You didn't have to do that." She gazed into his eyes. "But thank you."

"Ah, it's no big deal. Taddy hates me anyway."

"Aye, I noticed. Why is that?"

"I don't know... I think I'm a pretty charming guy." She giggled. He looked around. "Nary a fella or da or brother to walk ya home?"

The smile faded from her face. Again she cast her gaze down, shuffling her feet. "Nay. I'm alone."

Michael didn't know what he had done to change things between them. He tried to regain their playful mood. "Well then, how's about this charming guy walks ya home?"

She stiffened. "Uh, nay. I'll be fine." She stepped into the street and started to hurry away, but she stopped, perhaps remembering her manners. "Thanks. I'll be okay."

He stood staring after her retreating figure. He usually had no problem sweet-talking a girl; and if he did happen to strike out, it didn't bother him. This bothered him, and he didn't know why.

CHAPTER TWELVE

Tad McGregor peered through slats in the blinds at the two as they stood in the circle of the streetlight, talking. Tess walked away from Michael and he hesitated on the doorstep before turning and heading down the street. "Good," he grunted. He turned from the window and shuffled back to his office.

On the way he passed the small pile of glass that still lay on the floor, flecked with Tess's blood. *I'll get someone to clean it up tomorrow,* he thought, tiredly. He liked being the one to tell people what to do. For years he lived in his father's shadow, terrified of his erratic temper and the beatings he would often receive when his da returned home from the pub, drunk. There had been a time when he had hated the place. But now that his father was dead, he had a new lease on life. *He* was the one telling people what to do, and he loved the way that made him feel empowered. He would cower to no one now.

He looked around at his pub. He was proud of his business. It was not the cramped, dark, homey pub his father built, filled with old men smoking pipes in front of the large fireplace. After his father left the place to him, Tad borrowed money and put in new lighting, a bigger bar, and in the end nearly tripled the size of the building. Friends warned him it was too big a bar for the little village, but he had confidence people would travel from the nearby city of Kinsale to patronize his place. *They'd better,* he thought desperately, recalling the meager receipts from the night's till.

He grabbed his jacket. It could get chilly at night on the Old Head of Kinsale, especially when the wind came off the coastal waters, and Tad's place stood on a barren cliff above the rocky shoreline.

His thoughts turned to Tess. She was a pretty young thing...maybe twenty or so... ten years his junior, his father's death leaving him one of the youngest pub owners in the county. Tad liked the fact that he could easily intimidate her. The fear he saw in her eyes he took for respect. He would be patient, but eventually he was determined she would be his. He would control her and she would do whatever he wanted her to do, and he already had some ideas about that. He snickered lustily. He closed the door to the pub, leaving alone as he always did, his mind full of Tess Flanagan and what he wanted to do with her.

TESS TRAVERSED THE street, slowing her pace as she climbed the hill. She lifted her shawl over her head to ward off the dampness, and to give her the sense she had disappeared. She wanted to disappear. Why did she tell Michael not to walk her home? She felt she could trust him...but she had felt that way before... She shivered involuntarily to shake off the memories. She allowed herself instead to think of Michael. She smiled as she thought of him clumsily wrapping her hand in the towel. She liked the pleasure of his company, and it had been years since she could say that about anybody.

She listened to the water tumbling through the gutters on either side of the street; its babbling sounded like music in the still night. The air smelled fresh, of wet grass and good, rich soil. She had made her way out of the village now and turned on the gravel path leading to her little farm and the cottage she lived in. She slowed her pace, there was no reason to hurry, no one at home to greet her, no one to tell about her first day at work.

The cottage door creaked as she entered. She reached for the candle and matches she kept on the low windowsill near the door. Once lighted, she held it aloft to illuminate her way to the fireplace. She stirred the embers there and lit a piece of scrap paper to get a fire started. She no longer could afford to pay the electric bill, but at least the house hadn't been taken from her yet.

The cottage was bigger than most in this part of the country, but nearly empty. Tess had sold off almost everything of value to support herself. The house consisted of one large room which now housed one bed, a small kitchen table with one chair, an oversized trunk, and a rocker in front of the large stone fireplace. She'd even sold the oven and refrigerator and had simply learned to do without. Despite the fire, the room was cold. She kept her sweater on and slid underneath the quilt. She lay on her side listening to the clock on the mantelpiece tick. It was the one frivolous item she had held on to. It didn't even keep good time, but it had been her father's, given to him by his grandfather. The ticking comforted her. It meant something else was out there; something making noise and moving. She did not want to think of this house completely silent, with nothing but the constantly blowing wind without. Moonlight shone on the clock's face and she watched it as it kept its lonely vigil in the night, slowly ticking off the time. Finally she fell asleep.

As always, the dreams came. She was cleaning the house; not the house like it was now, but the house as it was then, full of life and color. She had been the woman of the house for as long as she could remember, and even at sixteen, she had it down to a fine art. She enjoyed taking care of her father, and he adored her. It was a happy home then. She had picked fresh flowers and put them on the table and had a stew going on the stovetop. Biscuits were set to go in as soon as she heard the sound of her father's voice.

A sharp rap on the door startled her. She opened it to see two friends of her father's on the doorstep, Simon and Jacob. Well, not friends exactly, but men he had tipped a pint with at McGregor's pub.

"How do you do, Miss Tess?" said the one she had heard her father call Jacob, doffing his hat to her. "Is your father home?"

"Nay, but he should be back soon. Would you gentlemen like to come in and wait?" It was drizzling and their clothes were wet.

"That's very nice of you, Miss Tess, very nice indeed." She saw the two men exchange a glance and wondered idly what they had silently communicated to each other. "Mind if we hang our coats?"

"Nay, of course not." She took them and hung them on a nail over the fireplace that had held her Christmas stocking when she was a little girl. Suddenly a hand was next to hers on the mantle.

"You sure are a fine young lady, Tess." Jacob's voice was close and his breath reeked of whiskey. Was he smelling her hair? She moved quickly away, near the table where the other man had taken a seat. Without warning, Simon grabbed her hips and pulled her onto his lap.

"Come on now, little lady. We're gonna show you a good time." His hand reached for the edge of her blouse but Tess wriggled out of his grasp and stood. Before she could get two feet Jacob seized her by the shoulders and spun her, capturing her arms and trapping them behind her back.

Simon rose from the table, a depraved smile on his face. She struggled, but life on the farm had made the two burley men strong. Simon snatched the sides of her shirt and waited a beat, watching her eyes with a smirk. He ripped it open.

"L-let me go." Her fear was evident in her trembling words. "My father will be home any minute."

"You better hope he's not." Jacob reached behind his back and drew out a wicked-looking hunting knife and held it to her throat. Simon shifted his hold on her and caught her hair, yanking her head back brutally to expose her neck. She struggled to look down and follow what Jacob was doing with the knife. She thought for a minute they were going to kill her. And then she feared they would not. Jacob trailed the point of the blade slowly down her neck. When he reached her chest, he applied more pressure, drawing blood in a thin line between her breasts. Then in a flash he changed his grip and stuck his knife savagely in the table. The blade quivered and twanged...and that's where the dream always seemed to fast forward...she fought at first, but repeated blows left her stunned. She had concentrated on forgetting the details, on becoming completely unattached to the reality of what was happening to her...until her father entered.

And then the dream changed and she was looking at things through her father's eyes.

Jack Flanagan opened his front door and stood thunderstruck for several seconds. Simon had Tess's arms pinned above her head on the bed and Jacob had his back turned toward him, but was pulling on his pants. Tess was nude except for her torn shirt which covered nothing. The look on her face ripped into his heart; he had never seen such stark pain in someone's eyes before. And this, his Tess, his little lamb. She turned her head, appearing unable to bear her father seeing her like this, and she began weeping anew.

"Wh-what the h-ell?" he sputtered in shock. He turned, too late, to grab his gun off the pegs where it hung by the door.

Jacob reached from behind and slammed the rifle back in its place. "I wouldn't do that, old man," he growled. He turned Jack around, took hold of his jacket by the lapels, and pushed him into a rocker drawn near the fire.

"You sons of bitches!" He flew furiously out of the chair and swung with the strength of a younger man. Jacob went down in a heartbeat. Simon crossed the room in two long strides and threw Jack into the stone fireplace. He slid down, his eyes wide, a horrible rasping noise issuing from his mouth. Simon moved to attack him again, but Tess shouted and jumped from the bed, hurtling herself at him in a blind rage, and landing squarely on his back. She thrashed around, hitting him on the head and neck.

"Nay! Nay! Let him be!" she screamed.

Simon tried to throw her off, but she clung with a tenacity only desperation provided. Irate, he snagged her arm and tugged mercilessly. He jerked her arm out of its socket like pulling the plug on an appliance. Her body followed and she came crashing down in front of him. Naked and bloody, she threw her uninjured arm up to block the blows she knew were to come. He stood forebodingly above her.

"Simon, enough. Let's get the hell out of here." Jacob shook his head, rubbing his chin and feeling for teeth with his tongue. "I think the old yoke broke me jaw."

Simon chuckled coarsely. "I warrant it will feel a mite better after a pint."

And then they left. They just left.

But the dream didn't end there.

Tess looked at her father. His eyes stared blankly ahead; his breathing was labored. She turned back toward the bed where the sheet had partly fallen off the mattress. She stretched to reach it, her beaten body protesting every inch. She covered herself with the sheet, hurrying back to her father's side.

"Da!" He slowly turned his eyes to hers. "Da?" Suddenly his breathing, which had seemed to fill the whole room, stilled. His head fell back against the stones and his eyes remained open, but she could see the light going out in their depths. Sobs racked her already sore body as she clung to him, burying her head on his chest. "Nay, Da! Nay!" She placed a hand on his cheek. "Don't leave me alone."

She woke, as she always did, her face wet with tears. It was amazing to her how real the dreams felt. Even now it was as if her arm still ached from being wrenched from its place, her body, still tender from the beating, her heart still squeezed in her chest like a tired sponge. The shock, the humiliation, the sorrow...each fresh every night, like the whole thing happened seconds before. When would she stop being transported back to a time she so desperately wanted to forget? She crawled from the bed, dragging her quilt with her and laying on the braided rug in front of the hearth. She reached for the poker and stirred the fire, staring into its depths and listening to the clock ticking its sympathy well into the night.

CHAPTER THIRTEEN

Tess plodded down the street. It was still hours before her shift started at McGregor's, but she was compelled to get out of the house; somehow the cottage seemed more oppressive than usual. She sometimes wanted to be rid of it because it held such dark memories; but at the same time, she couldn't bear to leave it because of all its happy ones. Besides, it was the only home she had ever known.

She inhaled deeply, the smell of someone's burning leaf pile comforting her. She looked around to see a little girl across the street dragging a wagon, two doll's legs sticking straight up in the air from inside. For some reason, the unusual sight tickled her and she laughed out loud. She crossed the street on a whim to talk to the little girl.

"Hallo," she said, smiling at her. She bent to peer into her eyes. "Aren't you one of the O'Toole girls?"

"Aye, miss. I'm Kitty O'Toole."

"Ah, Kitty is it? Well, you have a fine doll there, Miss Kitty. But she seems to have missed her balance."

Kitty glanced over her shoulder at the upside down doll, and responded in a businesslike manner. "Oh, nay, miss. She's been naughty."

"Ya don't say." Tess chuckled, rising and ruffling the little girl's long, blond hair. "Well, I bet you're a good mammy."

Kitty sighed like she'd heard adults do, answering, "Yes'm, I do me best."

With that, she was off up the block, trundling her little miscreant after her. She turned at the top of the hill and waved. Tess waved back, the sun in her eyes making her squint. For an instant, the image of Kitty turned into another little girl; a redhead with a penchant for singing. The young version of Tess waved to her, the wind blowing her long hair loose from her pigtails. She blinked again and both the imagined child and the real child were gone,

Kitty having turned around the corner behind the low stone wall bordering the narrow street.

DESPITE HIS QUICKENING pulse, when he caught sight of Tess entering the room, Michael tried to appear nonchalant. He had never felt this way about anyone. He hadn't even had a teenaged crush before. His adolescence had been unusual, having been on his own after losing his mam at twelve. He'd known many women, in a casual sense, but had given them very little thought when they were absent. Even when making love to them, at times, he had been completely unaware of their existence. Now, here was this woman, whom he had barely talked to, who had refused to even let him walk her home, and he couldn't get her off his mind. He reviewed every word of their conversation, every nuance it offered, over and over again. And now as she walked through the door he found his heart leaping, and a smile spreading involuntarily across his face. He made his way across the room to her side.

"Hey! How's your hand?"

"Oh," she replied, startled, "much better, thank you." Her smile warmed him instantly. Her hair looked pretty, the sides pulled up and secured with a length of green ribbon.

"Ah, Tessie," McGregor roared, "you're early. Couldn't stand to be away from me, huh?" He leaned toward her, resting his elbow on the bar.

Tess seemed uneasy. "Bored at home, I guess." She looked down and fiddled with her apron. "It's okay to be here before my shift, isn't it?" she added timidly.

"Why, of course, darlin'," Tad returned. "A man would be a fool not to want a pretty, young thing like you around." His eyes hardened as he shifted his gaze to look at Michael. "McKee. I'm not paying *you* to look pretty. Get back to work."

He glared at Tad but turned without a word and headed back on stage.

Tess's gaze followed his retreating form regretfully.

When she turned back, Molly was staring at her, a hand on her hip. "Ohh, darlin', you should stay away from that one."

Her cheeks flushed. "What?"

Molly nodded after him. "That one's a real heartbreaker. He's bagged about every moving thing in this town. He *is* good in the sack, girl. I'll tell you that much," she ended dreamily.

Unsure of how to respond to this, Tess simply turned and walked away.

HOURS LATER, MICHAEL sat alone on the stage, as he had the night before, toying around with the keyboard. In the back Tad's adding machine clicked away as an odd sort of accompaniment. After a bit, Michael closed his eyes and was able to tune it out. He let the music he created roll through him, the piano keys becoming an extension of his fingers, the chords like his breathing, his heartbeat, his soul. Singing was the only time he let himself feel the emotions he usually kept hidden away; the anger, when he played his harder music, and now, the sadness and loneliness that sometimes threatened to engulf him.

This time he knew she was there in the shadows. He clinked the last few notes of his song and spun slowly on his stool to catch her form silhouetted in the footlights. She must have also gotten caught up in the mournful chords he had played, as she had that same kid-caught-with-his-hand-in-the-cookie-jar expression she wore the night before. She quickly headed for the door.

"Tess, wait." He jumped from the stage and followed after her. She froze a few feet away from him, turning hesitantly.

"I-I'm sorry. I was listening in again. I shouldn't have. You obviously were enjoying the privacy."

"Nay, Tess. It's all right. I knew you were there. I don't mind." The streetlights filtered in through the window, shining on one side of her face. Even in the dim light he could see she was blushing. It made his heart inch up in him even further. He cleared his throat to free his voice from its invisible blockage. He cocked his head toward the rear of the bar. "Taddy still countin' his copper back there?"

"Aye." She smiled. "I think I heard a coupla curse words. It can't be good."

"We best get out of here then, eh?" He held the door for her and they passed together into the welcoming light of the street lamp. They could hear the waves tonight, beating against the rocks below the cliff, the gusty winds off the water giving the air a definite nip. He pulled up his collar and asked tentatively, "Can I walk with you a bit, Tess?"

She nodded silently and they fell into step together.

He grasped around for a conversation starter. "Did you grow up here, in the village, then?"

"Aye. I've lived here all my life." She peered at his face in the darkness as they began the long ascent up the hill. "Where do you hail from?"

"Cork, mostly...and Limerick."

"What brought you to Old Head?"

"Needed a change of scenery, I guess." He shrugged and the conversation lapsed. They continued to trudge up the dark street. Sidewalks were a luxury not reserved for the small town, although they connected McGregor's Pub to O'Toole's Grocery, to the post office, to the ramshackle building where Michael rented his room. Besides this, there were none. Not even the road to the church was granted a sidewalk.

Michael finally spoke. "Did you know ol' Taddy as a boy?"

Tess shook her head. "Nay. He is much older than me. And I didn't get off the farm much."

"A farm girl, eh?" He tilted his head in her direction, giving her a grin.

She smiled. "Aye. I've milked a few cows. How 'bout you?"

"Nay, nay. I'm a city boy, born and bred. I wouldn't know a cow's udder from a bar tap."

Tess laughed at the odd comparison.

"You have a nice laugh. You should use it more."

"I don't often have something to laugh about. But you make me laugh."

His hearty chuckle rang into the still night, making her jump. "I guess I should take that as a compliment?"

She giggled again. "Take it as you want it," she teased in return.

"Ahh...and a sense of humor, too."

They came to a dirt lane bordered by low stone walls on either side. "Thanks for walking with me, Michael." She put her hand on his arm and heat rushed through his body. He didn't want their time together to end.

"This is your place?" he said hurriedly to keep her. He made out a cottage at the end of the lane and the indistinct shape of a barn in the background.

"Aye." She looked across the pasture herself as if to verify the fact. She hesitated then brushed a hand over her skirt. She glanced at him again, a question briefly flitting through her eyes; then she shook her head, appearing to have answered the question herself. "Thank you again. It was nice having the company," she murmured, peering into his eyes earnestly for a beat. She seemed to be struggling to communicate with him without having to speak the words.

But, alas, Tess, I have no interpreter with me. His heart sank a little. She moved away from him, releasing his arm. Reflexively he grabbed her hand for the briefest second before they parted, her arm trailing after her like a dress's train. She turned and without another word, hastened down the lane. He stood confounded, watching her skirt swish behind her in the dregs of moonlight fighting through the cloud cover. He sighed, releasing the air caught in his chest since they first set off down the path. When she turned off the lane and on to a pathway leading to the cottage, he shuffled over to the wall with his hands stuck in his pockets.

She twisted as she opened the door. He wondered if she could see him sitting atop the stone wall. Moments later, he saw a small flicker of light in the window. He knew by the way the light flitted, grew, and ebbed she must be holding a candle. He wondered why she didn't turn on the electric lights. He watched as the room then became brighter, with the same kind of blinking, dancing light; he guessed she had stoked a fire. He saw her profile briefly in the window. She seemed to be taking off her shawl. The shadowy Tess released her hair from its ribbon and shook it out; he imagined it glowing in the firelight. Her hands went to her blouse and for a fleeting moment he entertained the thought of watching her undress for bed. But at last he pulled his eyes away and began the downward climb into town.

He shook his head. *Idiot. Why'd you turn away?* But a voice answered, *"Aah, but it wouldn't have been right.* He had seen many women in the buff, had, in fact, done many erotic things with them. But looking at Tess in the window without her permission, no matter how much he wanted to, *now that would be a crime.* He laughed at his own inconsistency and drew his coat tighter, whistling to himself in the night.

"GOOD EVENIN', MOLLY."

"Not so sure about that one, Tess," she whispered out of the side of her mouth. "The boss is in a *fine* mood." She hefted a full tray from the bar and nodded down the hallway. "That banker man's here again."

Tess followed her gaze to a short, balding man who strode briskly along the back hall, carrying a filer full of cockeyed documents threatening to spill free from the folder's confines at any moment. Tad stuck his head out of the office and glowered at the back of the man. Seeming satisfied the man was, indeed, heading out the door, he spun and returned to his office, slamming the door behind him. The smoky glass rattled in the door's window, but remained intact.

"I'd stay out of his way if I were you," Molly warned. Tess nodded her agreement and busied herself taking drink orders. Hours later, as she was handing drinks from her tray to a table of local farmers, she heard a familiar voice address her.

"See, Simon. I told you our little Tessie was still here in town." The hair rose on her neck and she turned slowly, a sick feeling in her stomach. And there they sat, *as pretty as a picture,* she thought in horror. She froze, staring at the pair and wishing, illogically, they would vanish in a puff of smoke. Jacob laid a hand on her arm and she yanked it back as if burnt.

"Don't touch me!" she yelped, her voice frantic.

"TESS!" Tad bellowed from behind the bar. She tore her eyes from the two men at the table, though it was a struggle, to look at her boss. McGregor waved his arms with irritation, signaling for her to come over. She did so without hesitating. He frowned at her as she approached. "What seems to be the problem?" he growled.

"Uh, I...I...I..." She glanced back to discover Simon and Jacob leering at her. Tad grabbed her arm and yanked her to him across the wet bar. He hissed in her ear, "Now listen here, missy. Whatever the customer wants he gets, got it? I don't care if a whole table wants you to give them blow jobs...you just get yourself down on your little knees and say, 'Who's first?' You hear me?"

She nodded dumbly and he released her. She slid back to her feet, shaking. A drunk at the far end of the bar shouted something and McGregor hollered back, "I said I'd be there in a minute, hold your damn horses!" He moved off, leaving her alone.

Michael walked into the pub, his guitar in tow. Noticing Tess at the bar he sauntered over, leaning his guitar case against a stool. "Hey, Tess. 'Evenin.'"

She stared glassily ahead and lifted her empty tray without a word, treading off to wait on tables. He stood for a couple of seconds with his mouth hanging open, crushed. What could he have done to make her act like that? Maybe she was mad because she had seen him out the window of the cottage in the dark. Maybe she thought he was some kind of pervert Peepin' Tom. He snapped his mouth shut, staring after her as she moved away. Anger slowly replaced disappointment. What had he done, anyway? He had walked away like a gentleman. She had no call to be upset with him. Hot with frustration and confusion, he marched across the room without another glance in her direction. He joined his band members on stage and poured all of his exasperation into the music.

He was so absorbed in his playing he almost missed it. But it was like walking into a room and knowing a spider is on the ceiling without even looking. He suddenly knew, without seeing, that something was amiss. He scanned the room uneasily and that was when he saw the men grabbing Tess. He would have thought it was just another rowdy customer except for the expression on her face. She was struggling with the men, a look of sheer terror in her eyes. In an instant he took it in, her fear and desperation, the stubby fingers digging into her bare arms, keeping her trapped on his lap, unable to rise to her feet, the other man leaning in to kiss her neck, an evil smile plastered on his sick face.

Without even realizing he was doing it, Michael hopped off the stage. A white roar filled his head. He was barely aware of the band instruments stopping one by one behind him, or of idle chatter abruptly ending as customers caught sight of him charging across the room. In a few long strides he was by her side. It was like everything was moving in half time. He untangled Tess from the man's lap and delivered a wallop to his chin, knocking him and his chair over backward. He was on the other man in a flash, laying into him without stopping to breathe. Then Jimmy Flynn and McGregor were hauling him off and things came back to real time. People were shouting, McGregor loudest of all.

Michael looked around at Tess. She stood trembling, openmouthed, staring at the men on the floor. He followed her gaze and was surprised to see blood running along the creases in his knuckles. McGregor's voice suddenly became clear, like he had tuned it in on the radio.

"Get the hell out of here McKee! And don't come back!"

He stumbled away a few steps, then turned toward the stage. He grabbed his guitar and shoved it into its case. Getting another glimpse at his shaking hands, he held them out, observing the blood in wonderment. He swiped them across his jeans and hurried in the direction of the break room to get his coat. He looked back to see McGregor helping the men to their feet, apologizing and offering them a conciliatory beer. Tess still stood there, looking pale and shocked. The crowd parted in front of him, and then he was in the break room, alone and confused. He sat silently for several moments on the bench in front of the cheap lockers Taddy had gotten from an abandoned factory.

He didn't know how long he had been sitting there when he heard voices coming from Tad's office. The walls were paper thin in the old building and although the voices were muffled, he still could catch a word here and there. He recognized the first voice as McGregor's.

"...you're not better than anyone else here. Time you get to know that."

He heard the unmistakable sound of a scuffle. The desk thumped the wall several times and a high-pitched voice begged frantically, "Nay! Please! DON'T!

"You owe me, now, Tessie," McGregor threatened. "Now SHUT UP AND LIE STILL!"

His momentary calm left him. He jumped to his feet and barreled out into the hall. He threw the office door open and by the pallid light of the desk's lamp saw McGregor wrestling with Tess. His right hand was under her skirt attempting to lift her hips onto his desk while his left hand pinioned her shoulder against the coarse wood amid a pile of papers. The shoulder of her blouse was torn and pulled down, revealing her bra. Despite the fact she was dwarfed by his large frame, Tess fought ferociously to free herself.

Tad pressed his lower body against hers to stop her flailing legs and absorbed the buffets she offered, limited by their close proximity. "Ahh, there now." He gave a coarse laugh as he managed at last to get her mostly onto the desk.

Tess took advantage of the new positioning to try to drive her knee into his crotch. Shifting to avoid injury he shouted, "Damn it, Tess! Knock it off!" He maneuvered the hand he had on Tess's shoulder, grasping her to lift her a few inches. Then he slammed her back down with such force her head hit the table and she cried out in pain.

Tad glanced up to catch Michael standing there. He grinned. "Come on in, Michael. You can watch us if you like. But be a good boy and close the door." His momentary distraction cost him. Tess's searching hand found the base of the lamp and brought it crashing down on his head. He groaned and pitched forward, burying her beneath his heavy body. Panicky, she squirmed out from under him, causing his body to fall to the floor with a loud, reverberating thud. He landed on his shoulder, twisting to lie face up amidst the broken glass. The green glass of the lamp shade mixed with the white of the broken bulb to form a grotesque halo of sorts around Tad's bleeding head. Her hands flew to her mouth in horror as she took in what she'd done.

Michael took a step toward her but was startled by the sound of Jimmy Flynn's voice from behind him in the doorway.

"Now you've done it, Michael."

Tess's tear-filled eyes met Jimmy's and she shook her head vehemently. "Nay. It was my fault. I—"

"Tess." Michael shot her a warning glance then extended his hand to her. She hesitated, but then clasped it as he helped her to step over the prone form of their boss, her shoes making a crunching sound in the broken debris. He slung his jacket over her to cover what her blouse no longer did. With his hand on her shoulder he started to walk her out the door past the bartender, when he thought of something. "Wait."

As if not hearing him, Tess continued plodding in a daze as he turned back to the desk. Stepping over Tad, he rifled through his top drawer. He removed the gun he knew was kept there. The bartender leaned casually against the door frame, observing him. As Michael rushed past him, Jimmy put his arm out to block his path. Michael glanced at him sideways.

"I hope she's worth it," he commented suggestively before raising his arm to let him through. Without a word, Michael headed down the hall in search of Tess. The bulky bartender called after him, "How far do you think you're gonna get anyway, Mikey, before the coppers catch ya?" He shouted the last at Michael's back before the rear exit door shut behind him, "Drunk like you needs his pint."

CHAPTER FOURTEEN

The salty, fishy smell of the sea was so thick tonight it threatened to choke him. The weather had grown unexpectanly cooler, making the hair rise on his arms. Michael scanned the area in front of him, his heart racing. He spotted her across the expanse of grass at the edge of the cliff. She stood peering down at the white waters as they crashed against the rocky shore. A low, wooden rail warned people of the cliff's edge but could really not serve as a barrier should someone stumble. Tess trembled, swallowed by his jacket. He worried for a moment she would jump. The wind whipped her hair back into her face as she rubbed her wrist. As he got close, the moonlight illuminated a welt already rising there.

He immediately stepped forward. "Are ya hurt?"

She didn't turn toward him but shook her head slightly.

"Tessie..." He offered again. "We have to get out of here."

She remained frozen in her spot, staring blindly over the cliff. He moved a step closer and gently grasped her elbow. "Tess—"

She whirled around and his heart caught in his chest as he stared into her wild green eyes. Tears shone on her damp cheeks, glimmering in the moonlight like trails of scattered diamonds. "Nay, Michael," she said, her words coming out choked. "I have to tell them the truth. It's my fault. ...I k-killed him." She sobbed.

He looked at her sadly, begging her, "Let me help you."

The back door creaked open and light spilled out from the bar across the grass, startling them. He saw Jimmy Flynn's outline in the doorway. "They're out here!" he yelled.

Without waiting for a response, Michael took Tess's arm and steered her along the cliff's edge. He stepped over the railing and helped her to the other side as well. They stood on a narrow ledge. To the left a trail dropped off toward the sea. He led her skittering down the path, loose rock pebbling the beach far below. He had taken the pathway many a night when he was drunk and feeling particularly reckless. Tonight he hurried over it with only self-preservation and Tess's safety in mind.

They heard voices above them, coming from every direction as searchers fanned out along the top of the cliff. Their eyes met. They hardly dared to breathe. A flashlight beam ventured over the railing and along the cliff face. She clutched his hand, squeezing it until he lost feeling in his fingers. He tried to flatten himself even more tightly against the rock face, wishing it would somehow melt and absorb them. Several seconds passed and the beam of light was joined by another, and another, each swinging away, and then toward them again.

He grabbed a quick look at the churning sea below then closed his eyes for a second, and his stomach dropped. He took a deep breath before turning his head to look at Tess. Her eyes were closed and her lips were moving fervently, but she emitted no sound. He swallowed, wondering again why the sight of her affected him so. After several minutes a voice called out, "You won't get away with this, Mikey." Had someone seen them? He heard Jimmy Flynn mutter, "Wherever they are, we won't find them tonight." One by one the lights disappeared until only a solitary beam shone. It lingered a few minutes, its lonely light trying feebly to reach the waves below; then the searcher spun and left with the others.

He peered at Tess again. Her eyes were still shut tight, and her lips continued their silent litany. "Tess," he whispered. She didn't respond. "Tess." This time he reached over and took hold of her chin, slowly turning her head to face him. Her damp lashes fluttered open and his eyes strayed to her lips which were slightly parted, pausing in mid-prayer. He thought about kissing her, right there on the cliff, while people were searching for them above, and an all-but-certain rocky death waited below. But he knew it was wrong. She was an emotional basket case and he refused to take advantage of her vulnerable state. Instead he stroked her cheek softly, pushing back a stray tendril that had blown across her face. He shook his head, purposefully shattering his desire.

"It's goin' to be all right," he reassured her, his voice cracking. He saw in her eyes how desperately she wanted to believe him. She nodded and loosened her grip on his hand for a moment. Without another word, he led her carefully down the path to the beach.

When he reached the sand, his gaze traveled the long way to the top of the cliff and he was relieved to see no further sign of flashlights. Tess slipped off her shoes and carried them, walking along through the icy water; he let his sneakers get wet. Finding a large piece of kelp, and then a stick, he tried to erase all signs they had been there as they trudged along. They reached the makeshift path he knew would take them to the rear of his flat. While the path they took to the beach had been mostly small rock and even some sand, this path was broken here and there with bigger rocks, and was a murderous climb. How had he ever scaled it drunk? Looking back down, he shivered at the thought. Tess clambered below him. She seemed more put together now. Maybe having to focus her energies on the brutal path made her forget. Forget Tad lying in all that glass.

He shook his head. The bastard deserved it. But if she told her side of the story, no one would believe her, of that he was sure. Tad owned this village. And like most small towns, people could pull together in a crisis, or turn on one of their own like a pack of wild animals. And Tess had no one. No one to defend her. No one.

And if he claimed responsibility, he'd be sent up creek in a heartbeat. Mc-Gregor fired him in front of a room full of people. They'd have no doubt as to why he killed Tad.

He looked back at Tess and reached to help her the last several feet. She slipped her hand into his unquestioningly. As they began to crest the hill, he pressed her flat against the slope. "There's someone on the porch."

Of course they would have sent someone to the house, he thought belatedly. He poked his head up. Light flooded the lawn. *Damn that Mrs. Sheehan!* She had been his landlady for a number of years now. *That light's been busted for weeks and she picks tonight of all nights to get off her fanny and fix the freakin' thing.* He thought over his options. *I used to be a decent ball player in my time...before Mam died...*

Hefting a rock in his palm, he gauged the distance. He lobbed his missile through the air, hitting the base of the bulb with a sharp sound. The man on the porch jumped to his feet and paced behind the railing, inspecting the grounds, but the light remained intact. Michael closed his eyes, momentarily defeated, but even with his eyes closed he heard the humming of the bulb and sensed the flickering of the light. The man on the porch stuck his head out and craned his neck to see the light. It buzzed and sparked a few more times, and then with a loud pop, it went out. *I guess I hit it enough to loosen it.* The guard sat back down, seemingly convinced the bulb had burned out of its own accord.

Cautiously, they rose and crept along the side of the house. With the back door barred, and, he was certain, the front one as well, he had no choice but to go in through the windows of his apartment. As luck would have it, he'd done this many a night when he'd returned home late from the pub, unable to find his key, and afraid of the wrath of the widow Katy Sheehan. He motioned for Tess to stay behind a pair of scraggily mulberry bushes as he stole toward the foundation. The window creaked as loud as the yowl of a cat in heat as he opened it, and he held his breath in the still air.

After several minutes, he deemed it safe, and slid his legs through, flipping onto his stomach to grab the ledge. He dangled a few seconds before he dropped softly to the floor. Afraid of turning on the lights, he rummaged in the dark until he found what he was looking for. He plucked a small, intricately carved wooden box off a shelf in his nearly empty cabinets and opened it. By the pale illumination of a streetlight out front sifting through his dirty street-level windows, he counted his money. He cursed under his breath. Twenty-four Euros. That's all he had. How far could they get on that? He slammed the box shut and sighed, looking at the ceiling and clasping his hands behind his head.

After a minute or two he came to a decision. Resolutely, he grabbed the box and began searching for a knapsack under the bed. With a clink of bottles, he slid out a worn bag and began stuffing it with t-shirts and another pair of jeans. He snatched a tweed cap from the countertop and hit it against his thigh to dust it off. Putting it on his head, he quietly dragged a kitchen chair over to the wall, but he was still far short of the window ledge. He climbed the back of the chair, being careful not to push it out from under him, and balanced on the top. Grasping the edge of the sill, he grunted and hoisted himself, shimmying out the window to find Tess waiting along the side of the house.

"Michael." She smiled and squeezed his arm, her shoulders and face relaxing. He exhaled, having received all the reward he needed.

The still night was broken by a loud voice. "Seen anything, Collin?"

"Nay. You?"

"Nay."

"I'll tell you one thing, if it weren't Tad McGregor we were talking about here, I'd be home right now curled up in a warm bed with me wife."

"Aye. And even it bein' Taddy McGregor, I'm not long for this porch. I'll say that much."

"Aye." The two returned to their respective spots begrudgingly.

When he believed it was safe again to move, Michael whispered, "All right. Let's get out of here."

"Nay. This is not your mistake. I can't let you do this."

"I don't have time to argue the point with you. Come on." He tugged on her arm.

"Nay. This isn't right."

Over her shoulder Michael noticed a man shuffling uncertainly down the sidewalk in their direction. He pushed Tess into the recess formed where the chimney protruded from the wall and covered her mouth with his hand. Pressing against her, he tried to hide himself as well. Her eyes grew wide as she now heard the sound of the man's off-key singing as he approached the house. They tried to still their breathing. The man stumbled up the porch steps, knocking his shins several times.

"Sh-sh-shit!" he slurred, followed closely by, "Who the hell are you? ...Oh, Collin. Wh-wh-what are you doing here?" His attempts to straighten himself might have been comical if they weren't so pathetic.

"I'm not here for you, Amos, if that's what you're askin'. Not this time, anyways. I'm here for that McKee boy."

"What? Nay. That Michael's a good 'un, I tell ya. He'd share his last pint with ya, he would."

"Be that as it may, we're lookin' for him." Amos swayed on his feet and the lawman reached out to steady him. "Oh, come on, you old fool. Ta bed with ya." He kindly opened the door and helped Amos down the hall despite loud protests of, "I'm all right. Lemme go!"

"I'm sorry, Tess," Michael whispered, removing his hand from her mouth. She nodded, searching his face. Her eyes seemed to say, *Why? Why are you doing this for me?* Her closeness paralyzed him for a second. Her chest rising and falling with each breath, her heart thumping madly within her, her warm breath on his skin. Again, he fought the strange urge to press his lips to hers, to capture each breath from her lips and blend it with his own. But, no matter how strong his craving for her, no matter how dazed she left him feeling, a portion of him knew that was not what she needed right now. His better half winning out, he took her hand confidently, and without another word, he led her past the front door and up the long hill heading out of town.

CHAPTER FIFTEEN

Michael slowed his pace as they neared the outskirts of Tess's property. He could see the house was dark, but he didn't trust in its safety. They had steered clear of the road as they hiked out of town, scrambling over rocky terrain. Each had remained silent, preoccupied by their own thoughts.

Now he approached the house cautiously, pressing his back against the wall, and sliding to the edge of a window. He listened for several minutes, and then dared to peer in the glass. He saw no signs of movement and stole past it, guiding Tess behind him. He hesitated at the door then reached out and slowly turned the handle. He let the door swing inward of its own accord. It creaked, the sound cutting through the still night, making their hearts beat faster; but nothing happened. Taking a deep breath, he crossed the threshold and threw on the lights. The switch clicked, but the house remained dark. He tensed then remembered the candlelight from the night before. She had already moved to the window to retrieve the candle and matches, and in minutes the light revealed her empty home.

She stood, seeming unsure of what to do next.

"Tessie..." he murmured, "get your things together."

She looked at him blankly a moment then moved to a trunk at the foot of the bed and lifted out a few blouses and a couple pairs of jeans. She sat staring at the items gathered on her bed.

He nodded at her torn blouse. "Maybe you should change?"

Her head bobbed dumbly and he crossed to the window.

Staying out of view, Michael scanned the horizon for uninvited guests. He glanced over his shoulder. Tess had removed his jacket and laid it neatly on the bed. She untied her apron/uniform skirt and let it drop to the floor. Stepping out of it, she removed a pair of jeans from the bed. He couldn't help taking in the smooth, sensual curve of her bare hip, marred only by a thin line of black lace crossing it, before the denim robbed him of his view. Quickly, he turned back in case she lifted her head and caught him gaping at her. Raising a hand to the window, he released a slow, tremulous breath.

The fields outside remained quiet. The view was clear all the way through the gap in the stone wall surrounding the property to the road. Michael couldn't resist another peek back. He caught her eye as she was about to take the blouse off over her head.

"You'll have to turn around," she said matter-of-factly.

He looked away, chuckling quietly at her modesty, which seemed so out of place considering the circumstances. *I mean, come on. It's not like I haven't been around the block a few times, actually...quite a few times...* But even as he thought it, he knew this was different. Somehow she had a way of making everything new for him, and that revelation terrified him. He had promised himself a long time ago he would not care for anyone but himself...and yet here he was, drawn here by some power of hers she was completely unaware of possessing.

He faced the window but stared, unseeing. In his mind he saw them bent over the broken glass in the bar, he pressing the towel to her cut...the look of terror in her eyes as he opened the office door to catch Tad mashing himself against her, trapping her like an animal... her pale face on the edge of the cliff as she mumbled her silent prayer...her expression as she teased him on the walk home the night before, a smile dancing around her lips like a prizefighter, those damn gorgeous eyes stealing his breath away...and finally he saw that little bit of skin and silk he had glimpsed before the jeans slipped over her hip.

And then he saw them. Ten men, at least, breasting the hill, silhouetted by the moonlight like a posse from some American Western. "Uhh...Tessie? Do ya have a back door?"

"Nay. Why?"

He searched frantically around the bare room for a place to hide. He ran to her, scooping the clothes off the bed in one swift move. He seized her hand, blew out the candle, and bent in front of the fireplace. As in most Irish homes, the hearth was large and deep.

"Inside," he whispered, pushing her head down to avoid hitting it on the stones above. They flattened themselves as much as they could on opposite sides of the fireplace, their heads almost touching as they bent their necks to follow the inward curve of the flue. He prayed their shoes weren't showing, or at least the dim light would cover them. As he did, he heard the front door creaking open.

"I tell you I saw a light," a voice boomed loudly in the emptiness. He heard the *click, click, click* of the switch before the intruders figured out there was no electricity.

"Aye, sure you did. You eejit," another voice rejoined sarcastically. "I'm telling *you*, they're long gone."

Michael could see a portion of the hearth outside as a flashlight beam crossed it, heading perilously close to Tess's white shoe.

"Looky here," the first voice said, and the light abruptly moved away. "Her skirt."

Tess let a small gasp escape, but the searchers continued. "See, I told ya they'd been and gone. Let's get out of here. I'm not getting paid enough to be out on a cold night like tonight."

"Aye," the voice faded as the men left the cottage. "That McGregor sure pinches the pennies. Hard enough to raise blisters, I hear." The two men's low chuckles were the last thing to carry back to the fugitives.

They waited some time then crept out of their hiding place. When Michael was certain no one was about, he risked lighting the candle so Tess could finish packing her things into his knapsack. When she came to him, she seemed to have found her voice. "This'll be as far as you'll be comin', Michael McKee," she said as firmly as her nervous voice would allow. "You've been a good friend to me." A tear pushed past her eyelashes, and she swiped it away angrily with the side of her hand. "More than I deserve. And I'm certain to have gotten you into some hot water already for helping me, but—"

"Tess, this town holds nothing for me. I've been thinkin' of goin' for weeks now."

"But not this way, like some dog bein' hunted in the night."

"I've been in worse positions," he lied, grinning at her to throw her off track.

It had the desired effect. She sighed with exasperation, and before she could formulate her next thought, he led her out the door and into the night, where she dare not break the silence with another argument.

THEY TRUDGED ON SILENTLY through the dark along the roadways, ducking behind the low, stone walls lining them whenever headlights appeared through the gloom. It was at one of these intervals, when they chanced to stop in a rare streetlight shining down where they huddled, near the base of a small stone bridge, that he glanced back to check on her. She reached to touch his face softly, brushing at something. She caught herself, explaining haltingly, "Y-you have a smudge...from the fireplace."

His face grew hot. "Aye," he said, lamely. The car that had forced them to take cover rumbled across the bridge, and they were free to go on once more.

After what he felt for certain was many miles, he chanced to look at her again. She was concentrating on picking her way carefully over the shadowy ground, but he could see in her face her fatigue.

"How 'bout we stop for a rest?" He spoke the first words in hours.

"Aye." She sighed. They found a soft batch of heather, still within the protective arms of a wall's shadow, and sat. She removed her shoes and massaged her bare feet, which he noted were some of the smallest feet he had ever seen on a grown woman. He took a shoe idly to study its size and noticed the soles were nearly worn through. He peeked again at her feet, squinting in the fading moonlight, and discovered they were raw and bleeding in some places. How was she able to keep up at all? He was stabbed by a twinge of guilt for setting such a torrid pace.

He set the shoe in the grass, took his cap off, and slowly slid his legs out to recline, taking off his jacket to use as a sort of blanket. "I think I'll catch meself about forty winks or so." He folded his arms behind his head and laid them on top of the hat for a pillow.

"All right," she said, the word pitched high in surprise. She sat for awhile, wrapping her arms around her knees and staring at the glimmering surface of a nearby pond. He watched her, but when she turned around he closed his eyes and pretended to sleep.

After some time she spread out on the ground beside his tranquil form, curling on her side with her back to him. She shifted, trying to pull her sweater more closely around her. Now that their walking wasn't keeping them warm, he noticed how cold it had gotten.

"Tess," Michael called softly. She rolled over. "It's cold," he stated simply and lifted his arm and the jacket, inviting her into its warmth. She hesitated then inched her way over to him, laying her head, as he desired, on his arm. He made certain the jacket completely covered her far shoulder then fell back into his gentle breathing.

Tess's life was once again like an image in a kaleidoscope. When her father had died in her arms, it seemed like someone twisted the kaleidoscope, shifting forever the pieces of her life. Now again, with one fatal action, everything had changed. She couldn't quite wrap her mind around the fact that she was, at this very moment, on the run, wanted for the murder of Tad McGregor. Her brain felt like a computer that had been jammed by a cat running across its keyboard; there was too much information, and she couldn't sort through it all. She was numb. She listened to the steady breathing beside her, and despite her fears, before long the rhythm lulled her to sleep as well.

SUNLIGHT WARMED TESS'S eyelids, but she believed it to be shining in her window at home. She knew it must be late, but she stretched languidly, listening to a soothing, rhythmic thumping sound that seemed familiar, but yet she wasn't quite sure she recognized it. Her eyes flew open. She stared across Michael's chest at her hand on his shoulder. His hand lay on her upper arm. She realized she was asleep on the ground beside the road in the arms of a man she had met just days before. And then the brutal truth came back to her—she was running away from a murder.

She tilted her head slightly to check if he was still asleep. Much to her relief, he seemed unaware of her predicament. *I must have been cold and shifted my head onto his chest,* she thought in a panic. How to tactfully get out of this? Ever so cautiously she pulled her arm back. His hand slid to his chest. She stole a peek at him, but his eyes remained closed. Slowly, and without an ounce of grace, she slid out from under his other arm and sat. He seemed not to notice. She surveyed him. His hair was ruffled, his mouth hanging open a little, and she almost laughed out loud. She put a hand to her lips to smother her chuckle and crept off to the pond to splash her face with its cool water.

As she bent over, scooping handfuls of water, a soft bleating carried to her. Standing near a bush growing at the edge of the little pond were three sheep. Nervously, she searched the field for a farmer. Sheep stood in clumps of two or three, like children on the playground, or gossips in the churchyard, but there was not a soul to be found. Reassured, she tried to smooth her own rumpled hair as she returned to the roadside.

As she turned, she was frozen by the sight of a large ram standing over the snoozing Michael. The sheep sniffed him, tickling the slumbering figure with his velvety muzzle. Michael's face twitched and he turned over, his back to her, trying to curl up and go back to sleep. Suddenly he jerked and scurried away from the animal with a yelp. The ram took to its heels, kicking dirt into his face as a final insult.

Tess hugged herself, trying to keep the laughter from bubbling up, but she couldn't stop it. She doubled over, drawing his attention to her at last.

He turned over indignantly. "Huh. Some help you are. I guess ya'd've sat there and let that great beast...sniff me to death, huh?" The corners of his lips rose. "Blighter had some God-awful morning breath."

"I-I'm sorry." She straightened and tried to control herself. "It just looked so funny."

"Aye. I bet it did." He whipped his hat at her, but it landed far short in the grass. She picked it up and dusted it off then handed it to him, trying to look apologetic. Then they both became sober.

"Michael..." she started, but he seemed to anticipate her argument and quickly interrupted.

"We better get goin'." Without waiting for her response he donned his hat, swung the knapsack onto his shoulder, and took off across the field, calling over his shoulder, "We'll stay away from the roadways in the daytime."

BY THREE, THE PAIR was ravenous. They lucked into a clear stream early in the afternoon. It ran idly down a rocky hillside like a child's Slinky. But having nothing to carry it with, they gulped the water, and its revitalizing effects soon wore off. Now they lay flat against a slope, gazing down into the yard of a small farm as a beat-up pickup truck drove up to the house. A farm wife with her four small children exited the truck. She released the tailgate and started unloading a bed full of groceries.

"I think I spy our lunch," Michael whispered.

"Well, ya don't mean we're goin' to take it?"

"Of course, I do. Ya don't expect me to leave payment on her tailgate, do ya?"

When the momma and her four little chicks had trundled off with their sacks, they skittered down the slope. Michael peeked into the passenger side window as they shimmied past. *Damn. She took her keys.* He grabbed what appeared to be the fullest bag from the back of the truck.

They heard the lady of the house returning, chastising her idle children for not helping. They ducked behind the tire well, hoping not to be discovered, but as they did, an apple fell out and rolled several feet beyond the truck. They crouched, their eyes wide, as they helplessly watched it roll right past the mother's tennis shoes. Their luck holding, she was too lost in her tirade to even notice. Thinking they were out of the woods, they turned to leave with their purloined goods as a little girl rounded the corner of the truck. Her tightly curled blond hair bobbed as she sucked on a lollipop, staring at them with brilliant blue eyes.

"Ginny!" the mother barked. The little girl jumped. "You get your little fanny over here and lend me a hand. Right now!" The girl frowned at the pair, uncertain of her course of action. Tess smiled at her hopefully and waved. Michael mimicked her. The girl waved back cheerfully and skipped away. "Virginia Eugenia Shaw. I'm givin' ya two seconds..."

"Aye, Mama," came the tired voice of the little girl. A grocery bag crinkled and then it sounded like Ginny toddled off. More bags were gathered with a lot of grumbling about "when your da gets home..."

"Kelsey Anne. Is this your money on the tailgate?" The mother mumbled under her breath, "Child would lose the hair God gave her if only she had the chance." With that, she shut the back of the truck and headed inside.

THEY HIGHTAILED IT out of the farmyard and were well away from its inhabitants when they stopped to inspect the bag.

"Jackpot!" Michael called, drawing a bottle from the confines of the paper sack. "Ireland's best." He didn't wait to see what else it held, simply unscrewed the cap and took a swig.

Tess snatched the bag away. "I hope there's more than that in there." She fished out another apple and bit into it with relish. She recognized after a beat how wolfishly she was gobbling it and slowed, but he hadn't even noticed. He was in high spirits with his spirits. The sun had begun to set, and they were again leaning against the stone walls bordering the narrow roads of Ireland. She chewed on the apple, but her thoughts made her lose her appetite.

Michael's voice startled her. "What are ya thinkin' about?"

"Oh, nothing." She shifted.

"Doesn't look like nothing."

"....it's...that little girl..."

"The one in the farm yard?"

She nodded. "It made me think...did...Tad...have any children?"

His eyebrows rose. "Tad? Any kids? Nay, Tad and Helen never had any kids that I know of." He was studying her face. She was grateful it was the twilight hour, before the moon began to shine, the murky light making it difficult to see. But, try as she might, she couldn't keep it in.

"I didn't mean to, ya know," she cried, tears breaching the edges of her eyes. "I only wanted him to leave me alone. He—"

"Tess," Michael said sternly. "Ya have nothing to be sorry for. I saw...what he..." He struggled with his thoughts, becoming infuriated all over again. "I tell ya, if you hadn't, I would have killed the son of a bitch meself!"

"But...she's probably missing him right now." Tess sobbed.

"Who? Helen? Nay, Tessie, believe me, ya did Helen a favor. Tad used to sleep around on her and, if he couldn't find anyone to cheat on her with, he'd go home and beat her instead. Nay, Helen McGregor is one happy woman tonight, believe me." He took another shot of liquid courage and helped her to her feet. "I don't know 'bout you," he said, "but I ain't plannin' on spendin' another night on the ground. I'm gonna find us a real place to sleep tonight."

He turned to go, but she clutched his hand. "I don't know how to thank you for all you've done—"

"Don't thank me now. I haven't even found us a proper bed yet." He smiled at her and squeezed her hand and they walked on in silence.

CHAPTER SIXTEEN

"Aye?" The man answering the door eyed them suspiciously. His wife tried to peer out from behind his expansive shoulders.

"Excuse me, sir. I'm sorry to be interruptin' your evenin' here with the missus. It's only me and me gal Gracie, here..." Michael nodded at Tess. "We're on our way to Cork and we were needin' a place to stay. We won't bother ya for much. It's only that we are expecting a little one, aren't we sugar?"

Tess nodded uncertainly.

"Ain't she the sweetest lil' thing? And I don't want her to spend another cold night on the ground."

The man looked over his shoulder at Tess and asked slowly, "Headed to Cork, huh?"

Michael could see this one was going to need a little work, so he poured on the charm. "That's right, sir. You see, Gracie's daddy, he's a mean ol' cuss, sir, and he wasn't too happy about her gettin' knocked up. Ya know what I mean? So I thought it was best if we made a fresh start of things in Cork. Right, Gracie, honey?" He grasped Tess's hip and hauled her in to him, smiling to beat the band. She nodded again but when he took her hand her palms were sweaty.

The man's wife ducked under his arm to get a better look at them. She stared at the bruise on Tess's wrist. "Poor thing." she murmured. "How far along are ya, dear?"

"Um, a few weeks."

"Nay, Gracie, isn't it goin' on about six weeks now? I think it was about the middle of January when...it happened, ya know?"

"That's right, pumpkin," she replied, suddenly warming to her role. "It was about mid-January when we were visiting your Uncle Ollie."

The woman looked at her husband sympathetically, but he would have none of it. "Hold on a minute," he said gruffly, steering her back into the house and closing the door.

Michael and Tess looked at each other questioningly then stepped closer so that they could hear better.

"But, honey," the man was pleading. "I wanted to have some 'special time' with ya tonight?"

"We can still have 'special time,' Garvin."

"Nay, we can't," he whined. "Not with them in the house."

"Well...how 'bout the barn then? Would the barn be all right?" They heard movement behind the door, so they stepped back.

"You can sleep in the barn," the man said hurriedly, handing them a quilt, and closing the door.

"What the hell do we look like?" Michael grumbled. "Freakin' Joseph and Mary? No bloody room at the inn or somethin'?" He turned around and stomped off toward the barn, dragging Tess after him.

The barn was clean and cozy. He began to scramble up the ladder to the hayloft. He stopped halfway, swaying precariously. "Whoooaa."

"Are you all right?"

"I think I may have had too much to drink." He clambered the rest of the way and threw himself down two feet from the ladder. "Ugh. I don't feel so hot." He put a hand to his forehead.

"Let me help you." She sat in the hay, lifting his head onto her lap and gently massaged his temples.

He sighed. "Tessie, you're an angel."

He smiled at her with his eyes closed and promptly began to snore.

"Nay, I'm not." She sighed. "Nay, I'm not." She brushed the hair off his forehead and gingerly removed his hat and glasses. She stretched as far as she could, careful to not jostle his head in her lap, and was barely able to snag a bundle of hay. She shifted the bale closer to her, folded her arms, laying them atop the hay, and put her head down. Within minutes, she, too, had fallen into a restless sleep.

SIMON WAS WALKING TOWARD her through the dark. "Huh. Some angel. Maybe I should tell him what you're really like, Tessie," he jeered. She backed away, bumping into a solid figure. She turned with a scream as Jacob grabbed her upper arms.

"'Twasn't no angel that was with us, eh, Simon? Heh, heh." He pulled her closer. She broke away from him and ran into the dark, only to be captured in the burly arms of Tad McGregor, who held her tight despite the blood dripping from his head.

"Come on now, Tess. Ya owe me. Ya owe me."

Then all at once they were surrounding her, yanking on her, spinning her from one to the other in a circle. Their laughter sounded distorted, ghostly. Then, through the shadows came Michael. The men stopped taunting her, restraining her painfully as he stepped forward. Tad drew a gun out of his pocket.

"Michael!"

The gun went off, and he fell to his knees mere feet from her, staring at her in surprise and utter disbelief before pitching forward onto the floor.

MICHAEL OPENED HIS eyes. A mourning dove and his mate sat droning loudly in the upper door of the loft, the sun pouring in from behind the opening overlooking the farmer's rich fields. He felt around for his glasses in the hay next to him. His hand found his hat. Grabbing it, he chucked it at the pair of birds, who took off hastily, battering the sides of the doorway with their wings in a flurry of sound and motion. "Why can't we find a place without all these damn animal alarm clocks," he grumbled.

Tess moaned and shook her head slightly in her sleep. "Michael."

He sat frozen, listening for a second with intense interest.

"Michael!" she said more urgently. He sat and scrutinized her. Her face was tight, her breathing erratic.

"Oh, dear God!" she cried out in agony.

He took hold of her arms and shook her gently to wake her. "Nay! Let me go!" She struggled with him.

"Tess. Tess. I'm right here."

She struck out, hitting him solidly in the face. The contact seemed to finally wake her, and she gasped. "Oh, my sweet Lord! Michael, I'm so sorry." She began shaking and sobbing.

"It's all right. I'm all right."

"Nay, nay. 'Tis not all right. I struck you. You have to go back, Michael. It's too dangerous."

"Tess, I'm fine. You didn't hurt me."

"Nay. I had a dream. Tad shot you."

"Uhh...folks?" came a deep voice from below. "Everything all right?"

She hurriedly dried her tears on her sleeve and took some deep breaths. He squeezed her arms to reassure her and then leaned over the edge of the loft to peer into the face of their host. "Yeah, everything's fine. Gracie had a nightmare about her dad, is all." He gave him his best you-know-women smile.

"Ahh. Well...I'm goin' to Cork today to pick up me nephew at the train station. You want to come along?"

TESS SAT SILENTLY IN the back seat of the car, staring out the window as the miles ticked away. After a while, the combination of the heat in the small car and her lack of sleep put her under. She awoke when her body sensed the change of rhythm as they drove into town, slowing now to stop for streetlights and traffic. She couldn't believe her eyes. The biggest town she had been in was Kinsale, which had seemed huge to her with its colorful shops and restaurants. But Cork made Kinsale look like a mere speck on a map. Taxis and pedestrians swarmed the street in what seemed like even numbers. The cacophony of noise, bright lights, and one-way streets added to the city's busy confusion. After several failed attempts to reach the massive stone building housing the train station, each sabotaged by one-way streets going the wrong way, the party pulled into the shade of the huge edifice. She got out of the car slowly, mesmerized by the anthill-like quality of the people hurrying here and there, voices shouting welcomes, whistles blowing.

Michael, on the other hand, breathed in the dirty smell of the city like a familiar and pleasant scent, welcoming an old friend.

"I'll go in to check if the train is on time," the farmer said to his wife, hurrying through a set of revolving doors.

The kindly lady squeezed something into Tess's hand. "Here, dear—for the baby."

"Oh, nay, miss. I couldn't—"

"Please, take it before me husband gets back," she looked nervously over her shoulder, but then gave her an affectionate smile and a quick hug. As her husband approached she whispered, "Good luck."

Tess shoved the money into her pocket.

"Aye. It's on time, all right," he said, pleased. "Good luck to you both." He turned to shake Michael's hand.

"Thank you, sir."

"I don't know what we could ever do to thank you—" Tess began.

"It was our pleasure, little lady," the farmer replied, holding both her hands in his, showing his genuine warmth for the first time. He took his wife's arm and stepped away. They stood a moment then turned into the crowd and disappeared.

"How do you like that?" Michael intoned.

Tess looked at him and smiled. "I guess you finally grew on him," she teased.

"Me?" he said innocently, returning her grin. Then he became businesslike. "Well...I guess the first thing we do is find a place to stay." He extracted a piece of newspaper that had blown across the sidewalk and become plastered to his leg, ambling off to sit on a bench and inspect his find. "Ahh. Here it is." He gave the newspaper a sharp rap with the back of his hand.

"Here what is?" She came around to sit on the bench and view the paper from his perspective.

"Flat for rent. Cheap. 25 Oliver Plunkett Street Lower."

"Come on, it's not far from here." He popped up. Laughing, Tess shook her head and followed.

"Sounds perfect."

THE FLAT AT 25 OLIVER Plunkett Street Lower was suitable, if not perfect. They squatted to peer into the dirty windows. The room was cramped and old, but mostly clean. The prospect of a warm shower sounded irresistible to Tess.

"Paul Agostino," Michael called, recognizing the landlord the minute he saw him striding down the sidewalk in their direction. Agostino was seedy-looking, with greasy, thin, black hair and a slight build. He was probably in his early forties, but he carried himself like a much older man. "It's Michael. Michael McKee. I rented a flat on Bachelor's Quay?"

He tilted his head. "O-o-oh, aye. The guitar player. Hey. Didn't you stiff me on your last month's rent?"

"Nay, man. That wasn't me. You must have me confused with someone else." He ignored Tess's penetrating stare. "I paid you, I swear."

"Humpf."

"Listen, Paul, we need a place." He indicated Tess with his thumb.

Paul eyed her appreciatively. "Well, I guess I can show it to ya, anyways." He began to fetch the keys out of a deep pants' pocket.

"We have thirty pounds," Michael told him as he started to descend the few steps to the doorway.

The older man stopped and stared at him incredulously. "Well, I can let that cover your deposit, but what about your first month's rent?"

"I haven't got a job yet. But as soon as I do, I bring the paycheck straight to you." He emphasized his argument by pointing at him.

"Ach. That's not how I do business." He turned to shuffle off down the sidewalk.

"Wait. Please. I've got this." Tess opened her hand to reveal a crumpled wad of money. He came back and counted out fifty more pounds. He looked into her expectant face then over her shoulder at Michael.

"All right," he consented, handing him the key. They breathed a sigh of relief. "But you can only stay until I find someone to pay full rent—and I get to keep all of your money even if I do."

Michael knew he had no real choice. "Thanks."

Paul twisted to go, but then turned back. "Say. Do you still play guitar?"

"Aye, some."

"My brother's band needs a guitarist. Their guitar player got sent up river for beatin' his ol' lady with his guitar and strangling her to death with the strings."

Michael clapped his hands together. "That's great!" When they stared at him he added, "I mean...not for him...and definitely not for her...but...I could sure use the gig."

"They play tonight at Clancy's. You remember the place?"

"Aye. On Princes Street, off South Mall, right?"

"That's the place."

"Oh, but shit. I don't have a guitar."

"You had to sell your guitar? Well, never mind. My brother's got all sorts of guitars. He's a little nutty about them, but he'll lend you one. Tell 'em Paulie sent ya." He started to leave, but turned back, eyeing them with his head tilted in that peculiar way. "You two got anything to eat?"

They hesitated, exchanging a glance.

"Here." He pressed half the money into Michael's hand. He leaned in closer, cocking his head in Tess's direction. "Take her out to eat. She looks like a nice girl."

"Thanks, man. I'll never forget this," he called out to his landlord's retreating form.

"Just don't forget *me* on payday, ya hear?" he threw over his shoulder.

"I won't. I promise."

With that, Paul Agostino turned the corner, raising his hand for a final wave.

"Well, I'll be. The ol' cur does have a heart after all." Michael gazed at the key in his hand in wonderment a minute then turned and strode happily down the steps to open the door.

The room was almost exactly like the room he had left near McGregor's. Inside the doorway to the right was a pair of end tables separated by a shabby tweed-like pull-out sofa with the bed permanently unfolded. At the foot was only enough room to allow for the bathroom door to open. The hazy sunlight filtering in from the street-level windows dimly lit the rest of the room containing a beat-up recliner, a small, heavy wooden kitchen table suitable for two, and a simple kitchen setup. A long coffee table, which at one point must have stood in front of the couch, seemed now to be used as a bench of sorts for the table and so stood behind it along the far wall. Other than that, the room lay barren.

He sighed. "It's a bit of a kip, but it'll have to do."

As he closed the door on the noise and bustle of the street, the two stood awkwardly in the quiet of the small room.

Odd that we've just become roommates...

"Well-ell..." She stood frozen, seeming unsure of how to proceed.

"Aye." He sighed, moving over to the little table and setting the key on it. "Paul said I should take you out to dinner." He turned. "Would you be hungry by any chance?"

She smiled. "Famished, actually. But, Michael, I couldn't let you use your money—"

"It's not my money. It's the money the good farmer and his wife gave us for our baby."

Their laughter seemed to dispel any discomfort.

"Well, would you mind, instead, if we got some groceries and ate in? I would really love some shampoo so I can take a shower."

"Sure, sure." He grinned. "Anything you want."

TESS HAD TURNED HER back to the street and was examining the produce she found in a stand on the sidewalk when Michael saw them, a pair of middle-aged men, one short and podgy, the other tall and muscular, watching her from across the street. Were they only ogling her for ogling's sake, or were they trying to identify her? He eyed them casually, not wanting to alarm her, but was relieved when she finally made her selection, and they entered the relative privacy of the small store. "You go on ahead. I'll fetch a basket for us."

"Okay." She smiled in that open, innocent way she had. He let his eyes trail after her for a moment before again turning his attention to the men on the street corner. They seemed to be arguing. They glanced in the store's direction a number of times and finally stalked off around the corner and out of his sight.

He joined Tess again and stayed by her side until their shopping was completed. The cashier smiled at them and looked over from her work curiously from time to time. As he put their things in a brown paper bag, she commented, "You and your husband are new to the neighborhood, aren't you?"

He glanced at Tess with an eyebrow raised, his lips curling up in his amusement.

"Oh, nay," she said hurriedly. "We're not married."

"Oh, re-e-eally," she answered, peering again at him. She stepped over to help him bag the last remaining things. "My name's Bridget," she said coyly, shaking his hand.

Tess cleared her throat, her brow creasing, but the girl still focused her attention on Michael. "Here's my money," she said finally in a loud voice, forcing the cashier to at last turn her gaze from him, for a moment, at least.

"If you ever need anything...directions...or *anything...*" she offered suggestively.

"We'll be sure to call you." Tess said, grabbing one of their bags from the counter and hurrying out. The door's bells jingled to accompany a loud banging as the doorframe rattled in Tess's wake. Michael scooped up the other bag and rushed after her, but she was halfway down the sidewalk.

"Tess, wait." He covered the distance between them, falling into step with her, glancing sideways at her face. She stared ahead and kept walking.

"Tess, did I do something?"

"Nay, nay. I'm tired, I guess." They reached their steps, and she hurried down them without further explanation.

TESS IMMEDIATELY STARTED in on dinner. Despite the fact they had only one pan in which to cook both the noodles and the sauce, and only two plates on which to serve their spaghetti, they enjoyed the meal immensely.

Michael rose and took both the plates to the sink. "Why don't you take that shower you've been dying to take, and I'll clean up."

He had finished drying the plates with paper towels, as they were only able to afford the one towel she was using for her shower, when he heard the bathroom door open. Peering around the corner of the refrigerator he saw her. She faced the opposite direction, bent over, rubbing her long hair between folds in the towel, dressed in a simple white t-shirt and flannel shorts. He was admiring the smooth curves of her calves when she turned around and caught him gawking at her.

She looked down at herself. "What?"

He stared for a moment, trying to think of something to say. "Oh, nothing. Nothing. I thought I might go to Clancy's and check into that job. Will you be okay here, alone?" He was hesitant to leave her.

"Aye. I'll be fine." Her clean skin glowed, and she smelled like a field of wildflowers. He flashed back to a meadow near his home, as a child, full of wild daisies, and bluebells, and buttercups; his mother taught him the names. He remembered some of the flowers had even towered over his head at the time. He suddenly didn't want to leave.

"You'll make sure the door is locked."

"Aye. I'll be fine. Go on now." She walked him to the door with her hand on his back. He opened it a crack but stopped, turning to peer down into her pretty face again. He wanted to kiss her more than he had ever wanted to kiss a woman, but, inexplicably, he couldn't do it. To kiss her would cost him too much.

Even so, as he walked down the dark streets to the pub, he couldn't stop picturing her lips.

TESS CLOSED THE DOOR behind Michael and bolted it obediently. She turned to stare at the little apartment. It was the first time she was alone since she killed Tad McGregor, and even though she knew it was safe, nerves shook her. She had come to depend on the comfort of Michael's presence. She knew it was wrong. He should be back in Old Head right now with his old band instead of auditioning for a new one. Besides which, after so many years on her own, she thought of herself as independent, a solitary person, comfortably disconnected from others. But Tad's death changed all that. *I can't dwell on that now,* she chided herself and physically shook away the image of Tad lying on his office floor surrounded by broken glass.

She ambled over to the cabinets, opening them to examine their contents, even though she knew they were almost entirely empty. She came across the two plates and the pan that they purchased that afternoon. Running her hand over the surface of the plates she thought about how he washed them and tucked them away on the shelf. She smiled thinking about him then closed the cabinet hastily and turned around to lean on the counter. A sudden thought troubled her, why had she been so aggravated this afternoon?

Well, it's because that girl was such an unbelievably brazen hussy. Despite her best efforts, she began to fume about it again. *I mean, obviously I have no claim to Michael, I've only been knowing the man for a few days now...but she had no way of perceiving that.* Only it wasn't the girl's flirtatiousness bothering her. The thought of him perhaps taking an interest in the woman...it stirred up this sick feeling.

She allowed herself to think about him for a minute, about the way his arm felt around her as they stood on the farmer's threshold, pretending to be man and wife...about the goofy but contented look he had on his face when he fell asleep with his head in her lap in the hayloft...about how attractive his broad chest and muscular shoulders seemed when she woke next to him near the roadside, even now she could smell the pleasant fragrance of him, clean, but masculine...

Stop it! What are you doing? She could not afford to have feelings for Michael McKee. Especially after what Molly told her about him being a ladies' man.

Her eyes darted around for something to do, to take her mind off her present thoughts. She spotted the rag they borrowed from a neighbor, and the cleaner they purchased earlier in the day, and began to viciously scrub any surface unlucky enough to be within her reach, even though she had cleaned most of them as she cooked dinner. However, using the cleaner made her think of the shameless trollop behind the counter at the store where they bought it, and her temperature began to rise again. And so she continued to be a human pendulum of thought, thinking about Michael's charming smile, and then chastising herself; thinking about how he bent to help her pick up the glass she broke at McGregor's, and swearing off all thoughts outside of the thorough sterilization of the bathroom tiles.

Finally, worn out as much from the mental skirmish as from the physical work, she sat in the recliner to wait for Michael to return.

CHAPTER SEVENTEEN

"Paulie sent me."

"Oh yeah, my asshole brother sent ya?" the band leader growled.

Michael shifted his weight, uncertain of where to go next.

The big man's face broke into a grin. "Well, I guess you're okay then." He stretched out his hand. "I'm Tony, but me boys here call me Riff. This is Patty, Griz, and Tater." He nodded in their direction.

"Mike."

"So you play. Can you sing at all?"

"Some."

"Well, get up here, then. We've been without a guitarist for too long."

Michael played with them for awhile, and then they told him he should be singing lead, and he took the challenge. After about an hour and a half, he told them he needed to return home, thoughts of the two men on the street corner running through his head. Riff pressed thirty pounds into his hand. "You get the same each night you show. You've got some real talent, man."

"Thanks. And thanks for taking me on. I really needed a job."

IT WAS LATE WHEN HE finally unlocked the door to the apartment. The light from the hall fanned out as he opened the door and framed Tess in its spotlight. To his surprise, she sat curled in the recliner with the lights out. The invading light from the dirty hall bulb captured the peaceful look on her face. He held his breath for a minute, looking at her, then crept in so as not to awaken her. He stepped to the bed, not taking his eyes from her sleeping form. Taking his t-shirt off over his head, he considered his present dilemma. He could not sleep in the bed and let a lady sleep in a recliner; at the same time, he didn't wish to awaken her. His internal debate was ended when she raised her head.

"How'd it go?"

"Fine, fine. I got the gig."

"You did? Well, of course you did. I knew you would. They'd have been fools indeed not to have chosen you, Michael McKee."

"Well, thank you for saying so, Tess Flanagan. I'm sorry I woke you."

"Oh, nay. I was waiting for you." She smiled brightly.

"The place smells...good."

"A little bleachy, I guess." She looked around the small room despite the dark. "I may have gotten a bit carried away. There wasn't much to do."

"Oh, I'm sorry about that. I didn't think about the fact that you'd have nothing to do to entertain yourself."

"Oh, 'twas no big deal."

He realized how strange it was to be holding a conversation in the dark. He extended his hand to help her out of the chair. "You take the bed, Tess. I'll take the recliner."

"Oh," she said, as if the thought had never occurred to her. She placed her hand in his and he pulled her to her feet. They stood for a moment, within inches of each other in the dark, frozen, staring into each other's eyes.

He reached out and pushed a stray hair out of her face. "You were all right?" he asked, his voice feeling like syrup in his throat.

"Aye," she said breathlessly, her gaze dancing about his face. Then, as quickly as it had begun, the moment was shattered by some invisible force that lay within them both.

"I-I should b-brush my teeth."

"Aye. Me, too. You can go first."

After she disappeared behind the bathroom door he let out a huge breath and passed his hand over his face. He sat at the foot of the bed and let his heartbeat return to normal.

In a few minutes she returned, scrambling up the bed beside him and whispering playfully, "Your turn."

He laughed and headed into the bathroom.

When he came out, she was curled on her side on the naked mattress.

"Tessie," he whispered. "I have thirty pounds now. I could go get us some sheets."

"It's too late." She yawned. "Forget it for tonight."

"Okay." He made himself as comfortable as possible in the recliner, trying, unsuccessfully, to keep the creaking to a minimum.

After a few minutes, Tess flipped onto her back. Michael shifted his weight trying to get comfortable, but a spring or wire or something poked through between his shoulder blades, and he was keenly aware of the steel rods forming the skeleton of the chair. The mattress rustled. He smiled. Tess was wiggling her feet. She turned over violently and called out, "Michael?"

"What's wrong?"

"I can't sleep with you over there in that uncomfortable chair. Come over here with me and sleep in this uncomfortable bed, would ya?"

"Well...I can't hardly refuse such an inviting offer." He was hit with something soft. "All right, all right. Calm down, woman. What was that, anyway?"

He tumbled into bed next to her, and she giggled. "The postage stamp-sized pancake pillow someone left here." She quieted and turned her back to him to again lie on her side.

He sighed happily and shut his eyes, trying to relax. The flat was hot, and Tess had switched into a top with thin straps; this he could see in the light from the window. He, himself, had changed from his jeans into the only pair of cotton shorts he owned, and the bare skin of his right biceps absorbed the heat radiating from her back, mere inches away.

Several minutes passed before he dared to flip on his side and copy her position so he could see her better. The light from the street was actually quite bright, but luckily it fell upon the middle to lower part of the bed and did not bother their eyes. By this friendly illumination he was able to see her top had scrunched up under her when she turned over, and the small of her back was exposed. He had never thought much about this section of a woman's body, but the smooth skin was extremely attractive. He raised his gaze to the graceful curves of her shoulder blades and wished he could run a finger down there to give her a shiver, or better yet, his tongue...

His thoughts were abruptly interrupted when she shifted infinitesimally closer, pinning his arm uncomfortably along his side. *Even if me arm falls off, I am NOT moving.*

And then, something extraordinary happened. Without saying a word, Tess lifted her head slightly to give him room to put his arm around her. He hesitated only a split second, hoping he wasn't misinterpreting her movements, before he slid it cautiously into place. She laid her head back down, and he wrapped his other arm around her. She moved even closer, melting into him. He worried she would feel how excited he had become, but if anything she seemed to become more relaxed; and very shortly her soft breathing became rhythmic, and then he remembered nothing more except the warmth of her body and her sweet fragrance.

CHAPTER EIGHTEEN

The morning light stole away the darkness that had provided a degree of anonymity for them both. Michael awoke with his arms still around Tess. He relished the warmth and the closeness of her body. After about ten minutes, she stirred. She turned over gently, presumably trying not to awaken him. He reflexively closed his eyes. He had done this many a time, the morning after, when he woke with a girl in his bed. The girl would generally sneak out to avoid an awkward conversation, something he was unequivocally grateful for. But now, there was no way for her to sneak out, nowhere for her to go. He told himself he wasn't ready for any sort of real connection, even if that connection was only eye contact and an exchange of pleasantries after an evening together. Besides, he reminded himself, they had only been lying together, fully clothed, sharing one bed for lack of another. It meant nothing.

She slid out and entered the bathroom. He popped up like a child's punching bag, slipping out of bed. He collected his t-shirt from the floor where he left it the night before and slung it over his head hastily. She reentered the room and glanced from the empty bed to him in surprise. And perhaps relief.

"Good morning," he called out, a little too cheerfully.

"Good morning," she returned. She didn't look him in the eye, her gaze roaming over the room. She tucked her hair behind her ear in a nervous gesture he decided long ago was completely charming.

Somehow the small action erased his unease. "How's 'bout I whip us up some eggs?"

She smiled. "You know how to cook?" she asked teasingly.

"Well 'cook' may be a bit too strong of a word."

He set about his task and soon had a pair of plates heaped with steaming hot eggs in front of them. He longed for a slab of ham or some blood sausage to go with the meal, or even a cup of weak tea. Since he hadn't been drinking nearly as much as he had in the past, he found his appetite improved greatly. Had she not been there, he would have been tempted to finish off the leftover spaghetti they had stored in the spaghetti sauce jar the night before, deciding instead to display a rare sense of manners. He stood to clear the plates, but she stopped him.

"Uh, uh, uh. Nay. You've cooked, now I clean. Why don't you hop in the shower?"

He raised his eyebrows with a teasing grin. "Are you trying to tell me something?"

She gave him a little push in the direction of the bathroom. "Oh, get on with ya."

Tess cleaned the dishes and set them in the cabinet where he'd put them the night before. She was about to wipe the table when she heard him leave the bathroom. Looking over, her hand stopped mid-motion as Michael pulled on his shirt. She admired his build for a moment. He was not a burly, beefcakey one, but rather, slim, muscled, and toned. She always thought those over-conditioned guys who walked around with their arms held out from their bodies by their projecting muscles looked like buffoons, cartoon-like apes. Cavemen. But his physique was hard, chiseled, defined, without being blown up. She longed to run her hands along his shoulders and down his back...

He glanced in her direction, and she concentrated on some invisible spot on the table.

They spent the rest of the morning frugally trying to work out what best to do with the money Michael had earned.

"Shouldn't some go to Paul?"

"Aye, that's a good idea. I'll give him ten and promise him ten tomorrow and every night I work."

After they determined what to do with the remainder, they set off together for the corner store. Michael stopped outside the store to gaze at the headlines in the newspaper machine.

"You sit out here and read the paper. There's no reason for us both to have to do this," she added, waving their list. As she turned to go into the store, she noticed a "Help Wanted" sign leaning against the front window. She glanced back at Michael, who already had his nose buried in the paper, then snatched the sign out of the window and headed straight to the checkout.

The same woman from the day before stood sullenly behind the counter, paging through a magazine from one of the nearby racks. Tess spun on her heel, determined to avoid any unpleasantness, but then she caught sight of Michael outside. She took a deep breath, looked at the sign in her hands, then slowly turned around and marched toward the counter.

She laid the sign in front of the woman, who she now remembered was named Bridget. "I'm looking for a job."

She glanced up from her magazine. "Aye, so?"

Tess struggled to keep a smile on her face and her voice agreeable. "I saw you were needin' somebody."

"Hey, weren't you in here yesterday?" Bridget interrupted. She searched behind Tess. Her face brightened, and then she shifted her gaze back. "Do you...have any experience?" she added hopefully.

"Well...not really."

"Well, it doesn't matter. It ain't exactly brain surgery." She offered her hand. "The job is yours."

A bit later Tess stepped out of the door with two bulging sacks of groceries. Michael quickly folded the paper and stuck it under his arm, reaching for one of the bags.

"What do you say to a picnic for lunch, to celebrate our new jobs?"

"That sounds...*jobs?*"

She grinned at him. "Paper or plastic?"

He cocked his head. "Well, I'll be damned."

The day turned out to be a glorious one. The sun shone brightly and was accompanied by the perfect gentle breeze. They packed sandwiches and fruit in the brown paper grocery sack, along with some cookies she splurged on. He carried the new sheets she'd purchased and found a fairly private spot in the shade along the banks of the river to spread them out.

He stretched out on his side next to her. She had chosen a green sundress that set off her eyes from the dwindling knapsack that morning, along with strappy sandals. Somehow the fair weather, and the friendly company made the food taste even better. After he polished off the best-tasting ham sandwich he had ever had, and the most perfect apple, he lay on his back with his arms folded underneath his head and closed his eyes, letting the light filtering through the trees' leaves bathe his eyelids in warmth, the breeze kissing his skin as it passed.

"So, Tessie...tell me about yourself."

Tess laughed at the odd question. "What? Am I to have a job interview now, after I already got the job?"

He kicked her playfully. "Come on now, girl, humor me."

"But, what do you want to know?"

"Well...you lived in that cottage in Old Head all your life?"

"Aye. After me mum died when I was eight, my dad and I worked the farm together. He took care of the crops. I took care of the animals. Not much. A few cows, a goose or two...a handful of chickens..." Her voice trailed off.

Michael opened his eyes to watch her as she talked. The light breeze lifted her beautiful, gleaming red hair then dropped it in turns. She wore a distant look on her face, like in gazing out over the water of the River Lee she was looking back over the years of her life.

"What was he like? Your da?" he asked quietly.

"Oh, you would have liked him. He was wise and sensitive...'Course he *was* my da, so I worshiped him. But he really was a man worth knowing, ya know what I mean?" she ended sadly.

Michael nodded and looked out over the water, thinking of his own da and how unlike her da he was.

"He was a fantastic storyteller," she continued. "He would sit in his rocking chair in front of the fire each night—especially on winter nights when there wasn't a lot of work to be done—smoking his pipe; and he would tell me these wonderful stories." The corners of her pretty mouth turned up as she thought about him, and her eyes shown, reflecting the warm circle of firelight that had enfolded the two of them. "The stories would unwind from his imagination like the smoke curling from his pipe to the ceilin'. Funny stories, stories about leprechauns and banshees, about Cuchulainn, you know, the legendary hero?" He nodded. "Or Fionn and the Fianna, who were the distinguished warriors and guardians of all of Ireland." She wrapped the rest of her sandwich then paused, staring off again. "And he would get to laughing." She laughed herself. "He had this funny habit of telling a joke or a funny story, and he would get laughing so hard, you couldn't understand nary a word he said. But it didn't matter. I knew all the stories by heart at any rate. And it wasn't the stories. It was the way he would tell them." She stuck the sandwich back in the sack. "Sometimes he would put up his pipe to play his fiddle, and I would clap and laugh and dance until I would tumble on the rug at his feet, all out of breath." She sighed. "After Mum's death, we two became the world to each other." Her voice caught, and she looked down.

"What happened, Tess?" he asked gently, sitting up.

"He went away." Her voice was barely a whisper. The breeze blew back her hair again, and he could see a tear slip unchecked out of the corner of her eye and roll slowly down her creamy cheek. As so often happened when he was around her, his heart squeezed. He reached out and brushed the tear away with the back of his hand.

She turned to gaze at him with her wet eyes, her lips trembling slightly. He slid his hand underneath her hair at the back of her neck, leaning closer. Her eyes moved to his lips then flitted back. He brought his other hand to trail his fingers over the super-soft skin of her cheek. He knew he was going to kiss her, and he knew it would change things between them forever, and he wanted the moment to last a lifetime. He slowly leaned in and feathered his lips over hers. Once started, he wanted nothing more than to taste her further. His mouth covered hers, and he lost himself to his senses; the feel of her skin on his fingertips, the warmth of her mouth. His tongue sought hers, and when they met, a sweet longing filled him unlike anything he had ever felt before. His mind vacillated between struggling to stay in the moment, to be aware of every sense in every part of his body, and an urge to rush ahead, to take it further. He had, of course, experienced these physical urges before, but never had they been coupled with this deep yearning to let go, to let down his guard completely.

Tess's memories of her father stirred up all the heartache and loss she had felt since his death. When Michael brushed her cheek with the back of his hand, she was momentarily surprised. She had forgotten he was even there. But when she looked into his eyes, all thoughts of her father vanished. As he leaned in to kiss her, she wanted nothing more than to feel his lips on hers. Even so, she was completely staggered by the intense hunger that overtook her when they touched. The feel of his tongue sent shockwaves through her body and she couldn't think clearly.

His right hand skimmed along her bare arm and moved to cradle her back, laying her gently on the sheet. She had one arm around his waist and one across his shoulders, clinging to him as he lowered her.

She slipped her hand under the thin material of his t-shirt. The skin along his back was strangely cool, and his muscles rippled beneath her touch. She ran her hand down, feeling the indentation of his waist, dipping a finger into the waistband of his jeans. He shifted so that he was not entirely on his side, and she felt the weight of him. He took his lips from hers, and she opened her eyes to protest. She saw the light coming from behind him and his face above her...and the image morphed into Simon's face, jeering at her. She was filled with an instantaneous, intense fear. Instinctively she pushed him away. Just as suddenly she could see it was him, and not Simon, with her.

"Michael," she mumbled, confused and upset, breathing hard.

"What's wrong?"

She sought to control the torrent of emotions sweeping through her. "I-I...we shouldn't be doing this." She glanced toward the sidewalk above the sloping bank where they lay. A few people ambled by, unaware of their presence below.

He followed her gaze and then took a deep breath. "You're right."

She sat up and smoothed her skirt, hoping he would not notice her trembling. He slid his hand down the arm supporting her in the grass. "Tess," he said, and again bent her head back to kiss her. This time his kiss was passionate, but less insistent. Her heart rose, and desire burned through her. This time it was he who pulled unwillingly away. "Weren't those the bells from St. Anne's? It must be 2:00. Didn't ya say you had to work at 3?"

"Oh, good saints in heaven! Aye." He rose to his feet and offered his hand to help her stand. She scrambled up the embankment.

"Take it easy. You've got plenty of time." He chuckled.

"You're right." She smiled back. "Sorry. First day and all." She shrugged.

They walked down the sidewalk, his arm across her shoulder. They chatted happily about this and that, and then fell into a comfortable silence. When they stopped to wait for a light, Michael turned to kiss her again.

He swung back to check traffic and caught sight of a pair of familiar faces across the street. His body tensed but he tried to hide his alarm from Tess. It could not be coincidence that, in a city as big as Cork, the same men he had seen watching them outside the grocery store, were now across the street, trying conspicuously to look casual. Michael scanned the area and noticed for the first time that a tide of people was heading past them on the sidewalk to their right. He peered down the street to the end of the block and read a banner strung over the boulevard. He grabbed Tess's elbow and steered her in that direction. "Let's go to the Farmer's Market."

"But, I've got to get to work."

He stopped briefly and turned to her, giving him an opportunity to peek over his shoulder at the same time. He leaned in and gave her a peck, squeezing her and whispering in her ear, "I haven't wanted to worry you, but I think we're being followed. And this isn't the first time." He heard her little gasp of surprise. When he pulled back she stared at him wide-eyed, but nodded slightly. He chanced another glance. The men hustled to change their direction and follow their quarry, but they were momentarily detained by traffic turning in front of them.

Michael and Tess took advantage of their followers' predicament and increased their pace, trying to disappear into the thick press of people headed toward the overflowing booths at the end of the sidewalk. Unfortunately, the taller of the two was able to spot them above the heads of the throng. Michael held Tess's hand, weaving in and out of the shoppers, always looking for a place they could duck into to be out sight of their pursuers, who now clearly knew they had been spotted. Now that the chase was on, the ante had been raised. The men were no longer simply watching them, but were, instead, actively in pursuit, raising the question: what would happen if they were caught?

He spotted a vendor ahead in the mass of people. With a large rolling cart full of ice and fish, the man was being given a wide berth because of his smelly cargo. Out of the corner of his mouth Michael explained his plan to Tess. He stepped into the vacancy left by the crowd and matched his step with the vendor. As he had hoped, the fishmonger turned to take his load down a wider aisle. They moved with him, crouching low alongside the cart.

The short, heavy-set vendor had thin, snowy white hair and wore a stained apron over his nearly see-through t-shirt. He looked at the strange pair slinking along next to his cart. "What the hell are ya doin'?"

"Playin' a joke on some friends," Michael replied. Tess smiled helpfully.

The fishmonger's tired eyes lit up, like a child learning about some new game. He searched around in the direction they came from. "You mean those two blighters hoppin' around over there? They look real mad." He laughed.

"Aye, I know. They can be real jerks sometimes. Won't leave me and me gal here time to ourselves alone."

"Ah, that's a shame," said the big man, sympathetically, looking from her to Michael. "Here, get behind this." He stopped beside a booth and opened a half-door in the side. They scrambled in. A rotund, but kindly looking older woman glanced in their direction as she bagged goods for a customer then turned back to finish the transaction. It seemed to dawn on her after a beat that it was somewhat peculiar to have a young couple crawling into the back of their booth. She gave her husband a questioning look. "I'll explain in a minute. Here they come," he said out of the corner of his mouth to Michael. "Hey, there," he called out to them.

"Nay." Michael tugged on the bottom of his apron.

"Any fish, today?"

"Nah, old man. We don't want none of your friggin' fish." They hurried on, oblivious to the proximity of their prey.

The man watched them out of sight and then smiled at his guests crouching in the dirt. "How's that?"

"Heh, heh." Michael chuckled. "Pretty good. We sure appreciate—"

"How 'bout gettin' away from them for good tonight?" He grimaced at the retreating figures growing smaller in the distance. It was obvious he didn't care for them at all. "I've got a van out back. It's stinky, but I could take you anywhere you wanted to go. I'm sure Gloria here can spare me, can't you me love?" His wife stared at him like he'd lost his mind. "Oh, come on." He threw his arm around her shoulder. "You remember when you and I used to sneak around behind your old man's back." He hugged her to his side, and she blushed.

"Oh, George." She whipped him with a towel she had tucked in her apron. She glanced at Michael and Tess, embarrassed. "Da never thought much of George," she explained. "But he was wrong." She reached to pull her husband's face down and kissed him on the cheek.

Now it was his turn to color. "Oh." He chuckled. "I don't know about that."

"You go and take these two kids wherever they need to go. Godspeed."

"Thank you, miss," they both murmured. Michael squeezed her hand. She blushed again and shooed him off with the towel.

"Go on, now. Get ya gone."

CHAPTER NINETEEN

Michael and Tess argued quietly in the back of the fishy van. He believed it was far too dangerous for her to go to work at the grocery store where he first spotted the men who had followed them; but she'd promised Bridget she would be there at three and refused to go back on her word. In the end they compromised. They asked to be dropped off in front of the store together, and Tess promised to walk on to Clancy's after work so he could escort her home after his night was over.

Despite being careful, he still was terribly nervous for Tess. He was so distracted, in fact, that he muddled some of his lyrics, but no one seemed to notice. Something else was bothering him, too. If those men had been cops, why hadn't they called for reinforcements, or flashed their badges, or drawn their weapons, or...something? Could it be that someone hired thugs to bring them in for killing Tad McGregor? But who? Helen McGregor was too quiet a woman, and who else would have an interest in catching McGregor's killers? He couldn't put his finger on it, but something wasn't right.

The boys in the band called for a break, and he was mulling over these thoughts more seriously when he overheard Griz say, "Uum-uum. Take a gander at the gorgeous redhead who just walked in."

Patty straightened with a low whistle. "The good Lord's missin' an angel tonight, lads. But she's way out of your league, old man. What that lil' hottie needs is a piece of the ol' Patster." Michael glanced in that direction to see Tess moving through the crowd with Bridget. He put his hand out to restrain Pat, who was about to jump off the stage and approach her.

"No way, man. That gal's goin' home with me tonight."

The rest of the members, who were listening in by now, joined in the laughter following his statement, amazed at the new guy's overconfidence.

Riff elbowed him in the ribs. "Man, keep dreaming, that lil' bird'll never give you the time of day."

"You think so?" Michael hurriedly returned, hoping she wouldn't address him too soon. "Ya want to put your money where your mouth is?"

Riff's eyes opened wide. "Well, well! Aren't you a chancer?"

All the men huddled together in earnest now, all eyes fixed on her. "What ya got in mind?"

He judged his audience. "Twenty pounds apiece says I can't take her home with me tonight."

"You're a eejit."

"Lad, you're touched. She ain't no Sheila, you can tell. Not that type at all."

"You're on."

"Aye."

He shook hands all around and hopped happily off the stage. He approached Tess and Bridget, careful not to appear too familiar with them with the watching eyes of the others on him. The girls had stopped to admire a unique feature of the bar. In one corner sat an enormous red, glowing juke box. "The owner had it sent over all the way from America," Bridget was explaining. "His brother has a tavern there."

"It has some great tunes," added Michael, fishing in his pocket for a coin and nodding hello to Bridget. He slid his money in the slot and skimmed over the playlist. He chose "You Send Me," by Sam Cooke and gave Tess a comical half bow. "Would you care to dance, miss?"

"Here?" she said, uncertainly. The floor had cleared when the band had taken its break. Instead of responding, he simply took her hand, steered her to a clear area between tables, and wrapped his arms around her. As he spun her around, he winked at his fellow band members.

The guys on stage sat with their arms crossed over their chests. Riff spoke for them all, loud enough for Michael to hear. "Well, I'll be damned."

He was enjoying himself immensely now. He hummed a few bars in her ear then, started to quietly sing the chorus. He pulled a little bit away to look her in the eye, and all of a sudden his playfulness left him. The wonderful scent of her...her closeness was intoxicating. She smiled, swaying easily with him to the music. She tilted her head, stretching onto the balls of her feet, and kissed him. A loud cry arose from the stage, and she turned to see the rest of the band alternately cursing and laughing and slapping each other on the back. "What's with those guys?"

He shrugged. "Who knows?" He sighed, not wanting to release her. "I have one more set to do."

"That's fine. I'll sit with Bridget." She glanced over her shoulder, and Bridget waved at them.

"All right," he said, his arms still around her waist. "Let me give you some money for a drink. Riff already paid me."

"Are you sure we should be spending it on a drink?"

He kissed her to silence her objection. "Get yourself a drink," he ordered.

"All right, bossy." She giggled and accepted the bill he handed her before trotting off to the bar.

He bounded triumphantly back on the stage to a chorus of shouts and slaps on the back from the unlucky quartet who had been watching them. He sat at the keyboard still awash in the glow of his pending victory, and addressed the crowd. "We've had several requests from folks in the audience, visiting our fair city from somewhere over-the-pond, for some more traditional Irish music. So being obliging lads..." He and the boys began a rollicking version of "The Galway Races." When they got to the verse that mentioned Cork, the crowd cheered wildly. He winked at Tess who was clapping and singing along happily. The "obliging lads" finished the set entirely with traditional Irish tunes, to the great delight of the crowd.

All through his third set, he noted a growing pyramid of shot glasses on the table between Tess and Bridget. Bridget sat chattering away, but Tess seemed to be hardly listening. Her eyes followed everything he did. After he finished for the night, he jumped off the stage and headed straight over to Tess, who sat languidly in her chair, a huge smile plastered over her face.

"That was fantastic!" she exclaimed, a little louder than was necessary.

"Uh huh. Who drank all these shots, may I ask?" He gestured at the little glass structure, his hands on his hips, and a teasing smile tugging his lips up at the corners.

"You sure can," she said, her speech slightly slurred. She stared at him a moment before adding, "Oh, you want an answer." She and Bridget giggled.

He looked from one to the other, amused despite of himself. "Aye, sweetheart, I do."

"Oh, well then...Bridget and I did." She stated with an air of pride, which set them off on another round of giggles.

"Did ya, now?" he returned with mock severity, crossing his arms in front of his chest. "You're potted."

"Am not."

"Aye. Ya are. Ossified."

"Well, you told me to have a drink."

"Yes, Tessie. *A* drink, *a* drink." He sighed. "You sit here, you goofy girl, while I go get my jacket." He kissed her lightly on the cheek, but then looked her in the eye. "And try to stay out of trouble."

"Aye, s-sir." She winked with a jerky salute. He laughed, but shook his head, proceeding to the break room at the back of the pub. When he came out of the room, with his jacket in hand, he was surprised to see Bridget waiting for him.

"You know, Michael," she said, running a hand up his arm. "I don't believe your girl, Tess, can handle her liquor." She gestured over her shoulder into the outer room.

He zeroed in on Tess, who sat smiling at nobody in particular. "I'd have to agree with you there."

Bridget took his cheek and turned him so that he was looking at her. "But I can. She'll be no good to you tonight..." she continued, pressing against him and placing her hand on the wall behind him. "But I, on the other hand..." she ran her tongue around her lips. He noticed for the first time her low-cut blouse and tight leather mini-skirt. Since she was, in essence, Tess's boss, he resisted the urge to tell her flatly he wasn't at all interested in what she was offering. That she had, for all intents and purposes, liquored Tess up to get her out of the picture for the evening, actually repulsed him. She slipped her hand beneath his jacket and partially around his waist. He pointedly removed her hand, and slid out from under her body. "There's somebody I need to take home." He strode off, leaving her open-mouthed in his wake.

The walk home took twice as long as usual, broken as it was by bouts of giggling, and Tess's ill-fated attempt to take a stray alley cat home. After finally getting her down the stairs to the front door, he managed to hold her up with one hand, and jab the key in the lock with the other hand, while promising her for the hundredth time the cat would, indeed, be fine without their help. After getting her inside, he took advantage of a moment of steadiness, and slipped out of his coat then threw it on the recliner. When he turned around, she had already kicked off her shoes and unbuttoned the top of her dress. A beautiful, lacy black bra accentuated her voluptuous curves, and she was beginning to slide the straps down over her shoulders.

"Whoa, whoa, whoa, whoa, whoa!" He found himself saying, hastily trying to return the straps to their former positions, while still unable to rip his eyes away from the sight of her gorgeous breasts.

"Michael, I'm not drunk anymore. The night air sobered me," she said steadily. And so it seemed. Or was he hearing what he wanted to hear? She stepped forward and kissed him with an intensity that stirred every part of his body. "Make love to me," she whispered pleadingly, her eyes searching his for an answer.

His resolve melted away, and he released his hold on her dress, letting it drop to the floor. He ran a finger under a bra strap then across the cool skin of her upper chest and across the inner curve of her left breast. "Mmm..." He breathed with pleasure, and she moved him toward the bed, nipping at his bottom lip playfully. Her nipple was hard under the thin fabric as he caressed her.

She swung her feet up, kneeling on the bed in front of him. He pulled his mouth away for a minute to catch his breath and ran his hand over her stomach to the smooth curve of her hip. He stuck two fingers underneath the thin line of her panties that had tantalized him so, however many days ago. He slid his hand inside the cloth and behind her, drawing her to him, both hands now cupping her flesh. Her hands were on either side of his face. Her tongue, in his mouth, was sending blinding pulses through him.

She moved her hands to his belt and began to battle with it, trying to release the buckle. He helped her, and within seconds his pants hit the floor with a loud clang. He yanked his shirt off over his head and flung it, who-knew-where, and he began tugging at his shoes. Finally, released from most of his clothing, he sought her mouth again.

He pushed toward her, and she shifted her legs so she was sitting on the edge of the bed. He climbed onto the bed so he was kneeling, straddling her. He felt the curve of her back and supporting her shoulders, he lowered her onto the bed. She wriggled higher onto the bed beneath him. Using all the restraint he could muster, he pulled himself away from her, again to a kneeling position. He wanted this to last all night, not to be over in a heartbeat. He slid his hands to the back of her thighs. Reflexively she lifted her knees, bringing her feet to rest against the metal frame of the bed. His hands glided down the length of the outside of her legs, examining the sensual curve of her calves, and then back up. He noticed a fairly long, jagged scar on the inside of her thigh. He wondered for a blink how she could have cut herself there, but it was in his brain then out as he discovered more of her.

He brought his head on the inside of her legs and kissed her inner thigh, touching the skin with his tongue. She let out a shaky breath, quivering with excitement. He continued to alternately stroke the outside of her legs, and kiss the inside, adjusting to start from her ankles, and inching upward, scraping his teeth and nibbling from time to time, his own excitement rising. He was amazed at how relaxed she was in his arms, and was feeling very masterful...until he realized she had become absolutely still.

"Tess?" he whispered in the dark. No response. "Tess?" he said a little louder, with a hint of desperation in his voice. *Nay! Nay! Nay!* He listened. All he could hear was the bathroom sink dripping and her quiet breathing. He let out a loud, frustrated breath and put his head in his hands for a minute. She had been his. And he had to go and get greedy and try to stretch things out. He was annoyed with Tess, though he knew it wasn't her fault. He was angry at himself and furious with Bridget. He cursed her silently for robbing him of his night. He lifted her heels from where they were braced on the bed's bars and stretched her legs out.

He slid forward to confirm what he already knew. Her hair was splayed out on the bed, her head turned to one side, a hand curled against one cheek. Her lips were parted slightly and still flushed. They turned up at the ends like she was hiding a secret, and she had a look of utter contentment on her face. Her lips were not the wide, full lips most women craved; nor were they thin and demanding. Her top lip was peculiar as it looked like it was drawn with an artist's brush, peaked perfectly, as if on demand they could make the cliché lip-print mark on the back of a Valentine.

He lowered himself to lie on his side beside her. He couldn't help but smile as he observed her, brushing her hair back from her face. He allowed his eyes to wander over her incredible body, glistening in the moonlight. He lay for a long time and watched her sleeping, her bare chest rising and falling, her stomach accompanying it. She was not a skinny, stick girl like some he had dated, poky and sharp; but at the same time, she wasn't in anyway plump, only endlessly silky and curvy.

He sighed again. "Ahh, Tessie." He breathed sadly, stroking her arm. Finally, resignedly, he got out of bed and walked around to the other side. He placed his hands under her shoulders and coaxed her sideways and onto the pillow. He gathered the sheet, twisted and discarded like a gnarled tree branch at the end of the bed. He shook it out, suspending it for a moment in midair, then letting it fall over her body. He carefully crawled over her to lie on top of the sheet. He thought he'd never get to sleep as keyed up as he was, but her warmth and gentle breathing quieted him and, eventually, he fell asleep.

CHAPTER TWENTY

Michael awoke to find Tess buttoning the dress she had unbuttoned for him the night before. She was working quietly, probably trying not to disturb him. Unaware that she was being watched, she stopped and rubbed her temples, a pained expression on her face.

"You must have one hell of a headache," he ventured.

She jumped, startled. "Oh. Aye. I think I may have had one too many drinks last night."

He sat up, smiling. "Try six too many drinks."

She colored. "I'm sorry about that..."

He changed the subject to save her further embarrassment. "Where are you off to?"

"Church."

His brow furrowed.

"It's Sunday."

"Oh, aye," he said as if the idea had just come to him. "It is, isn't it? Hold on a sec, and I'll join you." He jumped to his feet.

"You don't have to."

"Nay. I want to."

"Are you worried about those men?"

"Nah," he lied, buckling his jeans. "Want to spend time with my best gal, Gracie," he finished, throwing his arm around her shoulder.

ST. FINNBAR SOUTH WAS not far, but they still had to scurry in as the last bell rang. Michael stopped in the back of the church to stand with the other men, sweeping his hat off belatedly and nodding to the others. Tess hurried forward; then slowed her steps to genuflect solemnly before entering

145

her pew. The building gave off that peculiar odor of all the ancient churches he had ever chanced to be in, a strange mixture of incense, mold, candlewicks, and the rich, earthy smell of the farmers beside him. Its massive stone walls made the temperature inside a good ten degrees colder than outside.

As the pastor began the services, Michael was swept back to a time long ago when he held his mother's hand in church as a little boy. He stared around at the walls, the statues and placards. The music of the choir filled him with thoughts of angels playing harps. A strange sensation crept over him, a familiarity, and it brought along with it an extraordinary sense of peace.

He remembered, suddenly, looking up into his mother's face, as she gazed at him with shining eyes. *You're a good boy, Mikey. A perfect angel,* her voice said to him again. In his memory she reached to straighten his new tie. *Such a little gentleman,* she would sigh.

He shook away the memory and focused in on Tess, sitting several pews ahead of him. Her head was bowed, and the light from the stained glass windows played on her hair like fairies were dancing around each strand. A strange murmur was created by people moving as one to kneel. Many of the roughly dressed men around him lowered themselves to their knees on the hard stone floor. He remembered another scene from his childhood; this time, an oft repeated one. He peered around the edge of the pew, when his mother wasn't looking, to see all of the men kneeling in the back. It had always filled him with a sense of awe. To see those big men, their hands callused from the plow, or the fishing lines, humbly holding their hats and bowing before an unseen God.

Now he was one of those men. The cold marble was worn smooth and his head bent, forced by an invisible hand. His heart swelled, and tears sprang to his eyes. He lifted his head to search for Tess, who had again managed to make him feel things he would rather not feel, to climb outside of the numbness that had been his companion for so long. The men around him now were standing and moving forward for communion. He scrambled to his feet and followed them, discreetly wiping his eyes with the back of his hand as he rose.

More composed now, he took communion and followed the others, like a horse on a trail ride, toward the rear of the church. His eyes sought again for Tess in the many rows of pews, kneeling by herself near the back. Her hands were folded in prayer on the pew rail, her forehead resting atop her hands. At the last minute, he veered and side-stepped along the long pew to kneel beside her. She looked up in surprise, and he smiled and squeezed her arm. She smiled warmly back and hooked her arm through his. After the concluding prayer he stood with her while the priest processed by, his resounding bass voice getting louder as he approached, and fading again as he passed them. They sauntered out together into the bright sunlight, heading down the stone path and out the wrought-iron gates to the sidewalk.

They walked several blocks in silence. "Something bothering you, Tess?"

"Nay, nay," she said lightly, if not all together convincingly. He decided not to push her.

When they returned to their room she sat on the bed, playing absentmindedly with a thread she had picked off her dress.

"Michael?"

"Aye."

"Last night...there are some things I don't remember."

So that's what's bothering her.

"I remember...a cat, I think. A little black kitten I wanted to bring home?"

He sat beside her. "More like a mangy, grey hell cat. But aye, there was a cat."

"And I remember some other things..." The color returned to her cheeks. "I-I woke up with...did we...?"

"Nay, we didn't," he assured her.

"Oh, all right then." She breathed a sigh of relief.

"Well, you don't have to sound so happy about it," he said, hurt.

"Nay, nay. It's just that...if I had made love with you..." She dropped her eyes, but finished the thought clearly. "...I'd want to remember every second of it." She lifted her head and looked him straight in the eye.

He kissed her softly, and she smiled. "You were an animal, though," he teased. "I was lucky to get out with my virtue intact." She hit him playfully, and he threw up his arms to defend himself. She laughed and continued buffeting him until he was lying back on the bed with her on top of him. She kissed him quickly and jumped off.

"I have to get ready for work." She dug around in her purse.

"Nay. Not today," he whined.

"Aye, today," she said, businesslike, drawing something black out of her purse, sealed in a plastic baggy.

"What is that?"

She wrestled with the bag. "It's my uniform. Bridget ordered several, and just my luck, they had one that fit me." She brandished the skirt triumphantly then gazed at it in dismay. "That's not gonna cover much."

"I knew there was a reason I liked that Bridget." He grinned. "Try it on." She plucked out a second bag from her purse; this time with something white in it. She took them both into the bathroom but left the door cracked so she could talk to him. He craned his neck so he could get a glimpse of her through the gap. The dress pooled on the floor again. Her gorgeous bare legs stepped into the skirt. She shimmied it over her hips. He groaned and then tried to listen to what she was saying.

"I'll only be gone a couple of hours. Bridget wanted me to help with a big shipment. Why don't you lie down and go back to sleep for awhile?"

"M-hmm," he mumbled, already closing his eyes. He opened one eye when the bathroom door creaked. He gave a low whistle, sitting up. The skirt was much like the one Bridget had worn the other night, only made out of some form-fitting fabric instead of leather. The blouse was a silky, shiny white, clingy in all the right places.

She looked at herself, trying to stretch the skirt over her legs. "I don't know. Isn't this a little too hotsy-totsy for a grocery store?"

"You say that as if it were a bad thing. Come here," he purred. She smiled, shuffling over to stand in front of him. He put his hands on the back of her thighs and drew her closer.

She took his face in her hands, as she had done the night before, letting her red curtain of hair fall around them, and kissed him long and deep. Finally she pulled away. "I need to go," she said her voice thick. And then she was gone.

MICHAEL DID CRASH OUT for a few hours before a knock on the door woke him. He had been having some very erotic dreams about Tess, and he woke in a sweat and disoriented. Wondering who in the world might be on their doorstep, he cautiously approached the door.

"Hey, Mike. Ya in there? It's Paulie."

"Yeah, sure, Paulie. Wait a second." Rubbing the sleep out of his eyes, he slid the latch back and opened the door.

He came in, inspecting the apartment as he talked. "I'm not surprised to find ya getting some z's. I've lived with Riff's crazy hours long enough."

"Here, I'll get you your money," Michael added with a yawn.

"Oh, that's not why I'm here, Mikey...but I'll take it. I wanted to congratulate you on your little victory." He pulled a bottle out from somewhere in his coat. Taking two plastic cups from off its neck, he unscrewed the cap and began to pour.

"My victory?"

"Aye. I hear you bamboozled that brother of mine, and the other louts in his band, out of a pretty penny. But don't worry, I won't let on." He stopped mid-pour to turn and gaze at him, the bottle still posed over the cups. "That pretty little redhead was Tess, wasn't it?"

He nodded sheepishly.

Paulie offered him the drink, chuckling. "You're a smooth one, Mikey. I'll give ya that." He toasted his health and, true to his word, was on his way.

Michael knew sleep was no longer an option for him. With nothing to do in the flat, he decided to shuffle down to the grocery to bug Tess.

TESS HAD HER BACK TURNED to the door while she shelved magazines.

"I think you gave me the wrong change, miss."

She spun around and smiled. "Nay. You got exactly what you had coming, mister," she countered, smacking him lightly with a rolled up magazine.

"Hey, watch the merchandise," Bridget said crossly from where she crouched behind the counter next to her. Then her gaze landed on Michael, and she changed her tune. "Oh. Hey, Michael."

"Hi, Bridget," he said evenly. He then turned his attention back to Tess. "So when're you getting' out of here?"

She peered eagerly at Bridget.

"Oh, she's gonna be awhile yet."

"I'll wait then." He leaned against a stack of beer cases and whistled an idle tune designed to annoy Bridget.

It worked. After only fifteen minutes she could no longer find anything more for Tess to do. "Oh, feck off then!" she said peevishly. When Tess didn't move she added, "Go on, now. Get out of here!" Tess bounded out from behind the counter, stuck her arm through Michael's and headed out the door without a backward glance.

"So, what do you want to do? I've got a couple of hours before I have to go to Clancy's. Want to skip a few rocks?" he suggested.

She peered at the sky with a frown. The day, which had started out so beautifully, had clouded over. Her gaze returned to his face for a moment and relaxed into a smile. "Maybe for a bit."

He led her to a place he spotted earlier, much more secluded than their picnic spot of the day before, behind a clump of trees. They were in the middle of a huge city, but as hidden as they were from the view of any strangers, they may as well have been out in the middle of the country. Across the river was an abandoned rail yard, not a soul in sight. Tess kicked off her shoes and sat on the hillside.

Michael joined her and began to rub her leg above the knee where the mini-skirt left her exposed. He leaned in and kissed her, tenderly at first, but with a growing insistence. He could make out the outline of her black bra beneath the shiny white material of her blouse, and he flashed back to the vision of her lying still across the bed, the moonlight bathing her in its white glow. He wanted desperately to pick up where they left off. He leaned her back in the grass and slid his hand to the edge of her skirt.

Tess let him ease her into the grass. His urgency awakened something in her, but it wasn't passion. It was panic. Something triggered a horrible fear in her. Her mind was racing to catch up with her body, which seemed to be acting of its own accord. Her heart was pounding in her chest, and sweat flowed out of every pore of her body. She couldn't breathe. What was it? What was it evoking this unknown terror in her heart? And then, she knew.

It was the smell of whiskey on his breath. She was here in the arms of the man she had come to love, and with her next horrified heartbeat she was back there, sixteen years old, grappling with two drunken, grown men.

Simon asked for the knife again. Jacob locked both her wrists in one large hand, and wrenched the knife out of the table with the other, handing it to his cohort.

Tess, you might as well give in, or I'll have to cut my way in.

The blade stung as it cut into her inner thigh, and warm blood ran down her leg.

Her arms ached from being pinned for so long, and she hurt herself in her struggles, pulling muscles in her arms and sides. She was afraid. She couldn't breathe with the weight of him on her. She was going to suffocate. She was afraid. She was going to die here in her bed, and her father was coming home soon. And when she thought it was over...they switched places.

She couldn't bear it another second. Michael's touch was setting off a firing squad of nerves. She knew it was him, she knew she was safe, yet she could not stop to make sense out of things. She had to go. With all her strength she pushed him away, scrambling up the hillside to escape.

As Michael began to touch her, she shoved him, harder than he would have thought possible for someone so small. Her bare heels dug into the hillside and she crab walked a few steps; then flipped, using hands and feet, finding purchase wherever she could. A chill washed over him when he caught the expression on her face as she turned from him. A hysterical, almost animal-like terror shone in her eyes. Although she was looking straight at him, he turned to see if there was, by chance, something behind him to cause her frantic actions. He saw nothing but the peaceful water below.

"Tess," he called out. "Wait, Tess!" He grabbed one of her arms to keep her from fleeing, and she turned around and hit him full force in the chest, knocking the wind out of him with a rush. He released her and fell to his knees, doubled over and gasping for breath. He looked toward the slope, his eyes swimming, in time to see her slip and fall hard on her right knee. She hardly seemed to notice, just continued to clamber on until she reached the sidewalk. He glanced back; she hadn't even stopped for her shoes.

CHAPTER TWENTY-ONE

Tess ran. She ran for several blocks. Past sympathetic faces, past irritated faces, past apathetic faces, and she kept running. At some point, the sky finally relented, and the rain came bucketing down, but she was barely aware of it. After a time, exhausted, her breath coming in ragged gulps, she collapsed on a bench, blood running down her leg from the cut on her knee. As her breathing slowed, she became more and more aware of what she had done, how she had pushed Michael, perhaps even hurt him, and run away like a crazy person through the streets of Cork. Unable to hold it in any longer, she let herself go, great sobs racking her body, not caring about the strange sight she made curled up on the park bench. She was glad for the rain. Perhaps it would hide her tears from the curious passersby; but the sound of the rain splashing on the pavement was not loud enough to disguise her sobs. Minutes passed before she regained enough control to still her whole body. She sat like some bizarre statue while the world went on around her.

A woman splashed through the puddles toward her, a soggy newspaper held over her head. She bent, and peered into Tess's face compassionately. "Come with me, dear." She took her arm and led her in a building, up a flight of stairs and into a cozy apartment. She was numb, her movements hardly registering on her besieged mind. The woman wrapped a thin blanket around her and poured her a cup of tea. She put on more water to boil and returned to her side with a washcloth and a bandage. She laid a hand on her shoulder.

"There, now, lamb. That's better, isn't it?"

She nodded, wanting to form the words "thank you" on her tongue, but momentarily unable to do so.

"Do you want to tell me what happened?" her hostess asked quietly, while she cleaned Tess' leg.

Tess shook her head initially, but then the words started cascading out of her like the rain still running through the gutters. "M-michael...we were kissing...and I...I don't know. I sort of freaked out. I shoved him, hard. And I ran."

"I see, the boy was going too far," the woman said with an edge to her voice.

"Nay! Nay, miss. I wanted him to." Her cheeks warmed with her unwitting confession. She couldn't believe she was telling all this to a stranger. "It wasn't him. I love him." She sobbed. A thought entered her mind. "*They* did this to me," she said, more to herself than to her confessor. She began to sob anew. The older woman let her cry, patting her back from time to time, until she had worn herself out.

Like fog lifting, she became aware of her presence in a stranger's home. "I'm sorry to have disturbed you." Flustered, she attempted to rise. "I should go."

But the woman put a hand on her shoulder and said with a kind but firm tone, "Nonsense. You will stay here, m'dear, until you are truly ready to go."

She lifted her head to smile at the woman and recognized her as the fish vendor's wife. "Why you're...you helped me before."

"Aye, dear. You and your young man. Is that who was..." she cleared her throat, "kissing you?"

She nodded.

"But he didn't force you..."

"Oh, nay, miss. Michael would never do that. He could never."

"Then who is it that hurt you, child?" she asked delicately, laying her hand over Tess's smaller, cold one. Something in her tone reminded Tess of her own mother, what she remembered of her, anyway. It became clear that she needed to say it. So, for the first time ever, she put words to the awful thing that happened to her on that day. The woman listened without interrupting, paling during sections of the story, but never opening her mouth. When she finished, they sat in silence for several minutes. "And you've never told anyone this?"

Tess shook her head, looking at her hands. "Not until now."

"Well, I'm glad you chose to tell me, anyway." She nodded, rubbing a thumb over Tess's hand. "Do you think you could tell your young man your story?"

"I don't know." She muffled a sob.

"I remember, at the market. He had his hand on your shoulder, like he was protecting you. He seemed like a good lad to me. Maybe he deserves to know?"

Tess knew what she had to do.

MICHAEL STOOD FLABBERGASTED, bent double and struggling to draw air into his lungs. A single refrain rang through his head over and over again, oddly timing itself to his gasps. *What the hell happened?* One minute he was kissing an angel, the next he was fighting a demon. He knew that even if he did manage to carry himself to the top of the hill, Tess was long gone. He had heard her bare feet pounding the sidewalk between his loud wheezes.

After several minutes, his breathing came back to normal, and he staggered up the slope, trying to discern where Tess would have gone. Home was the only place he could think of, so he started off in that direction. The clouds let loose. "Great. Friggin' perfect," he muttered. Minutes later, when he came to the grocery store, he decided to duck his head in to see if she had returned there.

"Tess?" Bridget replied, confused. "Didn't she leave with you fifteen minutes ago?"

"Aye," Michael said, irritably. He pushed back his wet hair, his dripping t-shirt nearly transparent and clinging to his chest. She was staring at him with her mouth hanging open. "So she hasn't been back then?"

"Nay. Nay. She hasn't been back. What's this about?"

Michael sighed, holding the door open with one foot and leaning his hands on either side of the doorframe, his head hanging for a minute. He said tiredly, "If she comes by, would you please tell her I went to Clancy's? It's important," he added earnestly.

"Of course, Michael," she promised.

He stepped back out and continued to check up and down the street for any sign of Tess on his way to work. He ended up being early, so he ordered a beer. When it came, he stared at it and ran his hand over the sweaty outside surface of his glass several times, wondering how to fix things with Tess. He gave his head a shake and raised his glass while motioning to the barkeep with his other hand.

"A shot of whiskey, if ya please."

By the time Bridget got there he had his own personal pyramid going. He looked up as she approached. "Have ya seen Tess?"

"Nay." She raised a hand, and the bartender walked over. She gestured between the two of them. "Two more, please."

She hopped on the stool beside him. "It was a long day at work. I'm ready to tie one on."

He grunted in reply, turning back to his half empty beer. The shots arrived, and she clinked glasses with him then downed hers in one fell swoop.

She leaned closer, looking him in the eye. "You two have a row?"

"Nay," he answered quickly. His head swam, and he knit his brows together in concentration. "Well...yeah. Maybe. I guess." Had they?

She put a hand on his knee. "It happens."

He tried to focus on her, his eyes stinging from the smoke in the bar. Her skirt was hiked up a little farther than even the night before. The top pulled down. She was wearing more makeup. He slid off the barstool. "I'm going home to look for Tess." He swayed.

"Are you okay, honey?" Bridget asked.

He didn't waste his breath commenting, merely tried to choose the right pathway from the three that were shifting in front of him. He placed his hand on a few drinkers' backs as he stumbled forward. "Sorry... Oops! Sorry." Once he reached the locker room it took him several attempts to locate his locker and open it. He had retrieved his coat when she walked into the break room.

"Michael, you are in no shape to be alone tonight." She pressed against him, and he backed away until he stumbled into a wooden kitchen chair. He stared at Bridget, a little dumbfounded by her persistence. Her image swam in and out of focus, and for a minute, she was Tess. She wore the same uniform, which, in his condition, was a matter of much confusion.

She straddled his lap, taking his head in her hands and steadying it. With a drunken sense of wonderment he reached to touch the ends of her hair where they rested below her shoulders. It was soft.

He remembered how it had been before Tess. No complications, no thought at all, only a pleasant numbness. Physical satisfaction, nothing more. Why were the two of them having so many problems? Maybe Tess wasn't attracted to him in the same way he was attracted to her...maybe he had done something to really piss her off...his mind was reeling, searching for an explanation for her behavior, as it had been for the last couple of hours.

Bridget tilted her head, bending to kiss him. It was a practiced kiss, one practiced on many men before him; but right now it was what he needed. He needed the buzzing in his head to stop. He needed to silence it.

TESS HURRIED HOME. She stuck her head in the grocery store along the way, and Bridget told her she hadn't seen Michael. When she opened the door to the flat and called his name out, she received no reply. She went to the only other place she could think of, Clancy's. Not seeing him right away, she hunted down one of the guys in his band. The one he called Riff. She ventured up to him, "Hi. Have you seen Michael?"

He stared at her for a beat. She was wet from the rain that had started again and bedraggled. She shifted her weight uncomfortably.

"I saw him a few minutes ago headed for the break room to get his coat." As she turned he touched her arm. "He's...had a few to drink." He looked into her eyes, passing on a secret message. She nodded. As she walked to the back, she tried to decipher the look on Riff's face.

She opened the break room door, and images rushed at her like she had broken a vacuum on a sealed door. Bridget's long legs straddling his lap, their lips locked together, her fingers in his hair then moving to unbutton her blouse...Tess backed out of the doorway, shaken, and turned to stumble down the hall and out the back exit.

CHAPTER TWENTY-TWO

Michael reveled in the kiss for a minute. It felt solid. His heart didn't race the way it did with Tess. He wasn't worried about what would happen next. He had done this before. Casual sex was part of his skill set. He was not moved by her closeness, not moved by her at all. It was all familiar to him…and yet it had changed.

This was not what he wanted anymore. He didn't want to play it safe with his heart anymore and be swallowed by the emptiness that was his life. Bridget moved her hands to unbutton her blouse, and it was as if he was waking from a dream. He put his hands on her forearms to stop her, and then heard someone in the doorway. He shifted to see Tess's shocked face as she was turning to escape from what she had seen.

He jumped out of the chair, sending it crashing to the ground. At the last second, he remembered Bridget, and saved her from being dumped rudely on her keister. After lowering her safely to the floor he stepped over her, running out the door.

"Tess! Wait!" He opened the back door to the alley to find a steady downpour, water cascading out of the overfull gutters and onto trash lining the two brick buildings on either side of the alleyway, beating off plastic trash bags and tin cans like an alleyway rhythm section. It was dark except for the blaring white light over the door he exited from. He ran several yards down the alley, still calling her name, although she was clearly not there. He stopped, miserable, bending over with his hands on his knees to catch his breath.

"Dammit!" he yelled over the sound of the beating rain. It was the second time she had run away from him today, and this time he didn't think she would ever return. "Dammit," he said again, quietly. The rain and exertion had sobered him instantly. He turned around to trudge back inside, ready to give Bridget hell for what she did. He knew it wasn't entirely her fault. But he also knew it would make him feel a little better, if only for a moment.

That's when he saw her there, spotlighted by the bulb over the doorway. She was huddled with her back against the brick building, partially hidden by a large trash bag. Her arms were wrapped around her legs, her head flung back, and her eyes closed as the rain pelted her mercilessly.

"Tess, my God!" He rushed to her and bent in front of her, taking her arms.

"Don't!" she screamed, jerking her arms away as if his touch seared her.

"Tess..." He had no words. "I'm so sorry. I—"

"Nay. It's fine. I have no claim on you. No right. I—"

"But Tessie, you have," he blurted out without thinking. Suddenly he knew it was true. His voice softened. "Don't you know? You claimed my heart long ago. Bridget just..." He shook his head. "I was confused...and I had been drinking. It meant nothing, absolutely nothing. I swear."

She searched his face. She wanted to believe him. He could see it in her eyes.

"Please, let me take you home. Let me take you home so we can talk...just talk," he reassured her.

She seemed undecided for several moments, but then nodded weakly.

He helped her to her feet, shirking his jacket off to wrap it around her shoulders. "I'll grab an umbrella. You won't leave, will you?"

She shook her head.

He dashed inside and in a few minutes, they wandered, wordless, down the street, dripping wet under an umbrella. Each was sorting through the events of the day. After they entered the flat, she moved over to sit on the edge of the bed. She watched as a puddle grew from the water dripping off her hair and clothes. He stood right inside the door for several minutes, trying to find the right words to explain what happened. He walked over at last and sat next to her. As he was about to say something she spoke.

"Michael," she said tentatively. "I have to tell you something. But...I'm afraid to tell you. Terrified, actually." Her voice choked, and the tears running down her face fell to join the pool already on the floor.

"You can tell me anything. You know that." He took her hands in his.

"I know. I know." She nodded her head. "But this..." Again emotion strangled her words. He was silent. What could she have to tell him that could be so awful? Finally, she took a deep breath and began. Her voice was hollow, like she was trying to distance herself from the words she was saying.

"It happened when I was sixteen. These men my father knew came to the door. It was raining. They had been drinking. They said they came to see my father." She broke off, and he could see the struggle on her face as she tried to speak. He wished he could help her, but he didn't know how. He simply squeezed her hands and waited. "They grabbed me," she said at last, her voice high and tight. "I tried to get away, but they were so strong...and they had a knife." A weight sank in his stomach. "It was those men—those men at Mc-Gregor's."

Michael stared at her blankly. "You mean the ones I punched?"

"Aye." Tess nodded. She took another deep breath. She seemed to be lost for a minute, dazed. "They cut me." Not even seeming to realize she was doing it, she trailed a finger between her breasts. "And they kept hitting me. They...t-took off my clothes. I couldn't get away from them." A single sob escaped. "They *hurt* me. They...raped me," she ended with barely a whisper. She broke down, and he drew her into an embrace.

He couldn't fathom what she had been through, a girl, all alone in her cottage... It made him sick. He wished more than anything in the world he could take this from her, make it all go away; but he knew he couldn't. It made sense now, her nightmares, her reaction to the men in the pub. Of course she had been horrified seeing them again. He stroked her hair idly. *What do you say to someone who just told you they had been brutally raped?*

"Sh-sh. I'm here. It's all right now. I'll make everything all right." His words sounded lame in his own ears, but they seemed to comfort her, for she quieted.

Raising her head off his chest, she searched his eyes. She sprang up and put several feet of distance between them before whirling about to meet his gaze. "My da..." Her voice shook, and one solitary, fat tear ran down her face when she closed her eyes. "My da c-came home." And he could see this was the cruelest part of it all, to have him walk in on what they were doing to her. She swayed, and he made a move to steady her, but the motion seemed to startle her. Her eyes flew open, and he froze, unsure of how to approach her.

After a breath, she continued. "He tried to stop them, but they pushed him into the fireplace." Her pained expression told him the rest before she said it. "And he died in my arms."

"Oh, Tess."

"They just left. They killed him, and they left." Her bitterness was palpable.

"And you never told anyone?" he asked quietly.

"I was sixteen. Who would have believed me?" She pushed back a mass of wet hair with a shaky hand. Now she had told her story, she seemed drained as she shuffled over to the bed and sat. "Do you want me to leave?" she asked dully, staring at the floor.

"Wh-what? Why would I want that?"

"Michael, I'm not thick." She looked at him now, agitated. "I know this...changes things. I mean...what man would have me after..." She gestured meaninglessly in the air.

"What are you talking about?"

"Do I have to say it?" she screamed in near hysterics. "I'm...damaged."

Now he jumped to his feet. "*Damaged? Damaged?* Why would you ever think a thing like that? That's not true. It's..." A light dawned on him. "Wait...*they* told you that, didn't they? Those bastards told you that!" She nodded tearfully. "Tess, *you* are not damaged. *They* are damaged. *I* am damaged. But *you* are not damaged."

He paused a minute, trying to gather his thoughts. She sat silently. He lifted her face to speak with her earnestly, emphasizing each word. "Nothing they did to you could ever change the way I feel about you. If anything, it makes me love you more." He moved over and sat next to her. "After all you've been through... I mean, most people would hide themselves away from a world that had been so cruel to them."

"Well, I did. That night at McGregor's, that was the first time I had left the cottage in months. I had to come out. I had sold off practically everything I owned, and I needed money for food. But you can see how good that turned out. I killed a man, and now you and I are on the run. It's been easy to forget about that, living here with you, but I killed a man."

"That was an accident."

"Aye, but that little accident made you an outlaw."

"I made my choices, Tess. And I'd make them all over again."

She stared at him a moment. "But after what I did today..." She shook her head.

"That's over."

"But it's not, Michael." She stood and paced in front of him, getting increasingly upset. "Not for me. It's never over. It'll *never* be over." She stopped in front of him. "I love you. You have to know that. And I...want you, too. But sometimes certain touches, certain smells, set me off...my God...I see their faces. No matter how hard I try to block it out."

"And that's what happened today?"

She nodded, sitting next to him again. "I'm so sorry."

"It's all right. I understand. It's not your fault. We'll work through that. I don't care how long it takes. For that matter, I don't care if we ever make love. Of course, I want to, don't get me wrong..." he said teasingly, smiling at her to make sure she understood, "but...it's not all about that."

She smiled sadly. "Oh, come on, now. After all this we have to be open with each other. No more secrets. Molly told me that...well...you date a lot of women." He knew it could hardly be called dating. "You don't really think you'd be happy without an intimate relationship?"

"I don't know," he said honestly. "But I do know I'd be miserable without you."

She reached to stroke his cheek, staring at him in wonder. He froze, his chest tight with the love he had for her, for her breath-stealing beauty. Slowly she craned her neck to kiss him.

He kissed her back tenderly, feeling like a great heaviness had been lifted from them at last. She leaned back against him, exhausted by the events of the day. They sat without speaking for several minutes while people passed above on the sidewalk, unaware of the drama that had unfolded beneath their feet.

"Why don't we get out of these wet clothes and get some sleep," he suggested finally.

He let her use the bathroom first. She came out looking fresher, wearing a t-shirt and pajama bottoms. "Michael, I don't know if I can go back to work at the grocery store."

"After what I said to Bridget when I went back for the umbrella, I'm not at all sure you have a job anyway. It'll be fine. We'll find something else."

"Can I burn these then?" She held her soggy uniform.

He laughed. "You can do whatever you want."

"Good," she replied, and threw them with a wet smack into the bathtub.

CHAPTER TWENTY-THREE

Michael came to bed a few minutes later, and she ducked under his arm so she could put her head on his chest. He gave her a squeeze and kissed the top of her head, and soon she fell asleep. He lay for awhile rubbing her arm and reflecting on all she told him. He thought about the leering faces of the men at McGregor's. The idea of them doing the things they did with Tess made him furious. His fists clenched and unclenched as he considered it. *And that pig, McGregor, made her serve those men. ...Of course, Tad had no way of knowing about them,* he reasoned, *but he knew she was uncomfortable with them. And then he had to go and try and have a piece of her himself.* The more he thought about those things, the more agitated he became. After an hour, he slid out from under her and got out of bed to pace the floor.

So what exactly upset her today? After several minutes an answer came to him. *It was the shot Paulie gave me. She said that they had been drinking. It was the smell of the whiskey.* He chided himself, guilt riddling him. He thought about their first days together, how skittish she had been at times, and wondered how she had ever trusted him at all. He thought about her terrified cries in her sleep the night they stayed in the hayloft. The more he considered it, the more riled up he became. And then he thought about what she had seen when she opened the break room door to find Bridget astride his lap. He stilled and gazed at her sleeping form in the bed. *Through all this she has managed to keep her heart pure,* he marveled.

He turned and stared out the window. His view was extremely limited by the angle to the street, but he looked up at the one streetlight he could see. Toward dawn, he crawled into bed next to her and fell asleep.

"I SEE YOUR GIRL'S BACK," Riff commented as they started to pack their instruments at the end of the night.

"Aye." Michael smiled, looking over at Tess, who sat at a table near the bar. Her silky, emerald green blouse accented her eyes, and her jeans fit perfectly. He decided they were his favorites.

"Good," Riff said, slapping him on the back. "Good for you."

Michael grabbed his guitar case and climbed off the stage, watching her as he moved toward her, weaving through tables. "I see you've got yourself a little mini-pyramid here," he said of her three stacked shot glasses.

"Aye, but I've been here all night. I'm not even buzzed, I swear."

"All right." He smiled. "You ready to go?" He offered her his free hand and helped her out of her chair. Not willing to stop there, he slipped his hand behind her waist and dragged her in for a kiss.

"Aye, I'm ready."

The night was beautiful, and they strolled home through the nearly deserted streets. "Man, I'm beat," he commented when he opened the door to their place. He plopped his guitar case on the floor inside the door.

"You've had a long night." She came from behind and slipped her arms around him. "Why don't you let me give you a massage? It might help you to wind down a little."

He smiled. "Well, I can hardly turn that down, now can I?" He sat on the edge of the bed, and she climbed on behind him, squeezing his shoulders. He closed his eyes and enjoyed the sensation as she worked the muscles in his upper back.

"You know, I could do a whole lot better if you took your shirt off," she said slowly.

Something in the way she said it made him turn around. "Are you sure you only had those three shots?"

"Um-hum," she answered innocently. "Don't you worry about me." She eased his shirt off over his head. He turned back around, wondering what she meant by that.

Her hands were exploring the muscles along his back, working her way slowly down. After a minute or two her touch seemed to have changed from strictly therapeutic to something else. "Mmm, that feels good," he couldn't help but say.

"Does it?" she rejoined in a low voice. All at once he was no longer tired. In fact, all his senses were heightened. Her mouth was on his neck, and he closed his eyes again. *God, I want her so badly. How am I ever gonna take things slowly with her?* Her tongue traveled over his skin, and he turned to find her searching mouth. The angle was awkward, and she slid around so she was standing in front of him. His hands naturally went to her hips and around behind her. Her kisses were urgent, and his willpower was deserting him. She pulled away from him, breathless, and brought her fingers to the buttons on her blouse. He brought his hands to cover hers.

"You don't have to do this."

"But I want to." She undid a button then a second.

He closed his eyes to muster his strength. "Wait. Wait! We should take things slow. You'll be the boss. That way you'll feel safe and in control—"

"Have you been thinking about this, by any chance?" she asked with a wry smile.

He frowned, but ignored her. "—and if there is ever anything I do that makes you feel uncomfortable, we'll have a signal, like—"

He couldn't finish his thought because she was kissing him again, deep, impassioned kisses. She stepped away and took off her blouse. Without looking away, she wiggled out of her jeans.

"Oh, what the hell?" He gave in, returning his hands to her hips. She giggled as he drew her in. But, true to his word, he let her take the lead. Never would he have imagined that giving over control to another could lead to such exquisite pleasure.

Tess was blown away by how not blown away she felt. Every part of her was relaxed and...happy. She was happy! For the first time in forever she wasn't scared, or lonely or heartbroken.

But, a voice inside her urged, *you should be terrified*. This was to be her first time. Shouldn't she be at least a bit intimidated by that? Michael was experienced, she, a novice. But it was clear that this—what they had between each other—was as new to him as it was to her. Maybe that was why she wasn't shaking. Why her heart felt open, not like it was caught in an ever tightening net. Her hands glided over his shoulders and back up. This was hers. He was hers to take. So lean and muscled. So beautiful. She wanted him just as much as he wanted her.

Her gaze lifted to his face. At the moment it reminded her of a puppy dog. Almost comical in his need for her, and his struggle to control it. Like a dog with a treat balanced on his nose waiting for his master to give the word.

But then again, it wasn't like that.

He said that she would decide what would come next, but she didn't want to master him, she only wanted to love him. Pure and simple. Tess knew it wasn't just his body aching for her, it was his heart, too. He was as broken inside as she. Maybe that was what made it work. They both needed to love one another and be loved.

And while this was true, at that moment, it didn't matter.

She didn't want to talk; she wanted to show him how she felt about him. Because words could only go so far, could only say so much. There were limits to how well they could translate the heart. She brought her hands to the side of his face, and her mouth down to cover his, soft, exploring. Her core melted in one long sensation. His hands moved up and down her sides, but waited. Waited for her to signal. She lifted a knee onto the bed, pushing against him and straddling his legs again. His breath was warm, and he tasted like beer and home and Michael. He was hard beneath her and moving. She pressed her heat to him, wanting him inside her, but not yet.

She pulled her lips away. "Lay down." Her voice was low and husky. He fell back, looking into her eyes as she tumbled with him, but she kept her arms extended, raised above him so she could watch. His gaze dropped to her breasts and then snapped back up to hers, almost apologetic. "It's all right, Michael." She lowered her head, her hair spilling around them, and brushed her lips over his. "Touch me."

Without hesitation his hands came up to undo her bra, which clasped in front. His fingers were strong as they glided over her skin, the thumbs grazing her nipples. He squeezed her as she filled his hands and then teased with his fingers, brushing over and then away. She threw her head back, moved her hips rhythmically against his crotch then came back to crush her lips to his. He trailed kisses along her jaw and down her neck, the feel of his lips and tongue on her skin made her wild. A strong desire rushed through her; she wanted his mouth to replace his hands on her breasts. "Taste me," she demanded, her breath coming in quick pants now. The wet warmth of his breath and then the sharp, sweet sensation of his sucking made her eyes roll back in her head, and she moaned. He lifted his hips and pressed against her, sliding along her body.

She wanted him on top of her, to feel his weight and know that it was him. There was still a niggling doubt, a small section of her brain that feared her reaction. Would panic seize her as before? Would she do something to hurt him? She gathered herself, let go of her fear and threw herself over to her side, flipping to her back. The bar along the side of the bed bit into her.

"Come on." She scurried up to the pillow and reached as he hurried after her to pull him down on top of her. He still had his arms extended, studying her face. They paused, the only sound their ragged breathing. She smiled, reaching down to yank at his belt and release it. She undid his button and slid her hands inside. Umm...she sighed in relief as she touched him. She stroked, and he closed his eyes, his forehead creasing as a noise escaped his mouth, something between a sigh and a hum. She removed her hand. She liked being in control.

"Take those off." He rose to his knees and struggled to be rid of the rest of his clothing as she raised her hips to take off her panties. He settled his weight back on her and peered into her eyes. She gave a slight nod, and he was inside her. Oh, so good! It felt so good, she'd been waiting forever for this, for him. He laced his fingers through hers and squeezed them as he thrust. She raised her head to reach for him with her mouth, and he answered her. His tongue probed as he drove into her, her body rising to meet his. He tore his mouth away and bent to again take her nipple into his mouth, scraping his teeth along it as he sucked then pulling back to twirl his tongue around it before tasting her again. He moaned and brought his head up to bury it in her hair. He was breathing more rapidly, urgent noises near her ear that increased her own passion. She cried out as he began his release and moved quickly to guarantee hers. With a final shudder, he collapsed on her.

She was glad of the dark as tears squeezed out of her eyes, rolling down to fall on her pillow. Her heart was full to overflowing. She raked her fingers along his back in long strokes. He'd banished the ghosts of her past. She was not fool enough to think they were gone forever, but no matter what they might face in the future, she had tonight. She was grateful for that.

He lifted up onto his arms. "You're all right?"

A smile spread across her face. "I'm great!"

He fell to the side and pulled her to him. She sighed. He passed a hand along her arm, slowly travelling from shoulder to elbow and back again. Moments later the words escaped her lips as she slowly slid into sleep, "I love you, Michael."

He rolled onto his side, stroking her face. "I love you, Tess."

MICHAEL BROUGHT HIS hand down to rest on her arm. Her eyes closed, she breathed rhythmically beside him. Her face, awash in moonlight, was so peaceful, so still...and without warning, a strange sensation stole over him. Ice poured through his veins. His hair stood on end, and he reached to flatten it. But he couldn't rid himself of the feeling that had descended on him unannounced. Creeping out of the bed, he stood by the window, as he had the night before. He rubbed his arms to ward off the chill and closed his eyes. He pictured Tess as he had a few minutes ago lying in his arms, and then the image changed into the face of another woman, from long, long ago.

He didn't know how long he had been standing there when her voice called through the darkness. "Michael?" She rose on her elbows, squinting. "What's wrong?" She bolted upright to a sitting position. "My goodness, you look as though you've seen a ghost."

"It's all right. Go back to sleep."

She looked at him strangely for a moment. "All right. Wake me if you need to talk." She sank back into her pillow and eventually closed her eyes.

He didn't want to talk about it. But looking at her, he thought about how she had told him her most painful secret. He scrambled back into bed roughly, and she sat up.

"When I was ten," he began slowly, "my dad up and left me and me mam. It was a real shock 'cause he always seemed to love her so much. But..." He shrugged. "There we were alone. Not that I minded too terribly much. We got along well, me and me mam. Not like me and me dad. The two of us fought like cats and dogs." He shook his head, remembering.

"Anyway, Mam, she would come home late, after working at the dress shop all day, and she'd be exhausted. But she would always have time for a game of rummy. Sometimes, if I had fallen asleep waiting for her, she'd even wake me up." He laughed, but then the smile faded from his face. "We lived in this old lighthouse out in the country. Crazy old thing, but I guess one of my dad's family was a mariner, and he built it. Anyway, it was old and broken down, but we had some fun times there."

"Then one night, I was about twelve, I woke and my room was full of smoke. It was on the second floor, but my folks' was on the first. Me mam was callin' my name. I stumbled down the stairs, and the heat rose, the flames crackled. The wood was popping." He closed his eyes for a second. "And then I saw her. She was like some demon, her nightgown all aglow, running toward the door. I ripped my old man's coat from off the hook at the bottom of the stairs." His face twisted in grief. "I ran across the room, but she opened the door. The wind blew the flames back at me, my eyes stung, and I lost sight of her for a moment. But she just stood there in the open doorway. I knew I had to do something so I charged at her, the coat held out. I tackled her. She was screaming."

He stopped and swallowed. His throat was dry. It ached, seeming as scorched as it had been that night. "God, I'll never forget the awful smell." He shook his head. "And then she stopped screaming. Just stopped. Seconds later she started this horrible moaning. I wrapped her in the coat as best I could and hitched the wagon. We had a car, but the gas at that time was more than we could afford. I laid her in the back as gently as I could. The moon hit her face, and, my God, it looked beautiful. But the jacket had fallen open, and her body...it was charred and mangled, it was hideous. Her face still looked pretty, a little smudged, but pretty. Her eyes kind of glazed over when I first lifted her, but for a second, in the moonlight, they were as clear as day. She looked me in the eye...and she told me she loved me."

His voice cracked a little bit, but he continued. "I told her it would be all right. That I would take care of her. And I drove like the devil himself over those back roads into town. I knocked on Dr. O'Dell's door and then I went to fetch her from the wagon. He came out in his dressing gown, and said, 'It's too late, son. There's nothing I can do for her now.'"

He stopped talking. He didn't cry; he sat there, stunned. "And I yelled at him. I cursed the old man. I screamed at him not to give up on her. Told him all she needed was a little help. But even a twelve-year-old could tell she was gone." He was emptied out.

"Oh, Michael." She took his hand, rubbing her thumb across the top of it and not wiping away the tears rolling down her face.

"We buried her the next day. And then I took off. I started walkin' down the road, and I never stopped." He lay back on the pillow, bending his free arm to tuck his hand behind his head, and stared at the ceiling, his eyes damp.

Tess was speechless. What could she say? Slowly, she lay down and turned on her side, curving her body to his and holding on to his arm. It was the perfect response to his story.

CHAPTER TWENTY-FOUR

When Michael woke, Tess was in the kitchen cooking. Bacon sizzled in the pan, and a pile of eggs steamed on a plate on the counter. She had even managed to toast bread without a toaster, in the oven. "I didn't know we had bacon."

"I snuck down to the grocery this mornin'."

"Did you run into Bridget?"

"I did."

"And what did you say to her?"

"I told her if she ever tried to lay a hand on you again I would beat the living daylights out of her," Tess answered sweetly.

"You did not."

"Aye, I did indeed."

"Well, I'll be damned. Never thought you had it in ya."

"Well, there's a lot of things you don't know about me, Michael McKee."

"Is that so?" He grabbed her as she passed and pulled her into his lap.

She giggled and kissed him then stroked his arm. "How'd you sleep?" she asked tentatively.

"Oh, fine, fine. Hey, I'm sorry about layin' that whole story about me mam on you last night."

"Nay. I want you to tell me that kind of stuff."

"Well, it's all in the past now, anyways."

"Nay. Those kinds of things stick with you. You wouldn't be human if it didn't."

Somehow the words made him feel better. They took a stroll after breakfast, it was a beautiful day, and then they came back to the apartment and made love again, with the footsteps of strangers passing by on the sidewalk above them.

Tess sat cross-legged on the bed in one of his button-down shirts, scanning the want ads for something suitable. He kissed her on the head. "I'd better get in the shower. Riff wants us there early today to work on a new song. You are comin' down, aren't you?"

"Of course. Wouldn't miss it for the world."

"Maybe I should see if Paulie could walk you."

"I'll be fine. I'll go around the dinner hour when there's plenty of people out on the street."

"All right. But be careful."

MICHAEL STRODE INTO Clancy's feeling lighthearted, until he saw an individual he instantly recognized behind the bar. He turned around to duck out, but he had already been spotted. "Well if it ain't little Mikey McKee."

Of all the joints in all the world, Michael thought morosely. *At least Tess is safe at home.* He wondered if he would ever get to see her again. If he could get to Riff, Riff could get a message to Tess, warn her not to come here. All of these thoughts were running through his mind as he watched Jimmy Flynn approach him.

Jimmy held out his hand. "Good to see you." He shook Michael's hand and patted him on the back.

"Y-you, too," he responded, confused. Wasn't he here to bop him over the head and drag him back to the proper authorities?

"Jesus, Michael, you look as though you've seen a ghost or something," he said jovially, thumping him on the back again. "You with the band?" He gestured toward the stage.

"Aye. And you?"

"Oh, I got a job here yesterday after old man McGregor closed his place."

Michael stared, trying to pick his jaw up off the floor. "Old man McGregor?"

"Aye. Surely you haven't forgotten old Taddie already? If I remember rightly, you gave him quite a wallop before you left," he added, rubbing his chin.

"Tad's okay?"

"Right as rain, other than being bankrupt. Hey, your friend is signaling you."

He looked over to where Riff was waving him onto stage like a 747 coming in for a landing. He glanced at his watch. "Oh, man. I've got to go. Well, nice seeing you again," he said, this time sincerely.

"Aye, Mikey, you too. I'm off now, but maybe I'll see ya tomorrow."

"Sure, Jimmy. See ya tomorrow."

AT THE APPROPRIATE hour, Tess strolled into Clancy's and plopped herself at a table to listen to her favorite singer. Halfway through his second set, Michael broke a guitar string and headed for the back to get one of the new strings he had brought out of his jacket. Riff took over leads for him. After fifteen or twenty minutes he and Tess began to exchange bewildered looks. Each had been looking toward the back of the room, waiting for Michael to reappear. She stood to go check on him.

"We'll be right back after a short break," Riff said hastily into the microphone.

"I'm comin' with you," he called from behind her. They hurried into the hall. But there was no sign of Michael. Riff checked out the break room and the men's room, but still, they couldn't find him. "Man, I didn't have a chance to say anything before but...some guys were here earlier today askin' questions about him. I didn't like the looks of 'em."

She stooped to pick something up off the floor. She showed him a package of guitar strings. "Riff?" she said worriedly.

"Let's check the alley." The big man grabbed the door handle and tried to open it. "Damn. Someone's jammed it shut from the other side." He started throwing his shoulder into it in a rage. He backed away and tried again. On the third try the door gave, and he was thrown into the alley.

Tess followed him out. "Michael?" She spotted a tennis shoe attached to a leg flopped over a trash bag. "Oh, my God! Riff!"

Riff had just discovered Michael's jacket on the ground, but he rushed in her direction. "Sweet Jesus! Somebody beat the livin' shit out of him."

MICHAEL FELT GOOD ABOUT talking to Tess about losing his mother. He had never spoken to anyone about it before and somehow, having told her seemed to demystify the memories of his mam's death a little. He had never realized sharing pain could lessen it. His thoughts were divided between that and a blow-by-blow mental reenactment of their night together. While reviewing his mother's death had reduced its power over him, thinking about their night of lovemaking had the opposite effect on him. He couldn't wait to be alone with her again. He was relieved he had been able to help her to forget what had happened to her, if only for one night.

She walked in and smiled at him in that way she had that turned his stomach inside out. She sat at a table and never took her eyes off him. He loved the way she got into his music. Suddenly a thought struck him. What would happen if Tess found out they weren't really wanted for murder, that Tad wasn't dead after all? With no need for protection, would she want to return to her cottage again, alone? *What if I don't tell her? Hell, she's gonna find out eventually when she sees Jimmy Flynn. Maybe I could take her away somewhere. Move to Limerick...* An off-chord on the guitar synched with his offbeat heart. He broke a string. He searched his case, but none were in there. Riff took over so he could walk to the back to get some out of his jacket.

He had fished the strings out of his pocket when he received a crushing blow from behind, sending him to his knees. Someone ripped his jacket out of his hands and threw it over him. Before his head could wrap around what was happening to him, he was trussed up in his jacket like a Christmas turkey and dragged out to the alley. Once outside, the hold on him loosened, and he was able to rip the jacket away and face his assailants. He recognized two of them as the men that had been spying on Tess outside the grocery. A third behemoth shoved a two-by-four underneath the handle of the door they came out of. *Hell, hell, the gang's all here,* he thought, wryly.

The tallest man addressed him. "Okay, McKee, give us what we want."

"I'm sorry fellas, but I'm not that sort of guy." WHHOOF. The shorter one punched him in the stomach. *Obviously these guys don't have a sense of humor.* He held his ribs reflexively. "I haven't," he choked out, breathing heavily, "the foggiest notion what you're talking about."

"Oh, come on now. Do you really think we're gonna buy that? Cut the crap, and give us whatever it is that your father gave you."

"My father?" Though no second blow had come, his shock was a punch in the gut. "What does my father—" The conversation was interrupted by a right hook. *Impatient little bastard!* He wondered idly why it was the little guy that was beating the crap out of him.

"Look Mikey, I hate to go all cliché on you and everything, but..." He sighed. "...we can do this the hard way, or the easy way."

He didn't even see the next blow coming. The gorilla behind him pounded him, and he fell forward. Once down, he could only curl in the fetal position and hope to protect his vital organs.

"We're...gonna...get it...one way...or another." The speaker punctuated each phrase with a kick. He would have responded if he was able to breathe, and his mouth was not full of blood. His vision was blurry, and all he could see was pavement and a trio of black boots hovering around him. A bizarre thought crossed his muddled mind, as he wondered if they all shopped at the same shoe store. He would have laughed if he hadn't seen a hand reach in the pile of garbage near his head and grab a section of pipe. He was jerked painfully to his feet. A crashing noise came from his right. Someone was trying to pound their way through the door.

"I'm gonna give you one last try." He hammered the pipe into his open palm. "Where is it?"

Metal crunched, accompanied by some choice curse words he knew to be Riff's favorites, and he turned to see the two-by-four under the door scraping against the pavement. When he whirled around, he saw only the motion of the pipe as it swung through the air and into his head.

CHAPTER TWENTY-FIVE

R iff and Tater half-supported, half-carried Michael back to his apartment. Riff told Tess he wasn't happy about Michael's insisting they not call the police or an ambulance. He was messed up worse than anyone he had ever seen in the frequent bar fights he had witnessed and participated in. In the end, he respected Michael's wishes.

He groaned as they laid him on the bed. His face was bloody and already swelling considerably. But until he knew for sure it wasn't bad cops he was dealing with, he wasn't about to alert any authorities.

Tater spoke up. "We've gotta get back, Riff. We're supposed to be on stage right now."

"Aye, I know," Riff said irritably. He hesitated then took hold of Tess's upper arms and squatted a little, looking her directly in the eyes. "Are you sure you're all right?" She nodded mutely. He glanced back over his shoulder at the battered figure on the bed. "Try to get him to go to the hospital, would ya? Talk some sense into him," he said loudly.

"Riff, thank you." She stretched to give him a kiss on the cheek.

"If you need anything…"

"I'll call you," she responded, holding up the little scrap of paper he had written his phone number on before they left Clancy's. She turned and stared at Michael in stunned silence as they left.

"Lock this door," Riff said gruffly, sticking his head back in. Again she nodded and moved to the door to secure it.

Suddenly the room seemed very quiet, with only her and Michael's labored breathing. A medical assistant friend of Tater's checked him out at Clancy's and said he had no broken ribs, but she would have felt a lot better if they had taken him to the hospital. There was no way for them to tell if he had any internal injuries. She moved over to where he slept, her heart aching over every wound. She had bandaged her dad several times when he hurt himself badly on the farm, but never had his injuries been as severe as this. She knew she had to get him cleaned up so she could assess his injuries. She wanted to check underneath his shirt, but she recognized taking it off over his head would be too painful, if even possible. She retrieved a knife from the kitchen drawer and began to saw away at the fabric.

To her surprise, he didn't awaken at all during the whole time she was doing it. This added to her worry. Maybe he had some kind of horrific head trauma. He was sleeping with what looked like comfort, and she decided the best thing for him was probably to sleep. She wet the torn pieces of his shirt and carefully wiped away any debris and dry blood she could find. When she'd done all she could, she sat in the recliner to watch over him.

TEDDY MCKEE WAS A BITTER man. His wife had been taken from him. His son was nowhere to be found. He discovered his best friend's body in a room that still smelled of his murderer's cigar. And then, as a final blow, his freedom was taken from him.

Before he could react, police surrounded the building, spurred there by an anonymous call. He was found over the body of his wife's lover, his fingerprints all over the syringe that killed him. He was sent to prison for fourteen years.

When he got out, he began to immediately search for the key, the key to the door that locked away Bradigan's invoices. He had not forgotten. Fourteen years hadn't dulled his memory; he had thought about it every day. The thought of revenge kept him alive behind bars.

Unfortunately Patrick Bradigan had not forgotten either.

DURING THE NIGHT, MICHAEL woke several times asking for pain relievers, but as soon as he took them, he would fall back to sleep. In the morning, Tess snuck out to get more medicine. She was unsure about leaving him, but since it was only to the corner and back, she decided to chance it. She managed to run the errand in less than ten minutes. She was opening the door when she sensed somebody behind her. She spun around, but was knocked roughly against the door, a hand clapped over her mouth. The man snarled at her, his chocolate-brown eyes boring through her, his forearm bearing down on her chest. Pressing her against the door he quickly reached to turn the knob, pushing them both inside the apartment and slamming the door behind them. Her gaze flew to her right, but the bed was empty. She prayed that Michael was somewhere safe. The stranger released her, and she turned to face him, stumbling back several steps. He advanced on her in a sinister way, his eyes, too, darting around the room. Oddly, something was familiar about the man.

"Okay, little girlie. Tell me where it is, and you won't get hurt."

"I don't know what you're talking about," Tess said shakily.

"Don't give me that!" he shouted. "The box, the wooden box I gave him."

"I don't know—" He stepped forward, and before the words were even out of her mouth, he gave her a vicious backhand that knocked her into the recliner.

Michael was examining the damage done to his face in the bathroom mirror when the door slammed shut. A loud male voice shouted beyond the door. A voice he recognized. His grip on the sink tightened. He stepped out of the bathroom as Tess rose from the recliner.

"What the hell are you doing here?" he asked icily. He glanced at Tess. Her wide eyes looked from one to the other, her mouth open.

"Well, well, well. Mikey." Teddy's voice cracked, and he shifted his weight as he stared at him. "I'd say it was good to see ya and all..." He didn't finish the thought. His gaze wandered around again, and he seemed to recover from his initial shock. "Real nice place ya got here," he added sarcastically.

Michael, not disturbed by any pleasant memories of his father, found his voice easier and came back with bitterness. "As good as any you put us in." He looked his father over. Prison had changed him. He was thinner, harder. His eyes—once open and frank—were slitted and glinted with an edge he'd not seen before. Michael's gaze shifted to Tess, and for the first time saw the red mark on her cheekbone. "You hit her, you bastard." As he said it, he charged at his father, but she stepped between them.

"Michael, nay. It's your father." She wrestled him back. "Stop! You're hurt!"

"Aye, Mikey," Teddy taunted. "Listen to your little girlfriend." But he looked from one to the other, appearing interested.

"You, shut up!" she said so sharply that both men stared at her.

Teddy glowered. "Listen. All I want is that little wooden box I gave you, and I'll be on my way and leave you two in your little love nest here."

"Why would I have kept anything that might remind me of you?" Michael saw that it hurt, and he was glad.

Teddy rubbed his chin, appearing to be chewing over something. "You got yourself quite a temper, Mike."

"Aye. I wonder who I got it from."

Teddy just stared at him, shifting his jaw from side to side. "I guess ya got a point there. Well, I suppose this little happy reunion is over." His eyes scanned the room one last time as he retreated toward the door. "But don't you worry. I'll be back for what's mine."

As Teddy turned to reach for the doorknob, Michael stepped forward. "Wait!" The jarring movement sent an unexpected wave of pain through him, and he gasped, bending over and putting an arm around his ribs. Tess grabbed his shoulders, trying to help support him. He concentrated on breathing for a second, but then raised his head, squinting as he drew a raspy breath. "What happened to you? I mean, you've always been a prick, but...what happened to you? You've changed." He waved his free hand in Tess's direction. "You'd've never hit a woman before."

Teddy looked at her. "Aye." He shifted his gaze back. "Fourteen years is a lot of time to think, Michael. A lot of years to gnaw over a cheating wife, a no-good, disloyal friend, a crooked justice system... Ach!" He threw a hand in the air. Shifting his weight he added, "And prison ain't no walk in the park, my friend. Every day, scratching for survival..." He stared off, but then started again. "I've seen more than you will ever know. Thank God! You just be grateful for that, me lad!" He raised a fist and shook it at him. And with that, he was gone.

Michael collapsed on the bed, his eyes squeezed shut to block out his agonizing injuries. The effort of sticking up to his father cost him.

Tess bent over him, obviously concerned. "Michael, are you all right?"

He opened his eyes and caressed her cheek. "I'm fine. Are *you*?" She nodded.

"Oh, God, Tess, I'm sorry. I didn't even know he was still alive." He sighed. "Any other day I would have killed him for touching you, but I'm so—"

"Nay! Don't say that! If your being hurt prevented you from doing that, I'm glad of it."

He opened his less swollen eye. "Woman, what a thing to say."

"I'm sorry," she said firmly. "But I won't have you fighting your da on account of me." She climbed to lie beside him, placing her head tentatively on his chest. He decided to drop it. How could he explain he wouldn't have had any problem punching the man who left him and his mam? Who wasn't there to help him save her on the night their house caught on fire? With a groan he wrapped his arm around her and sighed. "I can't believe I am even saying this, but Tess I think you need to get away from here."

"What?" She flew up, and the unexpected movement jostled him. He grimaced. "Oh, I'm sorry." She peered into his eyes. "You want me to leave?"

He played with a strand of her hair. "I don't want you to leave, babe, but it might be the best thing for you."

"I don't want to go anywhere without you."

"But here's the thing, Tess," he said it as fast as he could so that he wouldn't have time to change his mind. "I ran into Jimmy Flynn the other day, and he told me that Tad McGregor isn't dead. You didn't kill him after all, only wounded his ego. So you see, it's safe for you to go home now."

"Tad's not dead," she repeated slowly.

"That's right."

"I didn't kill him."

"Exactly."

"And these men that are following us..."

"Well, as it turns out, they were really after me. So no one is looking for you. You can go back to Old Head, and—"

Her jaw tightened. "So you think that I only see you as...some kind of body guard?"

Michael could see he had taken a wrong step somewhere, but he didn't quite know where. "Well...I...uh..." She continued to look at him balefully. He closed his eyes, exhausted. "Now Tess," he said sternly, trying to regain the upper hand, "I'm not going to argue with you about this."

"Good."

"Woman, you can be so difficult at times," he said sleepily. But when he drifted off to sleep, he had a smile on his face.

THROUGHOUT THE DAY and into the night Michael dozed on and off, his body shutting down for repairs. Tess stayed by his side, nursing him. They would occasionally argue about whether or not she should leave, but he found her to be as stubborn as he was, and the matter remained unresolved.

Around midnight he woke to find her gently shaking him. "Outside," she whispered, and he looked up to see several familiar pairs of boots through their window.

"Come on." He jumped out of bed, his body objecting adamantly to the action. Groaning he leaned over and extracted something from underneath the mattress then grabbed a kitchen chair and leaned it under the window on the north wall. He steadied the chair as she scrambled up it but she was still far shy of the window's lock. Stepping on the chair behind her, he managed to keep it balanced while pushing her from underneath.

He felt sure she would have protested this undignified exit had boots not sounded on the stairs, and something scraped in the lock. Spurred on by this she opened the window while leaning on her elbows on the narrow ledge. She had no sooner pulled herself through and turned around when he came nimbly through the window, knocking the chair over in the process.

They heard shouts of, "Hurry up! They went out the window!"

Their pursuers backtracked and took the easier way out the front door, which gave them only a small head start. They ran down the alley between their building and the next and through the gate in a tall chain link fence. He threw a look back. His father was being dragged along unwillingly by one of the others. He slowed a little, interested in his connection to the group, but he didn't dwell on it long, as the gap was being narrowed by those in the lead. He turned onto a street he knew led to the wharf.

Their followers' footsteps clapped against the pavement behind them, echoing off the surrounding buildings with a ringing intensity. He rounded a corner quickly and took advantage of being out of sight for a second by ducking into an abandoned warehouse. The building was black as night and smelled like fish and motor oil. The light from the narrow windows running along the roof line couldn't penetrate the velvety darkness. He held Tess in front of him, their breathing pounding in their ears. Footfalls ran past, and shouts filled the air. They were obviously not concerned about being heard in the deserted area.

The large door they came through moved back on its rollers. Standing in the light from the outside he recognized the image of his father. He was alone. Michael edged Tess deeper into the shadows.

"Michael," his father whispered loudly. He listened. The inky blackness did not surrender its fugitives. More noise came from outside. Teddy closed the door behind him. "Dammit, Michael, I want to help you."

Michael shot Tess a warning look.

She hesitated. "We're over here."

He closed his eyes and exhaled loudly. *This woman's gonna do me in.* She stepped forward.

"Michael, we don't have much time. Those guys will be back at any moment." His father had turned to look out of a crack in the door. "They'll figure out you're in here like I did. When they get close, I'll run out and distract them. You take your little filly here, and run the other way."

"Why?" Michael said, raising his eyebrows and crossing his arms over his chest.

"Look, I know ya've got no reason to believe me, boy, but I'm telling you the truth. Here they come. Make your decision." With that, his father opened the door wide and ran out. Michael could see three figures take after him on the run. He stepped out to get a better look. He saw them simultaneously draw guns out of their jackets with silencers on them like some sick trio of synchronized swimmers. He heard the high-pitched sound of their discharge, and saw his father's back jolt as he was hit. He stood frozen to the spot in horror.

"No!" he found himself shouting.

The three shooters turned their heads in unison to look at him. Teddy lifted his head, grimacing in pain, and yelled, "Dammit, Michael! Don't ruin the only good thing I've ever done in my miserable life. Run, man, run!"

Shots whistled past their heads. Tess screamed. Michael turned and ran blindly, gripping her hand. He realized, with dread, he made a poor choice. They were running down a gangplank poking straight out into the water, with no turns or chances for escape. Tess seemed to make the realization at the same time. They looked at each other in desperation. Having no choice, they barreled on. The three men's heavy boots thudded behind them now. Twenty feet ahead of them, the wooden pathway ended at the river. Holding hands, they ran, leaping into the air at the last minute.

Michael jerked his body as they fell, letting go of Tess's hand. The drop to the swiftly moving water seemed to take an eternity. They plunged deep under the surface but could still hear the _pocketa-pocketa_ noise of bullets hitting the water. She tried to follow him as he swam back through the murky water toward the shore.

My God! He's heading right back toward them, she thought in alarm, but she followed in his wake. Her arm scraped against something slimy, and she realized it was the algae-covered posts supporting the docks. Her lungs were threatening to explode when the pair finally burst through the surface to a shallow pocket of air under the pier. They frantically tried to quiet their breathing, but were surprised by the wail of sirens rupturing the former stillness. They could hear the men cursing and running, and the sound of them being chased. Tess looked at Michael and knew something was wrong. It took a minute for her mind to register the red water swirling around them was infused with his blood.

She swam out from the protection of the dock, trying to drag him with her. He still tried to feebly swim beside her, even in his half-conscious state. A policeman, who had probably stayed near the dock in case anyone tried to escape by boat, saw them surface and immediately called on his radio for an ambulance.

CHAPTER TWENTY-SIX

Michael opened his eyes to the blinding white lights of an overly-sterile hospital room.

"Oh, thank God!" Tess cried.

"Oh, I will. I will," a bearded clergyman from the other side of the bed answered. Tears were rolling down Tess's face. "Well it seems like your young lady here can't speak, so I'll tell ya son, you ruined a lovely Last Rites."

Tess leaned over him. "Michael, are you all right? How are ya feeling?"

"Whatever they gave me is making me feel a little loopy, but...not bad." He tried to skootch up farther on the pillows. His face contorted and sucked in a breath through his teeth. "Except when I try to move." He closed his eyes. "What happened?"

"Well, I'll tell ya what happened," inserted the priest, "you got shot in the back, that's what happened."

"You lost a lot of blood," Tess added.

"But you've got yourself a lovely young lady here, lovely. Cries a little too much." He chuckled as Tess circled the bed to hug him. "Ach. Don't do that now. Those vows, ya know? You'll be ruinin' my priestly image." He tipped his hat to them both and stepped out of the room as the doctor stepped in.

"Where'd you find him?" Michael asked, amused, but the doctor forestalled Tess's answer.

"Ahh, the other Mr. McKee. How are you feeling, son?" he asked soberly.

"Dandy," he answered sarcastically. "Is my da here?"

Tess and the doctor exchanged a look. He glanced at a monitor. "Your vital signs are all good. Incredible, really, when you consider what your body's gone through." The doctor paused, gripping the bed rail. "I'm Dr. Callahan. Your father is here, Mr. McKee, but I'm afraid he is in grave condition. He was shot four times and lost a large quantity of blood, although you wouldn't know it by looking at him." He sat on the edge of the bed. "I'm going to be frank with you, Mr. McKee, your father is in very bad shape. In fact, we're all amazed he even survived the ambulance trip, let alone the surgery. I think the only reason he's been holding on is to check on you. He's been asking to talk to you whenever he's conscious."

Dr. Callahan looked again at Tess. When she didn't protest he asked, "Do you think you feel strong enough to visit him?" Michael nodded dully. "Let me get some help here." The doctor headed out the door and came back in a few short minutes with two nurses. With Tess's help they were able to wheel Michael and all of his equipment into the next room.

Teddy McKee lay in his bed looking pale and haggard. He opened one eye with the commotion of people trying to fit Michael's bed into the room and immediately began speaking to him, even before he was completely in the room. "Son, son. How are ya doin'? Come to see your ol' man, huh?" He laughed, which set off a bout of coughing. When he recovered, he took up the conversation again, though his voice was weak. "Michael, I've got to tell you something." He reached a shaking arm through the bars of both beds to hold his hand. The doctor and one of the nurses began to leave the room and Tess, too, but he called her back. "Nay. Stay, young lady, you should hear this, too." The other nurse buzzed about, checking both men's equipment. He cleared his throat. "I've been doing a lot of thinking since I first laid eyes on you two. You reminded me of who I was in a better time...of me and your mam."

"Da—" Michael began to interrupt.

"Now, shut up, son. I'm trying to talk. Oh...sorry about that...old habits, you know. Anyway, I was always hard on you, Mikey, and I'm sorry about that. And I'm sorry about hitting you, miss." He reached his other hand out to Tess. "I can tell my son really thinks a lot of you." He squeezed her hand. Tess blinked back tears, looking away for a moment. His energy was running out, and his voice was little more than a whisper.

"I want you to know," his eyes gazed off, unable to focus properly, "I loved you and your mam, Michael. And I didn't leave you exceptin' because I had to. The folks I got mixed up with was bad folks, real bad folks, and they would have come after you two, and I couldn't have that. Besides, I knew I was a hard man to get along with, so I thought maybe it would be better that way." Michael could no longer contain his tears. "I was...there...sometimes, though. At your soccer games and such..." He trailed off, and Michael looked to the ceiling, tears streaming down his face.

Suddenly the old man grasped Tess's hand tightly. "Gabrielle," he called out. She looked at Michael, questioningly.

"That's me mam's name."

She moved closer to him. "Gabby," he said, sounding relieved. "Make sure you tell the boy...tell him to stay away from those mamby-pamby Wallace boys...and to do his best at school." An urgency filled his words. She seemed unsure of how to respond, but patted his hand and he quieted.

Sometime in the middle of the night, he left them.

TESS WHEELED MICHAEL out into the courtyard. "Maybe the sunshine and fresh air will raise your spirits some." She positioned him and locked the wheels. "It's beautiful out here, isn't it?" she said, sitting on a stone bench.

"Aye." He was distracted, as he had been for the past several days. He slipped the little wooden box from his pocket, turning it over and over in his hand. It had all been because of this box. What was its secret? It was about five inches across, seven inches wide, and probably another four inches deep. He'd always found it to be the perfect size for holding a wad of bills, or some loose change. It had been emptied, though, so he could examine it more closely. He had checked it for a false bottom, for some kind of mysterious writing, for any clue to why it was so damned important. He was set to be released from the hospital tomorrow, and somehow he felt it was critical to figure out the riddle before he left there. He had never discussed it with his father in the final hours of his life. It hadn't seemed crucial at the time.

"Michael, may I see it a minute?"

"Sure." He shrugged, handing it to her.

"It's lovely. Did he make a lot of these?"

"Not that I know of. He made mostly coffins for other people and furniture for us. He couldn't make furniture for other people, because once he had made it, he couldn't part with it. So he made coffins. We didn't have much use for those in the house."

Tess ran her hand over the carvings. They were mostly of leaves and vines, but in the middle of the lid was an oval section with an inlaid dove made of some sort of white stone. "Did he do a lot of inlays like this?"

"Nay. In fact I don't remember any other piece with inlay, except for me mam's nativity set." He frowned and held out his hand to get the box back. All of a sudden, he sat up excitedly. "Tess, do you have your key?" She slid her hand into her jeans pocket and pulled it out. He held the box up. "I wonder..." He stuck the tip of the key at the edge of the outline of the dove and began to try to pry it loose. After several minutes he had a large section up, but he couldn't get it off. He shook the box in frustration and something fell with a clink to the ground. They both stared at the strange two-pronged key on the sidewalk. She retrieved it and handed it to him.

"What do you think it's to?"

"I'm not sure."

"Well, it's pretty small. Could it be to a safety deposit box?"

"I don't think so. My dad had a real distrust for banks. He always said that people put their money in the bank to keep it safe from robbers, but that the real robbers were the crooks that ran the banks and charged all those outrageous fees. Except for my Daddo Quinn, my mum's dad. He liked my Daddo Quinn."

"Ahh. So probably not a bank then." She laughed.

"Nay. A post office box, maybe? But where?"

"Maybe the box itself is a clue," Tess mused. "The dove and vines could be a reference to Noah. But I've never heard of Noah's Bank and Trust. Is there a Noah Street in Cork?"

He jumped out of his wheelchair and hugged her, laying a big smacking kiss on her. "You're brilliant, Tess."

"There really is a Noah Street in Cork?" she asked, breathless from the unexpected kiss.

"Nay, nay." He danced a little jig. "My Daddo McKee's name was Noah."

"I don't think the doctor wants you doing that," she scolded. "Is your daddo still alive?"

"Nay, darlin' he's not," he said, gleefully.

"Al-l-l-l right," she responded, confused by his strange behavior.

"Do you think you could use your special powers to bust me out of this place today?"

She winked at him. "I'll see what I can do."

THEY STOOD IN FRONT of the mausoleum, suddenly unsure. Michael took Tess's hand, and they walked in together, looking for NOAH BREN-DAN MCKEE on one of the name plates.

"Here it is!" she squealed, jumping a little at the echoes she sent pinging off the white marble walls.

He drew the key out of his pocket. It glided perfectly into the lock. He opened the door. Inside was an urn and a bunch of loose documents. Michael started riffling through the papers.

She tried to peek over his shoulder. "What are they?"

"They are receipts. Receipts my father wrote for coffins. I don't understand," he said with an air of disappointment. He dropped a few on the ground.

Tess bent to collect them. "They're all for the same person, someone named Patrick Bradigan. Why would one person need so many coffins?"

"That's it. Holy shit! That's unbelievable!" He put a hand on her arm. "I read an article, not long after we arrived in Cork, about the trial of a man named Patrick Bradigan. He had been accused of smuggling drugs into the country. A shipment of coffins was confiscated by the port authorities. These coffins had false bottoms that concealed drugs that were being transported illegally. These papers tie Bradigan to those coffins. My father was making his coffins for drug runners, and he was trying to turn them in. We've got to get these to the authorities. This will be the final nail in Bradigan's coffin." He flashed her a grin. "Pun intended."

EPILOGUE

Tess stirred a pot of oatmeal on the stove in their big, white farmhouse and pressed the toaster's lever down with her other hand.

Her daughter entered the kitchen, urging a brush through her straight red hair one more time. "I'm leavin', Mam." She grabbed a piece of toast off the plate as Tess turned to put it on the table, stuffing it into her mouth.

Tess bent to kiss the top of her head. "All right, Katy-did. Have a great day."

She mumbled goodbye through her toast and left, but then stuck her head back in the door a second later. "And make sure Liam stays out of my stuff, will ya?"

"Of course, darlin'." Tess promised as Michael, sitting at the table, reached around his newspaper to steal another piece of toast from the plate she was setting down. She slapped at his hands while calling to her oldest, "I'll take care of Liam. You take care of Boots and Ginny."

"Aye, Mam."

A second girl, this one blond, wearing the same school uniform her sister had, crossed the kitchen, pushing her glasses farther up her nose. "Mam, nobody but you calls me Boots anymore. It's Beth."

Michael looked at Tess from the behind the safety curtain of his paper and rolled his eyes.

"Aye, I know very well what your name is, Elizabeth Anne McKee, since I gave it to you after twelve hours of the most excruciating labor pains I have ever been through."

Beth kissed her sweetly on the cheek. "Last time you told me it was ten hours."

"Oh, off with you then, Whatsyourname." She snapped the towel hanging on her shoulder at her and then turned around to dish out oatmeal. She spun a few seconds later with her bowl to offer it to the curly haired blond at the table. "Here ya go, Sir Liam."

Michael folded the top edge of his paper down to look at his son. "I don't know how we do it, you and I, in this house full of women."

"Me neither," the five-year-old replied in the serious way that so often made his parents laugh. Then he announced, "Da, I've been thinkin'."

"Oh, ya have, have ya?" He folded the paper and put it away, giving his son his full attention.

"Aye. I've been thinkin' that I want to be a musician like you when I grow up."

"Oh, now, lad. There's a gob of more things you can do that's better than being a musician."

"Why's that, Da? You've got everything you need. You've got Mam and all."

"The boy has a point." Tess smiled, crossing to give his head a kiss, and his curls a tousle.

"Aye, maybe..." He put his chin in his hand, giving the prospect his full consideration.

"Maybe?" she returned, getting out her towel and winking at Liam while approaching Michael from the opposite side of the table.

He sensed something was up and rose from his chair. "Woman, if you snap that thing at me you better make damn sure—" He glanced at Liam. "—oops, I mean darn sure, that you hit me." He backed away grinning, but when she made her move he sprang forward, catching the towel and yanking her to him. "Now you're in trouble," he teased, wrapping the towel around to trap her. Switching gears, he secured her with one arm around her waist and snatched Liam's spoon full of oatmeal and held it over her head. Liam was grinning from ear to ear, enjoying one of his parents' frequent playful moods.

"Michael Patrick McKee, if you so much as get one dab of that in my hair, I'll..."

"You'll what?" he said, nibbling her neck. She giggled. "What do you think, Liam? Should I put cereal in your mam's hair?"

Tess winked at Liam, shaking her head and mouthing "no."

"Now that's cheating. We're putting Liam in charge of this. If he says the cereal goes in Mam's hair," Michael smiled comically and nodded his head in an exaggerated way, "then it goes in Mam's hair. If he says it doesn't," he said in a voice that clearly expressed that this would be the wrong decision, "then it doesn't." He finished quickly, as if this wasn't a serious option at all. "So, okay Liam. What's it gonna be?" Michael sat with the spoon posed. Liam was glowing with his newfound power. Tess was still trying to break free from Michael's grip.

"We-e-l-l-l," Liam said thoughtfully, mischief in his eyes.

"Now Liam, remember who plays rummy with you every day after school," Tess coaxed, suddenly concerned.

"And remember who plays rummy with you every day after work." Michael countered. "And who plays catch with you." He knew he said the wrong thing the minute it came out of his mouth.

"Mam played catch with me all day yesterday."

"Aye, but who makes you fold-over jelly breads?" Michael tried another tack.

"You both do, but Mam's the only one who folds them right. I say...we let her go," Liam proclaimed with a wave of his arms to all those gathered in the kitchen, which was only the three of them.

"O-o-o-h-h," Michael said in mock disappointment, setting her free, but as he did so he accidentally tipped the spoon, releasing oatmeal down the front of her hair and dripping into her face. He looked at her with a mixture of horror and amusement.

"Michael Patrick McKee! Wait 'til I get ahold of you!" she screamed and began chasing him around the table.

Liam squealed with delight. "Get 'im, Mam!"

Michael knocked a chair over to try to block her, but she side-stepped it with ease. Knowing there was no way he would make it around the end of the table, he dashed outside instead. He didn't expect Tess to follow him out, so he was surprised by the shove from behind. He teetered for a moment like a man on the edge of a cliff and then fell into the animals' watering trough.

Tess laughed nervously, surprised as she was to see him sitting fully dressed in the water. "Oh, Michael, I'm sorry," she said, trying to suppress her giggles.

"Oh yeah?" He lunged at her and pulled her into the tub of water on top of him. He laughed and kissed her.

Liam stuck his head out of the kitchen door. "You two are mad." He turned around and headed back inside, letting the screen door slam behind him.

They laughed and kissed some more. "You better get up and change so you can get to work," Tess reminded him eventually.

"I'm not going to work today."

"You're not?"

"Nay. I took the day off. Told the boss it was our anniversary."

"But it's not."

"I know that, and you know that. But, darlin', he don't know that. And besides, I told him I'd come in on Saturday and help him out with that dining room table and chairs he has to make."

"You're a big softy," she said, kissing him again.

"Woman, I wouldn't count on it," he said suggestively.

"Michael!" Tess scolded in a whisper. "Liam's right inside the house."

"So let's go in the hayloft. You know he's watching cartoons anyway."

"Oh, come on," she chided. "Old women like me don't do it in haylofts."

"Well, you're not old." He kissed her. "Not yet anyway."

"You are so-oo smooth," she teased, sitting up and stepping out of the water.

"Come on," he begged. "I'll pull up the ladder so there's no chance of him walking in on us."

Tess glanced in the window, through the lacy curtains, to where she could see Liam already engrossed in his cartoons. She had once thought of her life as a kaleidoscope, and now she was grateful for all the pretty pictures it made for her. "Last one to the barn is a rotten egg," she challenged him at last, darting off without waiting for a response.

"Not fair, not fair!" He tried, awkwardly, to remove himself from the trough. But when he took off after her, he was grinning.

Note from author

Thank you for reading DAMAGE DONE, part of my REAL RO-
MANCE COLLECTION. I hope you enjoyed it! Now that you've read the
book, won't you please consider writing a review? Reviews are one of the best
ways readers discover great new books. They don't need to be fancy or long,
just a sentence or two honestly describing your opinion of/experience with
the book. I would sincerely appreciate it.

Want more from M.J. Schiller?
Page forward for
an excerpt from
ROCK ME, GENTLY
Rocking Romance Collection

CHAPTER ONE

It was seven-thirty, and he wasn't even halfway trashed yet. Knowing he needed to make up for a late start, Josh serpentined his way through the press of suntanned gamblers to the bar.

The muscular, dark-haired bartender appeared to be stuffed into the tux he was wearing. "What can I get you, Mr. Dunningham?"

Stardom had its perks, such as prompt service at the bars.

"I'll have a shot of tequila."

While the bartender turned to prepare the shot, Josh let his eyes roam over the crowd. He loved the ding of the bells and the calls of the craps table and roulette wheel, along with the smell of hot bodies squashed together in a greedy, hedonistic bunch. Yes, this was his kind of place. When he surrounded himself with lights flashing, buzzers going off, shouting, groaning, and cheering, it provided him with a lot of distractions. A sort of artificial life to make him forget about his lack of a real one.

Life after his meteoric rise hadn't changed much for him. He was still drinking every night like he had in his little hometown in Iowa, and trying to make it with the girls. The only difference was now it wasn't Falstaff or Pabst, it was Crowne Royal or Dom Perignon; that, and the fact that now the girls didn't need any persuading.

"Here you go, sir."

The golden liquid key to oblivion lay on the bar in front of him, with a slice of lime and a saltshaker. Without a moment's hesitation, he downed the fiery fluid, ignoring the lime and salt, and then brought the shot glass down on the bar with a satisfying sharp rap. He grimaced. "Smoooth!" His voice sounded hoarse. "Another, please. I'm behind."

"Yes, sir," the bartender replied with a grin. While his quick hands poured a second dose of the lethal liquor, another bartender sidled up and slammed a shot glass down next to his.

"Pour me one, would ya?"

Josh kept the amber stream under his surveillance as it poured into the newly offered glass, a liquid lifeline for some other poor slob. He watched with idle curiosity, the voyage of the little glass as it headed to the other end of the bar, accompanied by the standard accoutrements of salt and lime. A short blonde stood with her back to the bar, resting her elbows casually on its top, apparently interested in some action elsewhere. As the bartender approached, she turned around.

And his heart about catapulted out of his chest to do a belly flop on the bar. She was breathtaking. She wore her hair in a practiced tousled style, a stunning contrast of light and dark shades of spun sunshine. It was the kind of rumpled approach which made him think she must look good when she rolled out of bed, and more about what she would look like when she rolled into it. Her makeup was perfect; her look fresh, not done up. And her lips, man...her lips were so full and lush he could almost feel the drool pooling behind his own. She ran a fingertip up and down the side of the glass where it was sweating, and glanced around self-consciously.

Seeming assured that no one was looking in her direction, she licked the side of her thumb and poured the salt on.

Watching as her tongue ran the short gamut along her glowing skin, a single thought ran through his head, *I think I'm in love.* If the alcohol didn't soothe him, he was certain she would.

She knocked the shot back like a pro and sucked on the lime. The expression of sweet pain on her pixie-like face was classic. Though he couldn't hear it, he was almost sure she muttered, "Smoooth!" with a little shiver and a smile. She lifted her gaze, catching him watching. Her eyes were a pair of blue thunderbolts, electric, in a shade the contact lens companies had yet to capture. With a line of black around the edges of the iris and thick, curling lashes fanning out gracefully along the perimeter of her lid, his eyes were drawn to hers like a target.

Her eyes grew wide when she saw him, and she scrambled to remove the spent piece of lime, dropping it into her glass as her cheeks flushed red. Her gorgeous mouth hung open a second and he could see the glint of recognition in her eyes. BINGO!

A second benefit of his fame, and the best, in his opinion, was the way it moved the ladies. The money meant nothing to him. He hadn't even bought himself any expensive toys, except for one red Lamborghini. It was about the sex. The sex fed his lust for something beyond himself. It was the rush of power it gave him. The power he felt now as he strode confidently around the bar toward the girl.

THE SHOT BURNED ALL the way down her throat. Cassie McCallister snatched up the lime; it killed a little of the numbing sensation in her mouth, while still allowing her to feel the strangely comforting heat as it slid deep down inside of her. She grimaced, as always, at the acidic taste and the little shudder it sent through her system. "Smooooth!" she said under her breath, as was her custom when her friends bought her the shot. They often ordered it just so they could watch the effect it had on her. Always open to being the comic relief, she rarely turned down tequila.

Setting the glass down in front of her, she glanced up, having the odd sensation someone was watching her. She saw him across the room, tall, and beautiful, and...oh, my gosh...it was Josh Dunningham! She quickly spit her lime out. *I must look quite the picture with the dark green rind wedged against my teeth.* He flashed her a smile which had her knees shaking even more than the tequila, and she realized he must have watched her throughout the whole stupid ritual—salt, tequila, lime. He started ambling in her direction, and she dropped her gaze, feeling foolish.

AS JOSH WALKED TOWARD her, the blonde glanced down, seeming certain he was headed somewhere else. In fact, she appeared genuinely surprised when he stopped by her side. He spread his long legs out in front of him, resting on the stool next to hers, and propped one elbow on the bar, sure of himself, as he leaned in to talk to her.

But when she peered up into his face with a nervous smile, that feeling of power he felt when he first began his trip around the bar, deserted him completely. His heart started beating so loudly it replaced the sound of the amplifiers which was still ringing in his ears from practice. Unaccustomed to such a physical reaction to anybody, he almost couldn't find the words to speak.

"Hello," he managed after a beat, his deep voice coming out awkward in his own ears.

"Oh..." she stuttered, obviously mortified. "You saw me staring at you. I'm sorry. I-I'm not a stalker, I swear."

His amusement flushed away his momentary apprehension. "No. I figured that out. Stalkers generally, well...stalk people. I approached you."

"Yeah." She continued to peer down and fiddle with her glass, an action he found absolutely adorable. "But I *was* looking at you."

"Yeah," he said, feeling his old charm coming back to him. "Why is that?" He pitched his voice so it was as smooth and sweet as hot fudge, and flashed a cocky grin.

"Why wouldn't I?" she breathed, almost involuntarily, her head still down.

He chortled.

"Oh my gosh, I'm acting like a fool." She reached for her clutch on the bar, knocking her shot glass over and then diving to straighten it up. "I'll go now."

"Hey...hey, hey," he said, grabbing her elbows as she turned to go. "Slow down. We're just having a conversation here."

"Yes, one in which I am making a complete ass out of myself." He slid his hands down to her wrists as she pulled away, restraining her. She turned back to say, "I'm sorry."

He didn't understand why he did it, maybe because he just had to have a look at those fascinating blue eyes again, but he reached to curl a finger under her chin, lifting her face. "I'm not."

Although she seemed determined to hide it, he could feel her pulse race underneath his fingertips as she gazed up at him helplessly. She was at least a foot shorter than him, even with the sexy little boots she was wearing. The boots told him she was hot, but not easy, like stilettos would have portrayed her. He prided himself in being able to pin down a girl in less than fifty seconds, and knowing whether he would be spending the night with her or not. The sleek black jeans hugging her hips gave him the same information the boots had. They made her look extremely appealing, but not outright advertising it, like leather would have. Her silky camisole, a confusion of browns and purples, revealed a hint of full breasts, sending his own pulse racing. She was not what he would call a hard body, but was deliciously toned and feminine; her breasts were large but not sloppy, with inviting curves which dove mysteriously into the shadow of her top.

She shifted her feet, and he was overwhelmed by the sweet scent of honeysuckle. He found himself swamped by a memory.

He was walking to school, dragging his feet as he went, as was his general custom, when he came across the white and yellow honeysuckle vines covering his neighbors' fence. He set his books down and plucked one of the white blossoms. He pulled at the base of the flower like he had seen the owners' son do, and watched, in wonder, as the delicate green and white stamen slid out, peppered with yellow dust. He slid his tongue along it, tasting the sugary, honeyed flavor of the pollen. Delighted, he quickly pulled off a yellow flower to see if it tasted the same.

The innocent memory seemed, at the moment, highly erotic and he let himself imagine his tongue trailing down the girl, tasting her in a similar way.

She blushed, as if reading his thoughts, or perhaps having a few similar thoughts of her own.

"Let me at least—" He wracked his brain. She was nervous, he was moving too fast. What was it normal guys did with girls? "—take you out for a cup of coffee."

"That sounds nice, but I don't drink coffee."

"Come to think of it, neither do I." He laughed. "Pepsi is my choice of caffeine."

She nodded, a smile replacing her anxious look. "Diet Pepsi."

"A new generation, I guess." He shrugged, releasing her hands. He peered into her eyes, and knew he couldn't leave it at that. The blue of her eyes was like the sky on a crystal clear night after sunset, just before the stars come out, layer upon layer of unequalled blue. He tentatively brought one finger up to one of the velvety brown spaghetti straps at her shoulders, letting it glide underneath the fabric and wrap around it.

The move was bold, risky, even; but he hadn't gotten as far as he had in life by taking the easy way out. After all, he didn't even know the girl, and she seemed the type to run like a rabbit. And yet, it was as if he couldn't help himself. He let his eyes follow his finger as he fantasized about pulling the straps down, allowing the satiny fabric to disappear, so he could gaze upon those spectacular breasts. A ripple of desire ran through her as he cruised up and down the strap, the back of his finger against her silky skin. But when he gazed up into her eyes he saw a flash of fear. *I'll have to work for this one.* He hated to have to work, it made him feel somewhat vulnerable, but on the flip side, he also relished the challenge.

"What if I just buy you another drink?" he asked, a hint of huskiness slipping into his voice. Before she could respond one way or another, he raised two fingers to the bartender. Then, he turned his attention back to her.

Another shot or two, and she'll be mine.

JOSH DUNNINGHAM WAS talking to her. It was like a dream come true. How many nights had she fantasized about just that?

And, unbelievably, he was even more gorgeous in person, every little bit of his six-foot-five-inch frame. As he stretched his legs out in front of him, her eyes fought to take in all of his luscious length. He smelled fantastic, too, a spicy scent which screamed rock and roll. *They should bottle it and name it something like, 'Totally Josh,' and I could run the ad copy for it...*

She shook her head. *Get a grip. You're acting like some silly school girl.*

But then again, a second voice reasoned, *it is Josh Dunningham.* If a person could squeal in her head, she was pretty sure she just had. And then, she opened her mouth, and the stupidest things flew out. She felt like ramming her head against the bar, but he grabbed her elbows with his big, skilled hands, and all logical thought—that was, whatever semblance of logical thought she had remaining—abandoned her in a whoosh. He curled his finger under her chin and lifted her face, and Cassie found herself staring into his incredible green eyes, the kind of green which had her thinking of making love with him in the deep grass of some meadow...and the gold specks she saw in his irises were the sun, filtering in through the blades of grass as they rolled around...

She realized he was observing her, and her face grew warm, as she wondered if he could read her thoughts. Those smoky green eyes traveled to one of the straps of her top and he slid a finger along its length. The touch of his skin on hers in such an intimate way, made her just about come unglued, and then she was scared. She hardly even knew the man! What the hell was she doing? What the hell was he doing? And why was he doing it to her?

To find out what happened next, purchase
ROCK ME, GENTLY!

ALSO FROM M.J. SCHILLER

ROMANTIC REALMS COLLECTION:
TAKEN BY STORM
AN UNCOMMON LOVE
LEAP INTO THE KNIGHT
LADY OF THE KNIGHT
A KNIGHT TO REMEMBER

ROCKING ROMANCE COLLECTION:
TRAPPED UNDER ICE
ABANDON ALL HOPE
BETWEEN ROCK AND A HARD PLACE
ROCK ME, GENTLY
MIDNIGHT MELODY

LOVE AND CHAOS SERIES:
ROCKED BY GRACE
ROCKED BY LOVE
ROCK IT TO THE MOON
ROCK OF SALVATION

REAL ROMANCE COLLECTION:
UPON A MIDNIGHT CLEAR
THE HEART TEACHES BEST
DAMAGE DONE
BLACKOUT
HOMETOWN HEARTACHE

TAKE A CHANCE ON ME

DEVILISH DESIRES SERIES:
TO HELL IN A COACH BAG
DAMNED IF I DO
THE DEVIL YOU KNOW
SATAN, LINE ONE
PITCHFORK IN THE ROAD
SIN WORTH THE PENANCE
HELL HATH NO FURY
TEN MINUTES IN THE SIN BIN
DEVIL'S IN THE DETAILS
DEVIL'S ADVOCATE
HADE'S NIGHT

INSATIABLE FIRE SERIES:
BEATING IN TIME
LEAD ME ON
ROCK WITH THE RHYTHM
BASSIST'S INSTINCTS

OTHERS:
HEARTS FLUSH

ABOUT THE AUTHOR

Bestselling author M.J. Schiller is a retired lunch lady/romance-romantic suspense writer. She enjoys writing novels whose characters include rock stars, desert princes, teachers, futuristic Knights, construction workers, cops, and a wide variety of others. In her mind everybody has a romance. She is the mother of a twenty-seven-year-old and three twenty-five-year-olds. That's right, triplets! So having recently taught four children to drive, she likes to escape from life on occasion by pretending to be a rock star at karaoke. However...you won't be seeing her name on any record labels soon.

www.ingramcontent.com/pod-product-compliance
Lightning Source LLC
Chambersburg PA
CBHW061155170626
46809CB00003B/1104